THE S★MALI AFFAIR

JAMES LAWRENCE

The Somali Affair is a work of fiction. Apart from the well-known actual people, events, and locales that figure in the narrative, all names, characters, places, and incidents are the products of the author's imagination or are used fictitiously. Any resemblance to current events, locales, or living persons is entirely coincidental.

ISBN-9781072598244

DEDICATION

THIS BOOK IS dedicated to my wife and family. Without their support and assistance, it would not have been possible to complete this book.

ABOUT THE AUTHOR

JAMES LAWRENCE HAS been a soldier, small business owner, military advisor, and defense trader. He currently lives in the Middle East. He's the author of six Pat Walsh Thriller novels: *Arabian Deception, Arabian Vengeance, Arabian Fury, Arabian Collusion, Rising Sea* and *The Somali Affair*.

CHAPTER 1

ORONO, MAINE

A FRESH BLANKET OF snow covered the Town of Orono, obscuring its blemishes and lurking hazards. The crunch of Becky Anderson's footsteps echoed against the snow piles on both sides of the freshly plowed sidewalk. School was cancelled for the second day in a row. A late season blizzard crushed any hint of spring and brought the central Maine town to a halt with twenty inches of the heavy wet stuff. Although she was tall enough to start as a forward on her high school basketball team, Becky travelled as if in a labyrinth, restricted to the path and unable to see over the frozen walls of snow.

Two days of being cooped up in the house with her two younger brothers was more than enough incentive to make her jump at the opportunity to meet a friend for lunch. Pat's Pizza was only a quarter mile from her house, and she was looking forward to meeting her new Facebook friend for the first time in person.

Becky turned left at the corner of Mill Street and entered the parking lot. She cut through a freshly plowed section Pat's Pizza shared with the Black Bear Microbrewery and a few smaller local retailers. She could hear the backing-up warning signal of the plow as it worked on the opposite side of the lot. There were only four vehicles parked in the cleared section, it was a day most people chose to stay home.

Across the freshly plowed lot, she eyed the pizzeria's entrance between Margaritas Mexican and Erv's Barbershop. She entered through the restaurant's back door, into the dimly lit no frills dining room. After her eyes adjusted to the light, she found Hani seated up front, near the cash register. It wasn't hard to pick out her lunch date from the seven other patrons who'd braved the weather to lunch at what is universally regarded as the best pizza in Orono.

"You must be Hani," Becky said after walking up to the lone African girl in the dining room.

The girl rose and the two greeted each other with a hug.

"It's so cool you could make it out. Thanks for meeting me."

"I'm happy for an excuse to get out. I was going stir crazy at home. My brothers are climbing the walls, plus I know what it's like to move to a new town."

"How long have you been here?" Hani asked.

"Two years, just before the start of freshman year. My dad's a professor at UMAINE and we transferred from Florida State. I'm still getting used to the winters."

"This weather must be nothing like Florida," Hani said.

"We'd be in shorts right now."

"This is my first experience with snow."

"It never snowed where you lived in Africa?"

"Never."

The waitress came over and the two suspended the conversation to order. Becky was a member of her congregation's youth ministry and greeting new members was part of her responsibilities. The two talked about the church, the school and the town while they ate. After the meal Becky excused herself to go to the ladies' room. When she returned, the two finished their pizza and continued to chat. After a time, Becky began to slur and found herself feeling dizzy. She gulped down the remainder of her Coke to combat a wicked case of dry mouth.

"You don't look well," Hani said.

"I don't feel good."

"Let's get you out to some fresh air," Hani said.

Having already paid the bill while Becky was in the ladies' room, Hani assisted the unsteady basketball player to the exit. She guided a compliant and barely conscious Becky out the door and into the side door of a white panel van that was waiting in front of the restaurant.

CHAPTER 2

SIARGAO, PHILIPPINES

I FOUND AN OPENING next to a coconut palm to park my Honda 125. Puny, by most standards, the tiny motorcycle is a muscle bike in the Philippines. With my surfboard mounted on the right side of the bike, it was tricky turning into the narrow parking space. I came within two inches of clipping a scooter and dropping the line of bikes like dominos. I was wearing only a pair of swim shorts and flip flops as I entered the bar, which meant I was appropriately dressed. The Offshore is an open-air sports bar with a beach-sand floor, bamboo walls and a thatched roof. Its close proximity to the Cloud 9 Pier, great service and ice-cold beer make it a popular stop off spot for surfers. Cloud 9, in Siargao Island, is the most famous surf break in the Philippines and it draws aspirants from across the globe.

Happy hour was in full swing and the crowd was lively. I waved to Novy, my favorite waitress, and headed to the farthest corner, away from the rowdy crowd, where I knew I'd find Mike. I threaded my way through a mix of athletic young Europeans, Australians, Americans and locals who in equal measure were dividing their attention between the band and each other. I found Mike occupying the lone pool table, seemingly oblivious to the post-surfing celebration going on in the other part of the room. I wrapped an arm around his neck and put him in a mock headlock. He responded by handing me his pool cue. I was watching him rack the balls when I felt a tap on my shoulder. It was Novy with a bucket of San Miguel Lights. I nodded to an empty table and she deposited the load. She opened a beer and brought it to me. The bottle was freezing cold and after a day in the sun and salt water it tasted of heaven. I gave her the roll of pesos I had in my bathing suit pocket and she smiled before disappearing.

"You break," Mike said.

"When did you get in?"

"About two hours ago. I'm staying down the street at the Siargao Bleu."

"I would've met you halfway," I said as I launched the cue ball hard into the mass hoping for some magic. Despite the thunderous clash, nothing fell in.

"Migos has been raving about this place nonstop for a month. I wanted to see what it was all about."

"That guy came to the greatest surf spot on the planet. Spent exactly two hours in the water before declaring surfing a sissy sport for unemployed hacky-sack players and gender fluid frisbee footballers. Then he proceeded to hit on every unmarried girl on the island. Before he left, the villagers were locking up their daughters."

"That's not the story he's telling."

"He's a rookie on the board and Savage and Rodriguez are both pro tour material. He's ultra-competitive and I think he just needed to find something he could beat them at."

"And that something was picking up girls."

"Yup, welcome to the home of the Migos Olympics."

Mike smiled and proceeded to sink four balls in a row.

"I think I'm being hustled. What are we playing for anyway?" I asked.

"Whether or not your vacation ends tonight."

I managed to put a ball out of its misery, one that was already so close to falling into the corner pocket, it was defying gravity. My next shot went astray, which allowed Mike to go on another killer streak. This wasn't going to take long.

"What's up?" I asked.

"Al Shabab attacked the Maka Al-Mukarama Hotel in Mogadishu last week. They killed twenty-nine. The attacks are occurring less frequently, but they're getting much more massive in scale. In the last couple of years, they've racked up some serious death tallies. The last truck bombing in Somalia killed five hundred. Two cross-border attacks into Kenya, one against a mall and another against a university, each killed hundreds."

"What business does Al Shabab have in Kenya?"

"It's more target rich. They go after Christians; they have to go cross border because there aren't many still alive in Somalia."

"They only attack Christians?"

"Any infidels will do, but Christians are far and away the target of choice. Eleven million Somalis and they're down to less than a hundred Christians from a high of about ten thousand."

"How hard could it be to save such a small group?"

"The US gave it a shot with a refugee program in

the 90s. That was after the government fell and the civil war intensified."

"Why didn't it work?"

"Because none of the people who came out of the UN-run Somali refugee camps were Christian."

"Why?"

"They gamed the system. When the people in the refugee camps realized that declaring themselves Christian was a one-way ticket out of Somalia, they suddenly all became Christian."

"How hard would be to ask them a few questions to screen them?"

"The UN has its own agenda. They couldn't even bring themselves to make an effort to stop the few authentic Christians inside the camps from being killed."

"I imagine once word got out, the actual Christians avoided the camps."

"Exactly. Christianity in Somalia is finished. The refugee camps are long gone. The country's a disaster, it's a failed state. All that's left is a marauding group of murderers. The big bosses are fed up. They've decided that drone strikes and a six-million-dollar bounty on Ahmed Umar, the head of Al Shabab, isn't going to get the job done, now it's time for direct action."

"Sounds like a JSOC mission to me."

"DoD is very skittish about operating in Mogadishu. Nobody wants a repeat of *Blackhawk Down*. We have no assets on the ground."

"How are you targeting all of those drone strikes I read about?"

"Everything is being done from the air. Restrictions on

putting boots on the ground is why we haven't been able to locate Umar. Aerial imagery and SIGINT will only take you so far."

"What do you want me to do?"

"Find Umar and kill him."

"That's it?"

"That's it," he said as he expertly banked the eight-ball off a side bumper and sunk it into the corner.

"I'm done with this game, it's time to devote my attention to something I'm good at."

"What's that?"

"Drinking."

"One more game. This time for dinner," Mike said.

"If I must."

"And not one of those cheap Filipino food stands either."

"This town has some great restaurants. You'll make sure David Forrest gets everything he requests, so we can find your terrorist?" I asked.

"Already done. Clearwater has approval for everything coming out of Eastern Africa. If anyone can find our man, your Scottish professor is the guy," Mike said as he broke. I watched two solids drain into opposite corner pockets along with any hopes I had of redemption.

"Where are you taking me to dinner?" Mike asked after a game that was shorter than the first.

"How about we finish these beers. Then I'll go back to my place and find a shirt and then we can meet up at Kermit Restaurant."

"Place must be fancy if you need a shirt," Mike said.

"It's a bit pretentious, but the food is worth it."

"Where's Kermit?"

"About a mile down the road, it's not on the beach road, it's up on the hill inside the forest. Next door is a place called Jungle, tonight is party night, I promise to get you in trouble."

"What's party night?"

"Nightlife rotates in Siargao, every night a different bar hosts the festivities. Tonight's Jungle, by ten it will be crazy," I said.

"Do you think crazy is something that I'm after?"

"Bad choice of words. What you see and do every day is crazy. Hanging out, eating tapas, drinking beer and watching a bunch of surfers cut loose is normal, some would argue, even healthy. It might be therapeutic for you to see some people enjoy themselves who honest to God don't go to sleep at night worrying about terrorists and genocides," I said.

"Ya know, you might have a point. It might be fun."

"Exactly, bring us back to when our life was wild, fun and carefree," I said.

"That was more you than me."

"Not true, I still remember that brawl in the cantina at Howard Air Force Base."

"If that guy hadn't survived, you would've been court marshalled for murder and I would've been an accessory," Mike said.

"No kidding. He fell off a two-story balcony, landed flat on his back and got up and walked away. It was a miracle," I said.

"He didn't fall, you punched him."

"He swung at you first, it was a reflex and I had no idea the drunken clown was going to back pedal and tumble over the rail. Who does that?"

"No brawling tonight."

"There are no fights in Siargao, it's way too chill. Surfers believe in karmic retributions and Gaia the earth goddess. They only get mad when you steal a wave. Only fun and relaxation allowed. Let's enjoy it while we can, tomorrow we go back to the job."

CHAPTER 3

INDIAN OCEAN

MIGOS AND I were sitting on opposite sides of an MH-6 waiting for the launch order. The remote-control little bird helicopter was perched on the stern of the *Nomad* with its bubble cockpit facing outward toward the sea. The *Nomad*, my hundred-foot AB100 yacht, was holding position fifteen miles off the coast of Mogadishu. McDonald was on the stick of the remote-controlled MH-6 inside a QUADCON container that was essentially a stationary cockpit, set up against the side of the salon door. In addition to the little bird, McDonald also had the controls of a Martin V-BAT UAV that he'd been loitering over our objective for the past five hours. The payload on the vertical take-off and landing UAV was primarily a day camera and a thermal camera. Although it also had a two-pound Banshee 4G/LTE networking radio that allowed Savage and Rodriguez, who were manning an observation position, to stream video of the target to the iPhone-like com sets each member of the team carried with them.

"Is that him?" I asked after I sent a cropped photo I'd

captured off Savage's sniper scope video feed to David Forrest in Scotland.

"That's definitely Ahmed Umar," I heard David say through my headset.

"Savage, do you have a shot?"

"Not if we want to get out of here alive I don't. He's too close," Savage said.

On my phone, I could see the UAV day camera image of Umar. He was walking away from a mosque. He was walking down the center of a road, surrounded by a personal security detail carrying AK-47s and a crowd of the faithful leaving the mosque with him. Savage and Rodriguez were located on the roof of a nearby building. If they fired a sniper round at Umar, they'd get besieged by hundreds of Somalis who had an uncanny, proven ability to transition from sleepy third world citizens to an aggressive bloodthirsty mob in minutes.

"It's getting dark. Track him to where he puts his head down tonight. We'll hit him in the early morning while he sleeps," I said.

"Wilco," I heard Savage say.

Migos and I dismounted off the little bird and went into the cool air conditioning of the yacht salon where we could watch the sensor feeds on the big screen TV in comfort.

Hours later, the blades on the little bird were already spinning when Migos and I returned to our bench seats. The aircraft lifted off as soon as I clipped my retaining strap to the airframe and gave the all clear. It was two in the morning and the air was hot and damp. I was looking through a pair of white phosphorous PVS-31 night vision goggles that were mounted on my helmet. Skimming fifty feet above the waves at sixty knots towards the coast was outer worldly through the sepia-like picture of my night vision.

Ten minutes into the trip, the aircraft began to gain altitude. We leveled off at five hundred feet.

"One minute," McDonald's voice said over my headset.

"Executing," I heard Savage say over my headset.

We crossed over a sandy white beach. I looked toward the city and saw flashes from the 40mm HE rounds Savage was firing at a roadblock that was three hundred yards from his sniper position. Migos and I unclipped our safety straps and jumped off the little bird as it touched down on a flat building roof. We ran to the wooden roof access door as the aircraft lifted off to assume a loitering position above the fray. I pulled the handle and the door swung open toward me. Migos threw a fragmentary grenade down the stairs and as soon as it went off, we both chased behind. The building had three stories and two exits. One opened to the street and a second opened to a back alley. Savage was covering the front exit and Rodriguez the back. Our plan was simple, we were going to clear every room from top to bottom and if anyone tried to escape the building, they would be killed by one of our two snipers.

Migos and I split up in the hallway, I went right, and he went left. The building was narrow and there was only space for two or three rooms on each floor. I blasted the thin wooden door with the M26 MASS shotgun I had mounted underneath the barrel of my M4. I kicked what was left of the door open. Lying on the floor was a thin, grey-haired African man who'd taken the buckshot blast full in the chest. I sprayed the closets and bathroom with my M4 and moved back toward the hallway.

"Room's clear. Coming out," I said.

"Waiting on you," Migos said.

We met midway in the hall at the stairwell. Migos led the way down the stairs and I covered from behind. After the first flight, the stairs turned, exposing us to the enemy below. We dropped to the ground at the eruption of gunfire. Migos side armed a grenade as he lay on his stomach. The fragmentary grenade exploded. The room was pitch black and filled with acrid smoke as we descended the final flight of stairs with the aid of our night vision. I oriented on the muzzle flash from a man firing wildly from across the room. I triggered the MAWR device with the middle finger of my left hand which was wrapped around the handguard of my M4. I moved the IR laser onto the man's chest and drilled him with two 300 blackout rounds in the space of two seconds. I could hear Migos firing behind me as I continued to clear toward the hallway and room beyond.

I pulled the pin on my last grenade and rolled it toward the wooden frame door at the end of the hallway. I slipped behind the wall.

"Frag out!" I yelled.

The grenade exploded and I followed the blast through the dust and smoke. I heard gunshots behind me.

"Tangos trying to move up the stairs from the first floor. Frag out."

Another grenade explosion shook the room. My ears were ringing, and my eyes were tearing as I entered the room. I sensed movement to my right, and I swung my weapon and opened fire. I hit the man with two shots to the chest. I shifted my aim higher, placing the IR laser on the man's forehead for a millisecond before I pulled the trigger.

"Jackpot," I said

I walked over to the dead man and snapped a picture of his face with my phone camera.

"We need to get out of here," Migos said.

"Okay, just let me do a quick SE."

I searched through the dead man's pockets, all I found was an iPhone. I tried to unlock the phone, but it was password protected. I took Umar's lifeless hand and pressed his right index finger against the button on the bottom of the phone. It unlocked. I kept the phone open by opening the compass app while I finished my brief search. I quickly went through the rest of the room. The phone was all I was going to get. I ran behind Migos up the stairs to the roof. When we reached the top, the little bird was already waiting for us. We hopped onto our respective sides and clipped in.

"Let's go," I said to McDonald. The aircraft took off.

From above the scene we could see a crowd forming on the street in front of Ahmed Umar's safe house. Umar was clever, he'd only survived as long as he did by staying constantly on the move and by taking advantage of the security his clan provided. His people were the dominant tribe in Somalia and he never strayed into areas they didn't control. Relying on his clan for protection allowed him to keep the signature of his security force to a minimum. For us that meant the risk of an organized response from a security force was small. However, I had enough experience in Mogadishu to develop a healthy fear of the unorganized mob.

Random shots were fired into the night sky at the sound of our helicopter, but we were quickly out of range. The helicopter flew directly back to the *Nomad*. Migos and I refueled it and then McDonald flew it back to Mogadishu to extract Savage and Rodriguez who used our exfil time to move to their own pickup zone. Over the comm link, David Forrest used the UAV feed to guide the two dismounted operators around the excited mob and along the safest route to the pick up zone.

I removed my plate carrier and helmet and sat down on a chair in the salon to watch the UAV thermal camera feed of the extraction on the big screen. I still had Umar's phone in my pocket, and I checked to make sure it was still open.

"David, I have the target's phone, can you send me a message with the link that lets you download it?" I said to David Forrest at his computer center in Scotland.

"What's the phone number?" he asked. I gave it to him.

Moments later, I heard a ping and I opened up the message. Inside was a hyperlink. I opened the link and in doing so, began to stream the data from the iPhone to David and his all-knowing all-seeing AI powered supercomputer he called ALICE.

While the system downloaded, I kept the phone open. I occupied myself by scrolling through the messages, all of which were in a language I didn't recognize or understand. One of the messages below the link from David's was a video. Since I couldn't read the texts, I thought I'd have a look at the video. I hit the play icon on the black screen. At first, I couldn't tell what the video was about. Then it got lighter and the video showed the backs of three black men who had the distinct gaunt look of Somali men. Eventually the curtain of men parted and revealed another man. The fourth man was standing at the head of a prostrate girl, holding her arms behind her head. The girl was flat on her back. Her long blonde hair was wrapped in the hands of the man pinning her arms. The face of the girl was clear, it was a face of sheer terror. The camera panned to the left and revealed a fifth man. The man's face wasn't in the picture, only his body from the chest down. He had a concave chest and strong sinewy arms. The fifth man was raping the girl. The girl was struggling, but she wasn't screaming. The fifth man had his hand on her throat as he raped her. The light in the video wasn't good, but the girl seemed very young. It was impossible to tell where the scene was taking place.

"Look at this," I said to Migos as I handed him the phone. He viewed the video.

"What is that?"

"I have no idea. But it was sent to Umar from an American phone number," I said.

"That's an American girl?" Migos said.

"Probably."

"When was it sent?"

"Yesterday afternoon."

"We should get David to locate the phone that sent it. We should call the police."

"David should be able to do that, and Mike will know someone from the FBI who can find her. I'll get him on the case," I said.

CHAPTER 4

RED SEA

I WOKE UP IN my cabin. The steady hum of the three MAN V12 1900 HP engines and the noise and vibration of the yacht cutting through the ocean was calming. My cabin was on the lower deck, midship, forward of the engine room. Being in the middle allowed the cabin to encompass the full beam of the boat, which is twenty-two feet. It's a big ensuite cabin that has a sitting area, walk-in closet and deluxe bathroom. I hit the button on my night stand and opened the four window shades to let the mid-afternoon sun shine in. I was operating on only three hours of sleep. After Savage and Rodriguez returned, I took the first shift at the wheel and let McDonald rest, now it was my turn to spot McDonald. I threw on a pair of canvas shorts and a pair of flip flops and headed upstairs. I found McDonald where I'd left him, he was sitting in one of the two captain's chairs inside the wheelhouse.

"How're things?" I asked as I plopped down on the seat next to him.

"We're still a few hours from the Suez. The sea lane is getting crowded."

I checked the radar and located six other ships within a five-mile radius. We were on one of the busiest shipping routes in the world and it was to be expected.

"Is that coffee fresh?" I asked, pointing to the Thermos on the countertop.

"No, it's old."

"Are any of the galley slaves up yet?"

"No, just us."

"Why don't you get some rest. I'll take it from the flydeck."

I walked toward the stern to the back of the main cabin. I passed the dining and living areas of the salon and went out through the triple sliding doors to the stern deck. I climbed up the stairs and took control of the yacht from the helm station at the front end of the flydeck. It was a cloudless day and I pulled out a pair of wayfarer Ray Bans from my shorts pocket. After I made a fresh cup of coffee in the Keurig machine on the flydeck bar, I decided to check in with Mike. It was a little after seven in the morning in Virginia and I knew he'd already be at his desk in Langley. I used a sat phone.

"Where are you?" he asked.

"Off the coast of Jeddah, heading North to the Suez."

"When will you get to Cyprus?"

"Another three days is my guess. Did you send law enforcement to that location David gave us?"

"It was a crappy hotel in Nashville. Nothing was found."

"Are you on the trail? Do you need David's help to find her?"

"Beyond giving the information to the FBI, there's nothing more I can do. Operating inside the USA is verboten. We gave the info to the FBI, they handed it over to local law enforcement. The Nashville PD went to the hotel and didn't find any evidence of an attack. There are no reports of anyone fitting the description of the girl. They're checking missing persons reports and the hospitals. Nashville police and the FBI are doing what they can."

"David said the phone that sent the video is no longer pinging. He was also tracking two other phones that were in close proximity. All three went dead at about the same time. Since then, he has nothing."

"Burner phones get swapped out constantly, especially after a crime. We have an interest in learning why the Al Shabab leader would be swapping rape videos with someone in Tennessee, but unless law enforcement finds something, this is going to be a dead end."

"That video has been haunting me. I'm thinking of looking into this myself."

"It's better if you leave it to law enforcement. We don't want to get drawn into a domestic matter."

"I know. But as a private citizen who sometimes contracts with the Agency on overseas assignments, I think I'm allowed to look into a private domestic matter. I don't have the same restrictions as you, I wouldn't be breaking any laws, would I?"

"Technically, no. But I know how you'll react if you get your hands on one of those guys. A news headline that reads 'CIA Contractor Arrested for Brutal Murder' is not a great outcome from my vantage point."

"Okay, I'll give the boys in blue another day before I do anything rash."

"Fair enough."

I spent the next three hours dividing my time between piloting the *Nomad* and preparing for dinner. By the time Migos, Savage and Rodriguez joined me on deck, I had the gas grill on the flydeck filled with Memphis dry rub pork ribs and spicy chicken thighs.

"Need any help?" Migos asked.

"The vegetables and coleslaw are all downstairs in the galley. Can you get them?" I said.

"On it," Migos said.

"What's our ETA in Cyprus?" Savage asked.

"He has a date tomorrow night," Rodriguez said.

"You're probably gonna miss it. We're less than five hundred miles from port, but it's going to take at least another day or two to get through the canal," I said.

"That's what I thought," Savage said.

"When we get within range of Paphos Airport we'll fly the little bird in. That way, we don't have to take it with the *Nomad* through customs and to the marina. I can put you on that flight," I said.

"What would happen if customs discovered the weapons cache in the engine room?" Rodriguez asked.

"They go through it all the time. Usually with dogs and they never find anything. That false wall is very well made. But if we ever did get caught In Cyprus, we'd probably get arrested. It would be up to the US Government to get us out, which I'm sure they would. In many of the other places we put to port, we would be much less fortunate," I said.

"Cyprus knows what Trident does?" Savage asked.

"They know we're a US defense contractor and that we move weapons and ammunition. None of which is allowed to go any further into Cyprus beyond the secured customs area of the airport. Within the fenced-in area of our hangar at the airport, we're in the customs holding area and we can have pretty much anything we want there. Outside the fenced area, the existence of weapons is a problem. It would still be manageable if we got caught, but it would be an incident that would reach the State Department and the people we work for wouldn't be happy about that," I said.

"Why are we flying the little bird in?" Savage asked.

"The beautiful people at Larnaca Marina believe the *Nomad* is a pleasure yacht. It allows us to blend. Having a weapon of war perched on our stern deck would blow our cover," I said.

"Makes sense."

"We'll get through customs in the canal by paying the Egyptians to look the other way. We could get by the customs agents in Cyprus the same way, but it's our fellow yachters at the marina we want to keep things hidden from," I said.

"So, we keep them from seeing the little bird," Savage said.

"Right, after we get through the canal, you and Rodriguez can fly in with the helicopter and we'll catch up to you later," I said.

"Deal."

"And tell me what you think of my new rib recipe, be honest? I'm trying to replicate the ribs at Rendezvous in Memphis," I said.

"Rendezvous. Never heard of it," Migos said as he appeared with a tray full of corn, beans and coleslaw.

"If you ever find yourself in Memphis, it's a must. They're the gold standard of dry rub," I said.

"I didn't know you took this stuff so seriously?" Rodriguez asked.

"Barbeque and baseball are America's two greatest cultural achievements. They should never be treated lightly or taken for granted," I said.

"I'll remember that," Savage said.

"The season opens in less than two weeks," I said.

"Are you going to the Red Sox season opener?" Savage asked.

"It's in Seattle under the dome. I just might do that, great city, super venue. I'm planning to go to the US anyway," I said.

"What for?" Savage asked.

"I want to look for that girl we saw on the video last night," I said.

"I thought the agency and the FBI were on the case," Migos said.

"Not really. The agency can only pass info, they can't do any work domestically. The FBI appears to be doing nothing, just passing the buck to the local police. I think with the help of Dr. Forrest and his magic computer, I can do a better job," I said.

"Do you want us to come along?" Migos asked.

"No, it's okay. If I find the girl, I'll get the authorities involved. I shouldn't need any backup," I said.

"You'll call if you do?" Migos said.

"Of course," I said.

"When are you leaving?" Migos said.

"I'm going to give Mike and the Feds one more day, if they don't find her, I'll fly out of Cairo tomorrow."

CHAPTER 5

NASHVILLE, TENNESSEE

I ARRIVED AT THE Fairlane Hotel in downtown Nashville in a rented Ford Explorer. I was a little punchy and badly in need of a shower after twenty-four hours of air travel. The route from Cairo to Dubai to New York and then Nashville is not one I ever intend to repeat. I rushed through hotel check-in, went upstairs immediately to my room, showered, shaved and put on a suit. My next stop was the Metropolitan Nashville Police Department – South Precinct.

The police building was past the airport across the Cumberland River on the South Side of the city. It's a utilitarian single-story red brick building off East Trinity, surrounded by scrub oaks on undeveloped commercial lots. I walked into the building and was stopped by a female sergeant at the reception desk. I showed her my Department of Homeland Security credentials and asked to meet with the detective handling the rape incident at the Apple Inn.

I anticipated a long wait before they figured out what to do with me and I took advantage of the time in the waiting area to call David Forrest. It was very early in the morning in Edinburgh, but fortunately David is an early riser.

"Do you have anything for me?" I asked.

"Nothing you don't already know," David replied.

"What about the phones?"

"They were all burners; the video sender and his accomplices all disposed of their phones the next morning," David said.

"Can't you track other numbers called by the phones and then pick up calls and locations of the new burners?" I asked.

"That's what I'm working on now. For it to work, the callers need to have a contact number they call that isn't a burner phone. A vector. So far, no luck, the original burner phones are only leading me to more burner phones."

"If I go to the hotel and I get a list of every person staying at the hotel the night of the attack, will that help?"

"It should. I'll track every hotel guest and find their cell number on the date of the attack and then we can find out who's no longer using the same cell phone number. The people with new phones will most likely be the ones we're looking for."

"The Apple Inn has over a hundred rooms; it's going to be long list," I said.

"ALICE will have no problem working through a long list," David said.

"Should I get the security footage? Can you do something with that?" I asked.

"Once I get the names of the registered guests, we can run some facial recognition," David said.

"Why don't we just pull head shots of the people who look like Somalis and run facial recognition on them," I said.

"Sounds easy, but in that area of Nashville, they're mostly going to be Somalis," David said.

"I'm paying a courtesy call to the local police. I'll have that data for you in a few hours," I said.

"Standing by. Happy hunting."

I no sooner hung up with David when a police officer walked over and asked me to follow him. He took me through the security door and down a corridor to the Office of the Precinct Commander. The Commander stood up and walked around his desk to meet me when I entered. We shook hands, he was a solid looking guy with a bone crushing handshake.

"Agent McDermott, I'm Captain Greg Allison. I apologize for the wait; it took some time for our Federal Liaison to verify your credentials." I couldn't suppress a smile when I heard that, because I knew it meant Mike received a phone call and now knew where I was and what I was doing.

"That's my fault, I probably could've done a better job of letting some of my peers know I was operating in their sandbox," I said.

"What's this all about? Why is Homeland involved?"

"Two nights ago, video evidence of a rape involving a young girl and five black males was taken from a cell phone belonging to an Al Shabab terrorist leader in Mogadishu. The phone that sent the video clip to the Somali terrorist was geo tagged to the Nashville Apple Inn. The Joint Terrorism Task Force referred the investigation of the rape to the Nashville Police and I'm here to follow up," I said.

"We were told of a suspected rape and we were given the time and location, but we weren't given any information about Somali terrorists," Captain Allison said.

"The JTTF probably didn't think it was important," I said.

"It's important."

"I agree, that's why I'm here, to dive a little deeper into this thing. I understand from the little information you were given, you didn't get very far," I said.

"That's true, we didn't get very far. We already suspected Somali gang involvement. I don't think the new information you've provided is going to change much in terms of the investigation," Captain Allison said.

"I only gave you that information to allow you to understand why this case has Federal interest. I'm sure your officers have plenty to do, I'm not asking for any support or help in any way. I just wanted as a courtesy to make sure you knew I was here and why," I said.

"I appreciate you coming by. Agent McDermott, you have our full support. Whatever you need just ask," Captain Allison said.

"That's very generous. Did the FBI at least provide you with a picture of the victim?" I asked.

"No, they didn't give us anything except a general description that we took to the nearby hospitals and clinics."

"I'm going to give you a copy of the video. Where do you want me to send it?"

He gave me an email address and I texted David and asked him to send a sanitized copy of the video without any way to trace where it came from.

"You'll have the video in a minute. If you can circulate the girl's picture, maybe we can find out who she is," I said.

"Absolutely."

"Thank you for your time, Captain. If you don't mind,

I'm going to head over to the Apple Inn and ask a few questions," I said.

"I have the detective who handled the initial investigation standing by, I'll have her escort you."

"That's very kind, but it's not necessary," I said.

"I insist." I didn't want a chaperone, but could tell Captain Allison was a no-nonsense guy and wasn't going to take no for an answer, so I figured, what the hell.

"Sounds good. Thanks again." I offered up my hand for more punishment.

On my way out the door, I was stopped by an athletic looking, short haired, blond woman in the hallway.

"I'm detective Grace Deforest. You must be Agent McDermott."

"Guilty as charged. Are you the detective who's going to be accompanying me?"

"I am, do you mind if I drive?" she asked.

"Not at all." Without another word, she abruptly turned and headed down the corridor at a fast clip. I chased and was a full ten steps behind by the time we reached the exit. My phone rang as we entered the parking lot.

"Mike, what a surprise," I said.

"Didn't we talk about how the Agency couldn't get involved in this," Mike said.

"We did. Remember we agreed about contractors being different from employees and why my 'we' is different than your 'we'," I said.

"The minute you used CIA supplied credentials that were given to you for a totally different purpose, that contractor-employee separation disappeared. What were you thinking?" Mike said.

"I thought I was avoiding trouble. I didn't think it would be an issue," I said.

"This could be a problem for both of us. You need to get out of there before this blows up. The Intel Committee would fry my boss if they ever got wind of this," he said.

"I can't. If I don't at least make a show of it, the local PD will become suspicious and that will triple the risk," I said.

"Make it quick and be gone."

"I will. David has some ideas on how to track the attackers. Once we get the scent, I'll turn it back over to the locals," I said.

"Good. Now I'm heading upstairs to explain to the Director why a knuckle dragging contractor known for stacking bodies and creating mayhem is playing Columbo in downtown Nashville."

"That should be a pleasant conversation."

"You have no idea."

The drive to the Apple Inn was a short one. It was only six miles from the police station and on the same road. Grace and I rode in silence, I tried to start up a conversation a couple of times, but the best I got out of her were curt monosyllabic responses. Grace didn't seem hostile or anything. She just seemed to be aloof. One of those rare people with no interest in relationship building with the likes of me.

Grace parked the sedan under the cover of the lobby entrance and we both walked into the hotel. The older woman behind the check-in desk recognized Grace.

"Livian, this is Agent McDermott. We're here to ask some follow up questions from our meeting earlier."

"Pleased to meet you, Agent McDermott. Would you like a coffee or a tea?"

"I'm fine, Livian, I don't want to take too much of your time, just a couple of quick questions. Can you tell me who was on duty Monday evening at 7:30?" I asked.

"I wasn't at reception; I leave at six. It was the night desk manager, Cesar. Frank Belonus is our General Manager and he was still on duty; he usually leaves at eight. I can give you a list of the housekeeping and maintenance staff who were on shift if you want."

"I do. I have a picture of the five attackers and the victim, and I need to know if anyone saw them. If they did, I'm hoping they can identify the room, which would be very helpful in identifying them, especially the victim. If you give me an email, I'll send a link to the file over to you," I said.

Livian gave me an email and I had David send a close-up face shot of the five rapists and the victim to Livian.

"That poor girl," was all Livian said as she looked at the tormented face of the young victim.

"Do you recognize anyone in those shots?" I asked.

"We get more than our share of Somali men; I don't know if I would recognize any of them. I would remember the girl. I definitely didn't see her," Livian said.

"Can I have a copy of the guest information for everyone who had a reservation at the hotel that day?" I asked.

"Yes of course."

"Just download it on a USB and while you're doing that, is there someone who can show us where the security video footage is kept?"

Livian picked up her phone and called the General Manager. It only took a minute for a heavy-set middle-aged bald man to come out of the office door behind the counter. Grace introduced us.

"Mr. Belonus, I'd like to review the security footage from the day of the attack, can you show us where to find it?" I asked.

"Agent, I don't mean to be difficult, but I need to see a search warrant before I can do that."

"No, you don't, Frank. All you need to do is give us permission. And if you don't give us permission, I'm going to start to think you're hiding something," I said.

"It's not my policy, it's the ownership. We can't provide you anything without a warrant," he said as Livian slid a USB across the table and I palmed it. She obviously wasn't familiar with the company policy.

"What's that?" Frank asked.

"Nothing, Frank. Now take me to the security room, before I bring a dozen FBI agents into this place to find out what it is you're hiding."

"I'm not hiding anything."

"If I have to get a warrant, then I'm going to use the hell out of it. Much easier for you if you cooperate. Livian, show Frank here the picture of what happened in his hotel." Frank looked down at the image on Livian's computer screen. His face registered shock and disgust.

"There's not a judge on the planet that wouldn't give me anything I asked for. Especially after they saw the video of that poor girl getting attacked in your hotel," I said.

"Come with me," Frank said as he turned and led us down the corridor.

He walked us into a windowless room that was occupied by a single uniformed security guard. The guard stood as soon as we entered. He was an alert older man who looked like he may have been a former policeman or soldier in his youth. The guard had a grey close-cropped crew cut and his uniform was starched with a perfect gig line.

"Sir, can you show me where the video files are from Monday?" I asked.

"All of the footage is stored in the hard drive."

"How many days before it overwrites?" I asked.

"Every five days."

"Did you pull the footage from the day of the attack?"

"No."

"Where's this hard drive?"

The guard got out of his seat and walked over to the console and pointed to a rectangular box the size of a toaster.

"Thanks," I said as I unplugged it and picked it up.

"What are you doing?" Frank asked.

"I'll return it as soon as we're done analyzing it," I said.

"You can't," he said.

"It's too late to protest, you already gave us permission to search. Didn't he, Detective Deforest?"

"Yes, he did, and now that we've discovered evidence it's too late. What are you going to do with the video?" Grace asked.

"I'm going to put all this video footage and all of the reservation data in a big fast computer and what's going to come out is our bad guys," I said.

"Just like that," she said.

"That's the plan."

"You're not kidding."

"No, not at all. We're going to use the register and run the name and phone number of every guest in the hotel. Then we're going to geo locate every single cell phone belonging to a registered guest in the hotel at the time of the attack.

Then we're going to run every person on this security camera footage through facial recognition. Next, we're going match who is who and then we're going to match them to the faces of those attackers I showed you. And then, with your help, we're going to hunt them down. How's that sound?"

She smiled. The ice queen smiled; I mean a great big beautiful smile. It totally changed the way I felt about her, she genuinely cared about what she was doing. "You can do that?"

"To be honest, I can barely use my iPhone, but I know a guy with an artificial intelligence powered supercomputer who can do that and a lot more. I'm pretty sure we'll at least have some suspects to chase down by tomorrow morning," I said.

"Awesome," Grace said.

CHAPTER 6

NASHVILLE, TENNESSEE

I SENT THE REGISTRY data and set up the transfer of the security footage. While the video data was downloading to David's computer, I took a nap. I was still operating on an Asian time zone and I was asleep before the sun set. When I woke, it was after eleven at night, but it was morning to my internal clock. Since I couldn't get back to sleep, I decided to do some work. I powered up my laptop and booked a ticket back to Cyprus. Then I checked my email for the suspect list I was waiting for from David Forrest.

The response from David was disappointing. None of the images we had of the rapists matched any of the registered guests, which wasn't surprising, because despite what you see on TV, a lot can go wrong with facial recognition. What was surprising and most disappointing was that the plan to identify the suspect by tracking the people on the guest list who changed out phones since the attack was a failure. All of the phones associated with the registered guests were still active. Which meant none of the rapists were registered guests. This was a disastrous development.

I walked out of the hotel into the cool spring night. It was a Friday night and I was alone and a little frustrated with the investigation. Downtown Nashville is a lively place with lots of restaurants and bars that are open late into the early morning. I walked down the block looking for a place to eat. As I sauntered past Jeff Ruby's Steakhouse, I heard a live band knocking out a Nirvana song and caught a whiff of steaks on the grill. I was sold.

I was lucky to get the only open table; the restaurant was packed. It was almost midnight and the young waiter told me they were about to close the kitchen. After a brief scan of the menu, I ordered the crab bisque and a bone in filet with grilled asparagus. The waiter rushed off to place the order and that gave me time to study the wine list.

After consulting Vivino, my phone app wine mentor, I settled on a 2015 Paul Hobbs Cabernet despite a curiously high reliance of the word cassis in the reviews. I wondered how that many people could know what a cassis is, much less what one tastes like. Unless my wine IQ is in the bottom ten percent, I don't think they do. I think it's an example of group think. My theory is that after a guy writes a super pretentious review with lots of obscure references, subsequent reviewers plagiarize bits and pieces to look smart. Having failed miserably at finding the rapists, I felt renewed confidence after solving the case of the purloined wine review. When the wine came it was outstanding, which made me think the first reviewer knew what he was talking about. Between the food, wine and band, my prospects for an enjoyable evening were looking up.

I was midway through the Napa Cab bottle, toying around with different sensory references to impress my nonexistent Vivino followership. Smoked wood, dark chocolate and black cherry were all I had at the time, but I was making progress. The waiter removed the scant remnants of my steak dinner and the band started up a new set with the song "Hotel California" from the Eagles. The music got me thinking of hotels, which reminded me of Frank Belonus, the General Manager at the Apple Inn. Frank was hiding something. He didn't seem like the type to go into business with Somali gang bangers, but it was clear he didn't want anyone looking too closely at his operation.

David was up already; it was early morning in Scotland. I called and reminded him that I was on a short leash from Mike. David was already aware of my plan to hand off the suspect list to Nashville PD in the morning and fly out in the afternoon. I told him it was time to get more aggressive. I asked him to send me Frank's home address. When I received the reply a few minutes later, I messaged for some background on Frank's living situation. Turns out, Frank's divorced and lives alone in a small townhouse on the outskirts of Nashville.

I ordered a double espresso while I pulled up Frank's housing complex on my iPhone. He lived in a middle-class suburban neighborhood with nice lawns and parks. It wasn't the kind of place that would require excessive security precautions. I paid the bill and headed back to the hotel to get my car.

It was almost 2 a.m. when I parked in front of Frank's townhouse. A motion sensor turned on a light that was mounted on the garage roof as I walked to the front door. I rang the doorbell and a dog began to bark. It was the yappy bark of a small dog. I waited fifteen seconds and rang the doorbell again. The porch light came on and I saw a shadow behind the window curtain next to the door. I removed my Department of Homeland Security credentials and put them in front of the peephole. The door opened a few inches to the limit of the chain lock.

"Do you know what time it is?" Frank said through the narrow opening.

"The law never sleeps. I have more questions," I said.

"I'm going to submit a complaint to your supervisor, this is harassment. Come back in the morning."

"It will only take a minute."

"No. I'm calling the police."

I drove my shoulder into the door. The chain lock snapped, and the door crashed into Frank, knocking the portly hotel manager flat onto his back. An orange and white sheltie ran up the stairs, barking madly as it retreated; clearly not the bravest of beasts. Frank started to get up. I leaned down and jabbed him in the nose with a quick left, which sent him flat again. I closed the door and dragged Frank by the collar of his bathrobe around the corner into a small kitchen. I sat a stunned Frank at the kitchen table. A trickle of blood was leaking from his nose and I tossed him a dish towel to stem the flow.

"Who are you?" he asked.

"We need to be reasonable about this. The veins in your neck are bulging, you're gasping for breath, your face is beet red. You're in terrible shape. You look like you're about to have a heart attack. You're clearly no fighter. And me, well, I kill terrorists for a living. And right now, based on all of the information I have, you're on the side with the terrorists," I said.

"What are you talking about?"

"Some problems are too serious for you to talk yourself out of. You're linked to Al Shabab, one of the worst Al Qaeda affiliates in the world. If you don't explain what the heck you've been up to, I am going to hit you another twenty or thirty times and then if you still don't talk, you're going to find yourself renditioned, wearing an orange jumpsuit in a prison cell at a black site in a remote third world country ending with 'stan', where you can expect to be interrogated daily by a sadist from the former Soviet Union. So, how about you tell me how those Somali gang bangers got into one of your hotel rooms without ever registering," I said.

Frank's facial expression was a mixture of fear and desperation.

"I rent rooms sometimes for pocket money. I had no idea they were going to bring in a girl and rape her."

"I'm not interested in your side hustle. I need to know everything about who you gave the room keys to."

"I didn't rent the room to any of the guys who were in the photo you showed me. Once or twice a week, I rent a room to the same guy. He's a Somali, an older man who pays me in cash."

"Did he tell you why he needs the room?"

"No, and he's not always the person who uses the room."

"He's the one who gave the rapists the room key."

"He must have."

"What's his name and where do I find him?"

"His name is Hodar. I don't know his last name and I don't know where he lives."

"How does he contact you?"

"He calls me on my cell."

"Let's start with his number."

"Can I get up?"

"Go ahead."

"My phone's upstairs in my bedroom."

I gestured for him to move, and Frank got out of the chair and headed up the stairs. I followed. I grabbed him by the back of the neck as he was entering the bedroom. He had a surprisingly skinny neck for fat guy.

"Where do you keep your guns?" I asked.

"What guns?"

I squeezed his neck hard.

"In the safe in my closet," he choked out.

"Okay, first open the safe. I'm going to need to relieve you of your weapons."

"How did you know I had a gun?" he asked.

"This is Tennessee, right?"

He opened a sliding closet door and spun the combo on a small safe. He handed me a box. I opened it and inside was a 1911 Colt .45. It was stainless steel with a customized grip and sight. I could tell by the heft it was loaded, I dropped the magazine out of the well. I pulled back the slide and a round ejected. I reached across my body and snagged the round in the air with my left hand before it landed.

Frank showed me the contact number for Hodar on his cell. I texted the number to David and asked him to find the location and owner the phone.

"Why does this guy named Hodar rent the room in cash?" I asked.

"I don't know. Most of the guys I rent to use the rooms for meetings they don't want their wives to know about," he said.

"How many other guys pay you cash on the side for rooms?"

"Five to ten every month."

"Don't the people at the front desk suspect?"

"I give the guy who works the night shift a cut, plus I have a lot over him. He's not a problem."

"How much does this side hustle of yours pay each month?" I asked.

"Four, sometimes five hundred dollars. People who pay cash pay higher rates."

"The privacy must be worth it."

"Must be," he said.

"Just in case, give me the numbers for the rest of the guys on the cash plan." It took several minutes for me to transfer the contacts to my phone.

My cell phone vibrated with an incoming message. I read it.

"Time for me to go. If you haven't figured out already, your phone calls and texts are being monitored. Don't contact Hodar. If you do, then your status is going to change from witless thieving stooge to terrorist accomplice and I'll be coming back to pay you a visit. Understand?" I said.

"Yes."

"I'm going to need some extra rounds for this .45, where do you keep your ammo?"

Armed with two additional nine round mags, I got into the truck and headed out.

I drove to Louise Drive in South Nashville. It's a multizoned area near the railroad tracks with small unattached homes, retail and industrial buildings. If the restaurants in the vicinity were any indication, the population was a mix of ethnicities. White Castle burger, Gojo's Somali Café and Pedro's Mexican were all within a stone's throw of each other. I parked in a dark lot next to a furniture store. I checked my phone and oriented my location to where David Forrest pinpointed Hodar's phone. I committed the image David sent me of Hodar's face to memory and got out of my truck.

Hodar lived on a side street, perpendicular off the main drag. The street was quiet and there was no traffic. The area was dark with only a single street light at the intersection to the main drag, on the opposite end of the street where Hodar lived. I found the house David gave me. It was a tiny single-story house. The kind I've heard referred to as shotgun homes in the south, because you can shoot someone with a shotgun in the back door from a firing position at the front door. I'd guess the size at nine hundred square feet with at most three or four rooms. I hopped the short chain-link fence surrounding the lot and walked into the yard. A late model fully loaded Toyota Land Cruiser was parked in the driveway. The truck was worth more than the house. I walked around the place. Shades were pulled down on all of the windows and I couldn't hear anything from inside. After a complete walk around, I moved to the back door. I removed my lock picking kit and went to work. It took only a few seconds to open the door.

I slid the .45 out of my back waistband with my right hand and pushed the door in with my left. The kitchen was dark. I could hear the hum of a refrigerator and see a small table setting with only two chairs. I left the kitchen and entered a small hallway and then moved into the living room. To my left was a closed door, which had to be the lone bedroom. I approached the door and reached for the door knob.

As I touched the doorknob, the door exploded toward me. I dropped to the ground as a second shotgun blast blew a hole in the door at waist level. While on my side, I raised my pistol and fired three shots blindly through the lower shotgun hole and then rolled across the door threshold to the other side. Another shotgun blast ripped through the wall next to the door where I'd just been lying. I pivoted on my knees back to the door and, looking this time, fired a shot through the bottom shotgun hole at a pair of legs. I watched a man drop and I jumped up and crashed through what was left of the door into the room. A shotgun blast fired high above me into the ceiling. I closed on the wounded man before he could pump another round into the chamber.

The man was fumbling with the shotgun, trying to rack another round while lying flat on his back. I stepped hard on the gun and drove it into his face. Then I dropped all 220 pounds of my body weight onto his abdomen. The impact of my knees connecting with his solar plexus took the fight out of him. I pulled the shotgun out of his hands as I stood back up. The man was barely conscious, and his right leg was bleeding badly. I fixed a tourniquet with his belt and threw the man onto my left shoulder. He didn't weigh more than 130 pounds. I ran out the back door and hopped the fence. Lights were coming on and dogs were barking at the neighboring homes. I stayed in the woods behind the houses until I reached the end of the street and then I crossed to the parking lot where I'd left my truck.

I pushed the man into the front seat and pulled onto the road. I could hear sirens as I took off down the road. I drove South on I-65 to Radnor State Park and parked in the lot near the lake under a streetlight. The man had begun to stir a few minutes earlier and I silenced him with hard right jab to the side of his face. I dragged the man out of the passenger seat and laid him on the parking lot asphalt. The bullet had hit him in the right leg, just below the knee. It tore through bone, which is sheer agony. The bleeding had stopped with the help of the tourniquet, but he was shivering and clearly in shock.

"You need to get to a hospital," I said.

"Don't kill me," he said, shaking from the shock-induced hypothermia.

"I want to take you to the hospital, but first I need some information."

"Okay."

I showed him the image taken from the rape video.

"I'm looking for this girl. Where is she?" I asked.

"She's gone."

"Gone where?"

"I don't know."

I kicked the man's bullet wound. He screamed.

"Let's back up. What's the girl's name?"

"Becky."

"Becky what?"

"I don't know."

"Where's she from?"

"Maine, somewhere in Maine."

"Is she a runaway?"

"She was taken and brought to Nashville."

"By who?"

"Lady Outlaws."

"What are they?"

"A gang, they sell prostitutes."

"Becky from Maine is a prostitute."

"Yes."

"Where's Becky now?"

"I don't know, I told you."

I hit the man again.

"Look, I'm growing tired of this. You know I'm trying to find this girl. You'll tell me everything I need to know to find out why this girl is in Nashville, who she's with and where I can find her, or I'm going to put a .45 hollow point through your skull. Is that clear?"

The man became noticeably more lucid. He looked at me with his face twisted in pain. What he saw told him clearly, I wasn't bluffing.

"The girl was taken by the Lady Outlaws. She was property of Somali Outlaws and brought to Nashville to work. I set up a meeting between Somali Outlaws and Somali Mafia at the Apple Inn. The Mafia bought the girl from the Outlaws and took her away. That's what was happening in the picture you showed me that was taken at the hotel."

"These men in the picture, who are they with, Outlaws or Mafia?"

"Those boys are local, they're Outlaws. They from around here."

"What about the people who have Becky now. How do I find them?"

"I don't know."

"What is it you do exactly? Why do the gangs come to you to set up meetings?"

"They pay me to help out once in a while. That's all."

"You're not the local gang boss or anything like that?"

"No, I just help out, earn some extra money."

"Well let's start with your contact in the Somali Mafia and then we'll get to these five guys in the picture," I said.

Hodar told me the names of the five suspects. He didn't seem sufficiently frightened of retribution. He also gave me the name and a phone number of the person he claimed was his contact in the Somali Mafia, a guy named Abdulkadir. It was an Ohio number. I took his cheap Nokia phone. I wasn't positive, but I had a strong feeling that Hodar was more than he was letting on. I wasn't completely certain Hodar was lying about who he was, but I figured better safe than sorry. Before I left, I shot Hodar in the head.

I sent a text to Detective Deforest: *I'm leaving this morning. Our analyst came up with the names of the five assailants. All live in Nashville.* I listed the names. The video would be enough to convict them, hopefully the names and pictures would be enough to find them. It would have been nice to hunt the attackers, but I was more interested in getting the girl.

CHAPTER 7

COLUMBUS, OHIO

I ROLLED INTO COLUMBUS, Ohio feeling tired. I'd been driving for six hours and it was coming up on noon. I decided to rest before doing anything else. I took a room at the Renaissance in Downtown and unpacked. My jet lag was an advantage, because it kept me alert into the wee hours. As a self-designated crime fighter, my prey was nocturnal, and I was already adapted. Before crashing I called David.

"What do you have for me on Abdulkadir?"

"For starters, he has two prior arrests. Pandering and robbery."

"He's been to prison."

"He served two years on the armed robbery charge in the state penitentiary."

"Did you send me his picture and background info?"

"I will, I'm almost done with the work-up. I'll send it once it's finished."

"Is he going to be hard to find?"

"No, not unless he's employing a ruse. I have good location data on his phone."

"What about the girl?"

"No luck so far. If they're advertising her, they're either not using her picture or they're advertising outside of the usual media for that sort of thing."

"I'm going to get some rest. Tonight, I'll visit Abdulkadir and ask him about Becky. Did you find her full name by the way?"

"Yes, Rebecca Anderson from Orono, Maine. Last seen at a pizzeria with a black girl of about the same age. I tracked the Facebook messages between Becky and her likely abductor. She was catfished by the Somali Lady Outlaws from the looks of it."

"If things go right, I'll get her back tonight. I'll be in touch in about five hours, after I get a nap and review what you're going to send me."

"You may want to consider bringing in the rest of the team, Pat."

"Why?"

"Abdulkadir has two convictions and he's been a suspect in several murders. The police came close to charging him once, but the witness disappeared. He's a violent gangster, he's going to be armed and I don't expect you'll be able to get him alone to interrogate him."

"That's good advice. Well intended, I'm sure. I'd rather not get any of the other guys in trouble with the government. What I'm planning to do tonight is going to stretch my charter a little bit."

"What you did yesterday did more than stretch it."

"Frank gave me Hodar. Hodar gave me Abdulkadir. Abdulkadir will give me Becky. I have no regrets."

"They found Hodar's body only an hour ago. The case has gone Federal."

"Why, he claimed to be a gofer for a two-bit gang? The FBI didn't lift a finger to find Becky and that was kidnapping, a major Federal crime."

"I don't know why. I saw a communication from DC to the Nashville FBI office approving the request. I thought you should know."

"Keep an eye on that. Maybe the FBI was using him as an informant."

"If he was part of an ongoing investigation, I don't believe the FBI Headquarters would have to give approval, the local office would automatically pick up the case. This is something else."

"Let me know when you figure out what that something else is, I'm hitting the rack."

I woke up hungry. It was almost midnight. Columbus doesn't compare to Nashville when it comes to late night dining opportunities. I decided to have a walk around and figure out my options. I threw on a leather jacket and a Red Sox cap and headed out. Once outside the lobby door, I turned left and saw a street sign that said Gay Street. I'm old enough to remember when that word meant happy. I'd never been to Columbus before and the city is a lot nicer than I expected it to be. I spend eleven months a year outside of the US and most of what I read in the media about the Midwest are stories of decay and despair. Columbus is neither. The streets are clean, the buildings are stately old brick and even in the cold of an early spring night, the potential beauty of the tree-lined streets is evident. It had a Norman Rockwell feel to it, no signs of decay and despair anywhere to be found.

I walked past a Steakhouse that was already closed for the night. The next place had a sign that said Tip Top Kitchen and Cocktails. It was a classic hole in the wall, but it was open, and I was hungry. I walked into the dingy bar area and was greeted by a friendly sandy-haired bartender wearing a Geeklycon T-shirt. Her name tag said Jenny.

"Is the kitchen open?" I asked.

"Do you want to eat at a table or at the bar?"

"I'll take a table."

Another young college-aged girl appeared and showed me to a table. The place was small, a bit on the quirky side and surprisingly busy. She sat me at a booth with the view of a red brick wall covered with pictures. The ornate metal lamp on the table must have been a hundred years old. If nothing else, Tip Top had character. The menu was classic American fare. I ordered the pot roast and a pint of a local craft beer that was called Jackie O' Mystic Manna IPA. When it comes to names, sometimes craft breweries try too hard.

I don't think I've had pot roast in a decade, and I don't know if it was the cold night or the homey atmosphere of the restaurant, but it was fantastic. I ordered a second Jackie O' and called David.

"Did I wake you up?" I asked.

"No, you said you'd be calling around midnight. I've been waiting for you." There was a sense of fatigue in his Scottish accent.

"Where's our guy?"

"He's in Westerville. Where are you?"

"I'm still downtown near my hotel. How far is Westerville from here?"

"It's fifteen minutes. I'll send you an address."

"Okay, let me know if he moves. Is he alone?"

"I'm getting his location by pinging his cell phone. He's

not in a good part of town and there are several bars close by. He's not alone," David said.

"How do you know?"

"I'm listening to the audio from his cell phone and I can hear three different voices."

"Neat trick, are you doing that with the Israeli software you were telling me about?"

"Pegasus is the name."

"What are they saying?" I asked.

"I can't speak Somali and they're talking too fast and on top of each other, which is making the computer translation unintelligible."

"What about the camera?"

"Phone must be in his pocket, there's no video."

I pulled into a parking lot beside a strip mall. Norman Rockwell's serene downtown was behind me and I was now in a rundown African ghetto. I parked in front of the Maverick Drive Thru Beverage Store. I got out and walked past the Suuqa Halal Market toward a restaurant bar called African Paradise. It was a small restaurant, painted lime green on the outside with no windows and only a single door. It was squeezed in between the EZ Pawn Shop and a Loan Max Title Loan Office.

The black windowless door looked too formidable to knock in and too difficult to pick. The hours posted beside the door showed the restaurant closed at 11 p.m. I put my ear to the door and called Dave.

"Are you sure he's in the African Paradise? Sign says it's closed and I don't hear anything from inside."

"His phone is there, and I can still hear conversation. I believe he's inside somewhere, you just need to find him."

I backed off the door and looked upward. It was a two-story building and the second floor had a small balcony. I decided that was a better way to enter. I walked to the end of the strip mall. Around the corner, I found an aluminum drainage pipe that offered a couple of decent footholds. I shimmied up the pipe and onto the roof. I walked along the top of the flat roof until I was above African Paradise. Then I hung from the gutter and swung myself onto the balcony rail and stepped down onto the balcony floor.

The door to the balcony was locked. I picked the lock and slowly opened the door into a dark office. I withdrew the Colt .45 from my waistband and cautiously entered the hallway. I heard a man's voice coming from downstairs. I made my way to the stairwell in the dark and crept down slowly. When I got to the bottom of the stairs, the voices became more distinct. It was as David described, three men doing the talking. I don't know why I wasn't able to hear them while I was outside the building, unless the exterior walls and door were seriously soundproofed. The men were loud and relaxed, it sounded like they were playing a game in the main dining room of the restaurant. The room was dimly lit. I had a picture of Abdulkadir, but given the light, I wasn't going to be able to recognize him easily. I decided to take my chances. I silently and slowly unmasked myself to the men in the room as I circled around the entryway from the hallway in a pie maneuver. The three men were seated around a table and in the faint light I could finally see they were playing dominos.

The first man to see me was a heavy-set bald man. He was the only man at the table seated in a direction that was facing me. He looked up from his dominos and immediately his right hand came off the table top. I shot him square in the face from a weaver stance ten feet away. The heavy caliber bullet snapped his head back and sprayed the two men sitting across from him with blood.

"Put your hands on the table and don't do anything stupid unless you want to wind up like your buddy," I said.

The men had to turn to see me. Both men in the poor light looked alike and I didn't have a direct view of their faces. They were both strongly built black men with Taliban-style beards. One turned his body to glare at me. The second man kept his back to me and focused his attention on the first man. I took two steps closer to the table and shot the second man at arm's reach. When the first man, the one who had been looking at me, turned to check on his nearly headless friend slumped across the table, I pistol whipped him. I flex cuffed the man as soon as he hit the floor and then I dragged him by his arms out of the African Paradise to my waiting vehicle. We drove to a golf course parking lot that I came across about half a mile down the street. I waited for the man to regain consciousness. It took a full twenty minutes. The 1911 Colt .45 pistol has the perfect weight and balance for pistol whipping, so I'd hit the guy harder than I'd wanted to. Next time I'd be more careful.

"What's your name?" I asked

"I'm not gonna tell you nothing. You gonna kill me anyway."

"I'm not asking you to trust me, but I do expect you to give yourself the best chance for survival. Don't answer my questions, you'll definitely die, one hundred percent guaranteed, no doubt about. Answer my questions and I'll let you go. I'm not after you, only what you know."

"I don't believe you. You just killed two men. Bro, I need a guarantee."

"I only shot your friends because they were drawing on me. It was self-defense. I need information. I'm a recovery specialist after a bounty. This is my business. If you help me, I'll repay you by letting you go."

"No way, I don't believe that."

"You don't have too many choices here. Make up your mind. Cooperate or die, you have thirty seconds."

I opened my door and got out. He was in the passenger side of the truck with his hands painfully bound behind him and his ankles flex tied together. I grabbed him by the ankles and yanked him out of the SUV. His back hit the parking lot with a flat smacking sound and then I heard his head bounce off the asphalt a second later.

I raised my pistol and aimed it at his right knee.

"Don't. Don't. I'll help you. My name is Abdulkadir."

I took out my phone and showed him a picture of Becky. Not the image of her being raped in Nashville, but a shot David had pulled off her Facebook page.

"Take me to her," I said.

"I don't know where she is," he said with a look of desperation in his eyes.

"You can find her."

"I need my phone."

I stepped on his throat and pulled the phone out of his right front pants pocket. He gave me the passcode and I opened the phone. I showed him the recent calls.

"Which one?"

"Aziz, call Aziz."

"You ask where the girl is, that's all. Once you get the location, I'll end the call," I said.

I called David. "I'm going to dial a number on Abdulkadir's phone. You need to record the conversation and get it translated before I make my next move."

"No problem with the translation. I just can't do it reliably in real time or when more than one person is talking," David said.

"Once you translate and confirm her location, I'll move. Also track Aziz's location. Okay, here we go," I said.

I dialed the number and the two men talked in Somali for several minutes. Abdulkadir signaled me with a head nod to terminate the call as I was holding the phone to his ear.

"Where is she?" I asked.

"She's working at the Day's Inn on Cleveland Ave."

"What's the room number?"

"216."

I called David. "Can you confirm room 216 at the Day's Inn on Cleveland?"

"Yes. That's what Aziz said."

"Is Aziz at that location?"

"Yes."

"I'm going to the Day's Inn."

I double tapped Abdulkadir before getting back into my car. As I stood over him with my pistol drawn, he was genuinely aggrieved that I'd lied to him about letting him go. I shook my head in amazement that a guy could be a kidnapper, human trafficker, pimp and slave owner and yet manage to be morally outraged when confronted with a lie.

The Day's Inn wasn't in the Somali section of Columbia. It was on the boundary between the nice part of the city and

Westerville. David had translated the call between Abdulkadir and Aziz but wasn't sure if Abdulkadir had warned Aziz. David said they may have had a panic word that he was unaware of. In situations like this, my philosophy is to rely on the principles of a raid, which are surprise, speed and violence of action. I drove fast to the hotel, parked in the front and ran up the exterior stairs to the second floor. When I arrived at the outside of room 216, the lights behind the heavy curtains were out.

The door didn't look very solid. I drew my trusty .45, took two steps back and kicked the door off its hinges with a running straight kick. A big body jumped up off the queen bed. The guy was in the shadows and he was moving fast. Still in the doorway, I fired two shots at the silhouette. The first round hit him in the chest. The second bullet caught him in the side of the head. He tumbled off the far side of the bed. A figure lay crumpled under the covers in the fetal position.

"If you're Becky Anderson, I'm here to take you home," I said.

A blonde head poked out at the top of the bed.

"Get dressed, we need to run," I said.

I was about to enter the room when I heard a door open off to my right. I dropped to a knee and spun as bullets whizzed over my head. I placed Frank's match quality knife sight onto the shooter's upper body and fired two well aimed rounds into his chest. When I jumped up and ran to the gunman, he was barely conscious.

"Are you Aziz?" I asked.

"Help me."

"Are you Aziz?"

"Yes."

"Who's the guy in the other room?"

"Customer."

I did a quick search of Aziz's hotel room and found there was no one else there. Then I went back to room 216 and collected Becky, who'd gotten dressed and was sitting on the side of the bed.

Minutes later Becky and I were speeding toward Highway 70 East on our way to Pittsburgh. I chose Pittsburgh as our destination, because I figured the police were probably not too far behind and I needed some drive time to arrange a charter to fly Becky to Bangor, Maine. She sat stoically with her arms folded across her chest for most of the trip. Eventually, on the outskirts of Pittsburgh, I managed to gain enough trust from the girl that she seemed willing to accept that I wasn't from a rival gang abducting her. We stopped at a mall when it opened, and I got her some decent clothes and shoes. We made it to the private terminal thirty minutes before planned take off. I gave her my cell and she called her mom. When her mother answered, she choked up and couldn't talk, she only sobbed, so she gave the phone to me. I explained to her mother that I was a US Agent and that we'd found her daughter. I told her that a charter would land in Bangor at 1:15 and that she should be there to meet her daughter. The mother was a mess. It was a thin story, but she wasn't in a state of mind to ask any questions. I walked Becky to the plane and wished her well. She looked at me with distant eyes, betraying no emotion.

"I'm really sorry this happened to you," was all I could think to say.

"Thank you," was all she said.

CHAPTER 8

PITTSBURGH, PENNSYLVANIA

AFTER SENDING BECKY off on her way home, I pulled onto Highway 76 and headed toward Harrisburg. I called the rental car company and arranged to dump off my Nashville rental at the Harrisburg airport. I booked a charter flight to Seattle, using a different name and credit card than the one I flew in with and just used for Becky. The light traffic and rolling hills of Western Pennsylvania made for a relaxing drive, which was a much appreciated departure from the intensity of the past two days. I was surfing radio stations when Mike Guthrie called.

"Are you out of your freaking mind? What did I tell you?"

I knew exactly what he told me, but I couldn't resist messing with him. "About what," I asked, "give me some context?"

"You know exactly what I'm talking about."

"I have no idea why your panties are all bunched up."

"Remember our last conversation, when you promised to get the info on the attackers and pass it to the Nashville PD and then get out of town," Mike said.

"Yes, and that's exactly what I did. I left Nashville the same night I got the info and I passed it onto the Nashville PD," I said.

"And then you proceeded to go on a multi-state murder spree. The FBI is looking for you."

"What do they want with me?" I asked.

"They're looking for the person who killed Hodar and Frank Belonus. Agent McDermott, Special Agent from the Department of Homeland Security, is a person of interest, because he's apparently the last person to see Frank Belonus, at least according to Frank's security system that captured an image of Agent McDermott kicking in his front door the night he died," Mike said.

"Frank was killed that same night?" I said in a surprised tone.

"Yes," Mike said.

"I didn't kill him. The FBI should watch the rest of the video footage, someone else must have visited Frank after I left."

"Maybe that's why you're a person of interest and not a murder suspect. Either way, they're looking into your Homeland cover and that's going to lead them right to the Agency's doorstep. When that happens, we're going to have a full-blown crisis on our hands," Mike said.

"I'm not going to apologize for rescuing an innocent girl the FBI couldn't be troubled to find. Tell them I went rogue, which you've already established is what happened," I said.

"This is DC politics, Congressional oversight and the violations of some very specific laws governing where the agency can and cannot operate. The problem is much bigger than you. We need to meet, where are you now?" Mike asked.

"About an hour northeast of Pittsburgh, heading to Harrisburg to grab a flight to Seattle," I said.

"Seattle?"

"Red Sox opener tonight, Chris Sale's on the mound. I'm excited. I have high hopes for this season," I said.

"Divert your flight to Eleuthera. We need you out of the country ASAP. I'll meet you there and we'll figure this out."

"What's to figure out?" I asked.

"We're missing something. Why the FBI involvement after Hodar's murder? How was the connection between the death of Hodar and the death of Frank made so quickly? Something is off on this," Mike said.

"Okay. See you at Governor's Harbor."

I drove in silence for a few minutes, then I called Grace Deforest.

"Detective, how've you been?" I said.

"I've been trying to reach you. So has the FBI," Grace replied.

"Sorry, I've been busy. Did you arrest those rapists yet?" I asked.

"Three of them so far, two are on the run, but we'll get them."

"You'll be happy to know that Becky Anderson is landing in Bangor, Maine in a few minutes," I said.

"Who is Becky Anderson?" Grace asked.

"That's the name of the girl that was attacked in the video taken from the Somali Al Shabab leader," I said.

"How did you find her?"

"Good solid police work by your partners in the Federal Government," I said.

"The agents here from the local FBI office don't seem to

feel the same way about you. They're not sharing everything with me, but they're definitely working with their management to force you back to Nashville for an interview," Grace said.

"I'd love to talk with them, it's just that I've been busy working on a more urgent matter. Being a crime stopper is taxing business. I'll be back in Nashville just as soon as I can to help those G-men out," I said.

"You need to get here fast."

"That's not going to be possible, at least for a while. Maybe I can just shoot them an email? What do they want to say to me anyway? I doubt they're going to apologize for rolling over on the Becky Anderson investigation."

"I've already told you more than I should. You need to return to Nashville and present yourself as soon as possible."

"I'll let my bosses make that decision, Detective. You know I'm just a foot soldier following orders."

"FBI and DHS don't get along very well, do they?"

"Interagency politics are not my specialty. Do you have any leads on the other two perps? I hope while you're watching the sideshow of federal agency follies, you're not taking your eye off the ball," I said.

"No, I haven't, but same as you I've been busy. We've had two murders recently."

"That's terrible."

"One of the deaths was Frank Belonus, the manager at the Apple Inn."

"Oh yeah, the guy who didn't want me borrowing the security camera footage."

"That's the guy. He was killed that same night."

"How'd he die?"

"Blunt force trauma to the head. He was beaten repeatedly by a pipe or something similar, he had a lot of broken bones and they weren't defensive. He was restrained and beaten," Grace said.

"That's grizzly. Where did it happen?"

"We don't know, his body was found on the side of a road in a ditch."

"I told you I thought he was hiding something. He didn't appear to have the skills to be working with gangsters. It was only a matter of time before it caught up with him."

"Very true, if that's who killed him. The investigation is still ongoing. The FBI has taken over the case. I'll look forward to seeing you soon in Nashville," she said.

"Absolutely, it will be great to catch up. Maybe we can have dinner."

"Goodbye, Agent."

I ended the call. I asked her to dinner, and she said "Goodbye, Agent", which is not *no*. I think Grace is warming to me. Nice to know I haven't lost my charm with the ladies.

CHAPTER 9

ELEUTHERA, BAHAMAS

I STOOD ON THE beach with a small six-and-a-half-foot surfboard tucked under my arm. The conditions weren't good. Swells of up to a meter, only eight seconds apart with a steady twenty knot offshore wind that was knocking them down early. I decided to make the best of it and jumped in.

I sat up on the board, past the break. I balanced my bulk on top of the little board, keeping it submerged about a foot below the water. The sky was partially cloudy, the temperature was eighty-six degrees and the water temperature was about the same. I could see the third floor of the house above the line of coconut palms bordering the beach. The rest of the beach was empty. The homes on this section of Banks Road aren't vacation rentals, they're estates that except for permanent household staff remain unoccupied most of the year. It makes for a fairly deserted stretch of paradise. The pinkish hue of the beach against the swaying palms was postcard perfect.

I picked out an incoming swell and cheated in toward the break. The shorter board was slow, and I paddled hard to get into position. When I felt the board rise behind me, I popped up and dropped into the wave. I shifted my weight forward and bent down, grabbing the board with my right hand as I cut left to stay ahead of the breaking wave. I managed a couple of short turns and then I bailed. It was low tide and I turned one hundred and eighty degrees to escape from being driven into the jagged edges of the coral that have cost me too much skin over the years. I flopped onto my board and began to paddle back to the break.

When I got back out past the whitewater, I sat up and rested my arms. It never ceases to amaze me how a five second paddle sprint, a ten second ride and a sixty second paddle through the surf can be so exhausting. I don't think there's any better way to work out and have fun at the same time. I stayed out in the ocean until I reached that familiar point of fatigue, where I could no longer generate the power necessary to catch an oncoming wave. I paddled in and called it a day.

With my board under my arm, I walked the path through the undergrowth between the beach and my home. The house has an infinity pool that looks out at the ocean through the palms. I've never used the pool, I'm not sure if anyone has, but it does look nice. On either side of the pool are pink stucco buildings. The building on the left is a guest house with two apartments. The guest house is home to my year-round tenants, Father Tellez with his sister, and the Filipino couple who maintain the property for me, Jonah and Maria. I headed across to the opposite building that was originally just a pool house and now is a pool house with an attached chapel. I rinsed the salt water off my board and then off myself using the shower attached to the outside wall.

Inside the pool house, I put my board on the wall next to what was becoming a pretty good collection of surfboards.

I walked along the patio tiles that made up the pool deck, toward the house. It's a picturesque back yard, with the pool, the acres of green lawn, the pink, white, yellow and purple flowers growing along the walls of the outbuildings and the surrounding palm trees. On the second-floor deck, I could see Mike and Father Tellez sitting down drinking what I assumed is Columbian Coffee, which is always a given wherever Father Tellez is concerned.

Maria brought me a bottle of Sam Adams as I sat down around the deck table with Mike and Father Tellez.

"Are you guys hungry?" Without waiting for an answer, I asked Maria to bring us some sandwiches. Surfing generates a hunger.

"I was just telling Father Tellez how you rescued Becky Anderson," Mike said.

"Any idea how she's doing?" I asked.

"We haven't had any direct contact. The story of her kidnapping and rescue made news in Maine and was picked up nationally."

"Have any details come out on her ordeal?" I asked.

"No, her family is protecting her. She hasn't given any interviews and neither has her family."

"What's happening on the Federal law enforcement front?"

"The FBI was given credit for the rescue. The problem was solved Director to Director between the Agency and FBI. The FBI in Ohio isn't going to be working too hard on finding out who rescued her."

"What's the FBI telling the public?" I asked.

"The usual, they were brilliant, heroic and saved the day," Mike said.

"That's one problem solved," I said.

"It is, but that still leaves us with the murders of Belonus and Hodar, both of which are being investigated by the FBI in Nashville," Mike said.

"I'm also interested in finding out who killed Belonus," I said.

"You're a person of interest in both killings. Which is why you need to disappear for a while," he said.

"The Nashville FBI office wants to interview me, that's not going to go away unless they catch Belonus' killer," I said.

"It may not go away even if they do catch his killer. Hodar's investigation is another matter entirely," Mike said.

"Do you know why that's an FBI matter?" I asked.

"No."

"David Forrest said the Nashville office was given approval to investigate from the Hoover building. I think that means the local office requested it," I said.

"The man was a criminal; he could be connected to another case."

"If he is, the case must not've involved the Nashville FBI office, otherwise they wouldn't have needed approval from HQ, according to David," I said.

"That's interesting."

"You should look into that."

"We're not going to look into anything from here on. We're in damage control mode. Your activities in Ohio are sufficiently suppressed. Nashville is a different matter. The arrest and trial of the Somali gang should consume all of the media attention. The existence of Agent McDermott just needs to fade away and eventually be forgotten," Mike said.

"Do you think that will happen?" I asked.

"The Director is counting on it. Only a few people within the Agency know what you did. The FBI Director was told that one of our contractors freed the girl. He doesn't know your name. He knows it wasn't a sanctioned Agency operation. The FBI is promoting the story that one of their undercover organized crime agents rescued the girl and for security reasons his identity must remain anonymous. The game plan is to tamp everything down and let the criminal justice system handle the rest."

"I'm good with that. I'll just continue to surf and chill in Eleuthera."

"No. I need to talk to you alone about a new task that should distract you for a while. Excuse us, Father," Mike said to Father Tellez as he stood to lead me up to my office on the third floor where we could speak in private.

CHAPTER 10

ABU DHABI, UNITED ARAB EMIRATES

FROM MY SEAT in the first-class section of the Airbus 380, I looked over the black waters of the Arabian Gulf. The Etihad flight from JFK had been in the air a little over fourteen hours and was on its approach to Abu Dhabi Airport. The only lights below were the occasional offshore oil platform. I had slept for most of the flight and for the last two hours, I'd been working on a decent Bordeaux the nice flight attendant kept my wine glass refilled with.

We finally reached land and the illuminated straight lines and clean geometric patterns of the road features below came into view on the flat desert floor. Air traffic control must have sent us into a holding pattern because instead of landing we orbited around the Abu Dhabi skyline. The first landmarks I picked up were the three curving blue Itihad towers and the gleaming white magnificence of the Presidential Palace and Emirates Palace Hotel nearby. We flew parallel to the beach road, which is called the Corniche in Abu Dhabi. I couldn't see the towers lined along the Corniche, because my window faced out to the Gulf and the scattered islands. I felt the plane bank right and saw the dense cluster of tall buildings on man-made Reem Island. Next came the lights of the Yas Marina, the Formula One Track and the cluster of adjacent hotels that make up the Yas Marina Complex. Finally, we banked right again and made our final approach into Abu Dhabi Airport.

The trip through passport control took less than a minute, the E-Gate system in Abu Dhabi is a modern miracle. My only luggage was a carry-on suitcase and a shopping bag which thankfully allowed me to skip baggage claim. I entered the premium lounge and Etihad had a car and driver waiting for me by the time I exited the lounge and the terminal onto the outside sidewalk.

The *Wayward Nomad* was tied up at the Intercontinental Marina in the Corniche area of Abu Dhabi. The team— McDonald, Migos, Savage and Rodriguez—sailed the boat from Cyprus to the Emirates and were all staying at the Intercontinental Hotel. It was forty-five minutes before the Mercedes sedan pulled into the Fish Market Restaurant parking lot. I spotted the *Nomad* right away; it was lit up and its clean racy lines outclassed every other boat in the marina. The Intercontinental Marina is shaped in a circle with a diameter of about two hundred yards. From above, the marina looks like a clock, with the slips at the perimeter appearing as minute markers. At the base, or the six o'clock, of the circle is the Fish Market Restaurant. At the nine o'clock is the Intercontinental Hotel and its adjacent outside restaurants the Chao Gao and Belgian Café. The twelve o'clock position is where the narrow marina entrance leading to the Arabian Gulf can be found, and at the three o'clock position is the entrance to the Bayshore Beach Club. Next to the entrance is a very nice Lebanese Restaurant, named Byblos. At one hundred feet, the *Nomad* is a full thirty feet too long to fit into the standard marina slip, which is why it wasn't backed into a slip, but was instead tied up lengthwise with its port side against the dock directly across from the entrance of the Bayshore Beach Club.

I tipped the driver and headed over to the *Nomad*. The weather was warm, and I could see a crowd on the top deck. It was a Thursday night, the first night of the weekend in Abu Dhabi. The restaurants were going full tilt and a live band playing at the Belgian Café across the water filled the air with soft rock music.

I waved to Migos as I stepped on board. I left the suitcase on the deck and made my way up the stairs to the flydeck. A group of four guys and three girls were seated around the table behind the flydeck helm station. The ladies were Arab and must have come over after a day at the beach club, because they were still wearing semitransparent bathing suit cover ups. The unique habit Lebanese and other liberal Arab women have of wearing make-up and jewelry with a bikini takes some getting used to. Migos did the introductions.

"Do you want a drink?" Chico Rodriguez asked.

"I'll help myself." I walked over to the bar and surveyed the damage. A bottle of eighteen-year-old MacCallum was open, most likely it was McDonald drinking the Scotch. Chico and Savage were drinking beer and Migos and the ladies were drinking white wine. I looked over and the ladies' wine glasses were filled with ice cubes. Not a big deal, except that genius Migos had pulled an expensive bottle of

Montrachet from the wine cabinet and then drowned the quality vintage with ice water. The man was hopeless. I hoped his Lebanese friends were worth it.

I poured myself a couple of fingers of Scotch.

"What's in the bag?" Migos asked.

"This is McDonald's birthday present," I said.

"It's McDonald's Birthday?"

"It was two days ago; he hit the big forty," I said.

"You're only forty?" asked Migos incredulously.

"How old did you think I was?" asked McDonald.

"You were a Master Chief when you retired as a squid, I figured you had to be at least forty-five," Migos said.

"I enlisted when I was eighteen and retired after twenty, I got promoted fast. You didn't have to get me anything, Pat," McDonald said.

I looked around and noticed everyone's attention was on me, so I began my gift presentation.

"What I have in this bag is the single greatest contribution to men over forty ever invented. This is an auspicious occasion, McDonald. I'm about to induct you into a very special society. It's more than a society, it's an order, a calling for men who've achieved financial success, guys who can buy whatever they want and who think they have everything they need. But before they joined this order, this special society, there was an emptiness. They couldn't understand why with all of their material possessions, they still felt like something was missing. I'm going to give you that missing something. You should wear these proudly, like a badge. A badge not only of achievement, but a badge of comfort. You're now an initiate in this order and I give you the greatest of gifts."

I reached into the bag and retrieved three gift wrapped packages.

"They're all the same, just different colors," I said.

"What are they?" McDonald asked.

"Open 'em up."

McDonald unwrapped the first package.

"Pants.... seriously?"

"Not just pants, McDonald. Those are stretchy pants. Orvis 5 pocket stretch twills to be exact, the holy grail of leisure wear," I said.

"This is a big deal to you, isn't it?"

"Just try them and you'll see. I'm wearing a pair now, just flew fifteen hours and I feel great. After this night, you're going to divide your life into two parts. Before you discovered stretchy pants and after," I said.

McDonald shook his head.

"Thanks, boss," he said with a half-smile.

"Stretchy pants for the over forties. Ladies, it's time to get out of here and find some night life. McDonald and Pat are going to warm up some milk and watch re-runs of the Lawrence Welk show," Migos said.

"Once you're worthy, I'm going to get all of you guys a proper set of stretchy pants. You'll see, this is serious stuff, it's life changing. McDonald, you should make an induction speech. This is a big moment. Migos, why don't you go downstairs and get some champagne so we can raise a glass on this occasion of McDonald's Birthday, the one that all of you forgot. I have a case of Dom down in the galley. And Migos, while you're down there maybe you could find some ice cubes and little umbrellas to go with the champagne," I said.

"I'm on it, boss," Migos said before he ran to the stairs.

"Do you think he caught the jab?" McDonald asked.

"Doubtful. You guys are welcome to raid the liquor cabinet any time you want. But putting ice cubes in a quality wine is too much, it's a desecration, you should've stopped him," I said.

Migos returned and toasts and birthday wishes to McDonald were made. The girls with Migos lost interest and disappeared. We moved the gathering across the marina to the Belgian Café because all of us were hungry. We sat outside at a table with a view of the *Nomad*. I ordered a rack of barbequed leffe-flavored pork ribs and a Delirium Beer. It was good to be back with the team.

"What happened in the States? Did you recover that girl?" Rodriguez asked.

I looked around to make sure nobody was in earshot.

"I did. The girl's been reunited with her family. The attackers have been apprehended and are pending trial. Overall the outcome was good."

"You should've taken us with you," said Savage.

"There's a fair amount of blowback from how I did it. The recovery got a little messy and there's a lot of static coming from Langley about it. It's better for all around that it was a solo rather than an organizational op. It's always easier to explain a rogue individual rather than a unit."

"That makes sense. Are you in any jeopardy?" Savage asked.

"The static will clear. But I've been sent away to prevent any further antagonizing," I said.

"What are we doing here anyway?" Migos asked.

"I'll tell you that tomorrow. Not here," I said looking

around. "Don't think I'm paranoid. Because of my history with them, UAE Intel always keeps a tail on me whenever I'm inside the country."

"This is where it all began, isn't it, boss?" McDonald said.

"What do you mean?" I asked.

"This is where Trident began, isn't it?" McDonald said.

"Kinda, I guess it is. I used to keep my old boat, the *Sam Houston,* in that slip right over there." I pointed to one of the yachts positioned nearest to the restaurant.

"How did you get into this business?" McDonald asked.

"It was an accident. When I retired from the Army, I started a building company. Home construction was going gang busters back then and I was just one of many enjoying the ride. Trident was originally a construction company in North Carolina. Then one day, everything changed. Bear Sterns went belly up, the banks shut down, the stock market crashed, and we had the Great Recession. I found myself unable to make payroll, so to keep from going under, I contracted out in Afghanistan," I said.

"As an operator?" McDonald asked.

"No, just an advisor. But while I was out there, Mike found me. He and I had been platoon leaders together in the Second Ranger Battalion and we'd known each other for a lot of years."

"That's when you started to contract for the Agency?" Savage asked.

"In Afghanistan, I was more of an asset than anything else. I supplied intel. Then, I left A-Stan and moved to Abu Dhabi and took a commercial job with a local company owned by one of the big Sheiks supplying defense items to the UAE Armed Forces."

"What happened to that job?" McDonald asked.

"It was a good position; I was COO of a leading company and we were doing well. So well that I bought a sixty-four-foot Azimuth Yacht and lived right here at the marina for a couple of years. Then one day, I was on the flydeck, drinking beer, watching a ball game and who walks onto my boat, but Mike."

"That's when things got interesting," Migos said.

"Yeah, it was a crazy time in the region. The geniuses in DC had just pulled all of our troops out of Iraq and ISIS was rolling over everybody, lopping off infidel heads and building a caliphate in the Levant."

"That wasn't that long ago," McDonald added.

"No, it wasn't. Anyway, the agency made a deal with the UAE to help with the support of forces that were fighting ISIS. We mostly supplied weapons to the Peshmerga. It had to be done clandestinely, much like how the situation is now in Libya. Congressional approval for the action wasn't possible, so everything was clandestine. I was offered a deal to become a CIA gunrunner and I took it. After that Trident remained a construction company in North Carolina, but it also became a Government Defense Contractor. We moved the headquarters to the Bahamas, we bought a couple of C130Js and we hired aircrews including Migos and Sachse, who are the only two still around from those days. It's been a good run," I said.

"Originally Trident was just in logistics then?" Savage asked.

"We didn't move into the operations business until recently. Logistics is still ninety percent of what we do and it's almost all of our revenue. But as you know, we help out occasionally when needed operationally."

"How long will Trident stay in business?" Rodriguez asked.

"I'd retire tomorrow if they'd let me. But they have a pair of handcuffs on me that I can't break. I'm not going anywhere. Because of what's going on in East Africa, Libya and Syria, we've never been busier on the logistics side. I sold one of the airplanes a while back and now I'm trying to find a replacement, we're that busy," I said.

"Why are we still in UAE?" Migos asked.

"The action is in the Middle East and except for Israel, the UAE is the only sane country in the region. The US partner for the Libyan operation is UAE. The US created the situation when we threw Ghaddafi to the mob. The US got the guy to give up his nuclear program and then after he unarmed himself, we let the poor guy get raped by a bayonet. The situation in Libya is bad and publicly, we can't decide what to do. Officially, the US isn't backing anyone. But on a clandestine level, the executive branch is backing Hafter, which is why we're making the weapons deliveries and not the US Air Force," I said.

"What about operationally?" McDonald asked.

"There are always going to be missions the Agency is unwilling or unable to farm out to the Department of Defense. Organically, the Agency's direct-action operational capability is almost all gone, they deactivated most of the SAD teams ages ago. The advantage of having Trident is just too great. I think they'll try to keep us around forever."

"That's good. Nice to know this is a long-term gig," Rodriguez said.

"It can be, but let's face it, it's not always the safest job," I said.

"Why did you dock the *Nomad* at the INTERCON. Nostalgia?" McDonald said.

"The better marina is at Emirates Palace, but I can't have you guys traipsing in and out of that hotel, it's too conspicuous and has too much security. The other option is Yas Marina, but I don't like the restaurant and entertainment selection," I said.

"We're here because of the restaurants," Savage said.

"Not just the restaurants at this hotel, but we have a good selection in the surrounding area. We also have a great gym, pool, beach club, dive shop and right down the road is the Corniche running trail. Plus, I know this marina like the back of my hand. I lived here for years, I know how to get around the security cameras and how to move things to the yacht surreptitiously. You'll understand why that's important when I brief you tomorrow morning," I said.

As I was speaking, I was watching Migos texting on his phone. My reference to the next morning was apparently the opening he was looking for.

"Well gentlemen, Savage, Chico and I have to run. We'll leave you two alone to allow further discussion on the near religious qualities of stretchy pants," Migos said.

"Where are you three going? I slept on the plane, I may want to join you," I said.

"The three lovely ladies you met earlier have invited us to join them at the Catch," Migos said.

"I don't want to hold that up. Be at the hangar in Darfur Air Force Base tomorrow at nine," I said.

After dinner, I returned to the *Nomad*. McDonald went to his room at the hotel and the three wild men went in search of love. It always takes me a while to adjust to the time zone when I return to the Middle East from the US. Despite it being almost midnight, I was wide awake. I cleaned up after the crew and then decided to catch up on my email.

In addition to my Trident email account that I use for personal and business communications, I have a CIA account given to me by Mike that's encrypted and is used for communication between us. The account is also where communications from my CIA alias are forwarded. The only item in the inbox was an email from Detective Grace Deforest of the Nashville Police Department:

"Agent McDermott, I left several voicemails and messages on your phone but have not received a response. A suppression hearing is scheduled in two weeks on the evidence you supplied. Becky Anderson is medically unable to testify and without her testimony, the video evidence is all that we have. In order to defend it, we'll need you to testify. The District Attorney's office asked me to contact you, we need your assistance."

I thought about the situation for a few minutes before replying. I was sitting on a leather recliner with my Mac perched on my lap. I got up, walked to the bar and poured myself a drink. When I returned, I replied to her message:

"Dear Detective, I apologize for the difficulty in communication. I'm on a new assignment outside of the US and it's not possible for me to testify. I'm not aware of the existence of any evidence that would suggest the video I supplied to you is inadmissible. I cannot imagine how or why the counsel for the defense believes that to be the case. However, just to be safe, I would suggest that you obtain a copy of the video file from the sender's phone records. I'm confident all of the defendants have had their phone records subpoenaed and I doubt it's possible for a judge to consider evidence gathered in such a way as inadmissible."

After I hit send, I took a sip of bourbon. It was Pappy Van Winkle and smooth as a baby's bottom. I couldn't think of any reason why the attorney representing the defense would think to question the legal providence of the video. I never told anyone the details of how I got it and I'm sure Mike didn't either. Without the video, the entire case would be based on the testimony of a seriously traumatized girl, who would no doubt suffer enormously at the hands of a competent attorney during cross examination. It was a very frustrating situation. I forwarded my correspondence to Mike to keep him in the loop, then I shut my computer off and sat back in the chair with my drink in hand to think.

CHAPTER 11

MEDITERRANEAN SEA

I PLACED A WASHINGTON & Lee travel mug on the console and took a seat at the helm station of the flydeck. I notified McDonald over the intercom that I had control which wasn't saying much, considering we were cruising on auto pilot. The *Nomad* had been steaming toward the Mediterranean for six days, including the two days we spent navigating through the locks of the Suez Canal. We'd transferred our assigned Egyptian pilot when we refueled in Port Said and were now on a route that would encircle the island of Cyprus clockwise and position us midway between Cyprus and Syria by midnight.

The weather was perfect, the skies were cloudless and the seas were calm. The forecast called for more of the same tonight during mission time, which was important because of the operating parameters of the Mini Harpy suicide drones, or what are properly referred to as loitering munitions. From the helm, I could see the top part of our cargo peeking up over the flydeck. The cargo on the main deck was covered with a black vinyl tarp. Underneath the tarp were two Mini Harpy launch systems stacked on top of one another. The dimensions for each system were about eight feet wide, twenty feet long and five feet deep. Each system held ten pods, five on top and five on the bottom, and inside each pod was an Israeli Aerospace Industries Mini Harpy Loitering Munition.

Before we set sail, the guys spent three days training under the tutelage of an Israeli Air Force Team at Darfur Air Force Base. We learned how to program a flight plan, launch and control the unmanned systems. Each Mini Harpy weighs just over a hundred pounds and has a warhead of approximately twenty pounds. The wings of the Mini Harpy are on a swivel. The fuselage and wing are both six feet long and while inside the pod, the wing is rotated so it extends the length of the fuselage. Once the UAV ejects from the pod, the wing scissors open, instantly snaps into flight position and gives the UAV the lift it needs to remain airborne. The L-shaped tail fin and the push propeller at the tail of the tapered fuselage give the Mini Harpy a sinister look. The electro optical and radiation detecting payload on the gimbal at the center of the bottom of the Harpy allow it to find targets, specifically radar systems. The Mini Harpy has two hours of endurance and a maximum range of sixty-two miles from its ground control station antenna.

We were running at fifteen knots north while the decoy *Nomad* was moving at twenty-two knots south of our start point in Abu Dhabi. At the moment the decoy *Nomad* was located in the Indian Ocean, somewhere off the coast of Sri Lanka. We swapped the *Nomad's* Automated Identification System (AIS) transceiver in Abu Dhabi and while the real *Nomad* was running dark, emitting no GPS or locating signals, our decoy was broadcasting to the world that the *Nomad* was on its way to the South Seas.

I pulled my iPad out of the chair side pocket and out of habit tried to connect, hoping to replay the Red Sox game from the previous night. I was instantly reminded that the yacht WIFI was shut off. Fortunately, I had the foresight to download enough material on my iPad Kindle App before departing to last me two weeks at sea. I don't know what was giving me more pleasure. Re-reading the Robert Parker *Spenser Series* or watching the younger generation suffer from internet withdrawals. I heard movement behind me and turned to find Migos approaching with a tray.

"I have your breakfast."

"Put it on the table, galley slave," I said.

"Very funny. This has got to be the lamest operation we've ever been on. Why are they wasting highly trained special operators like us on mission that could be done by any trash hauler in the Navy?" Migos said before slapping the breakfast tray down hard against the table top.

Savage exited the stairs with his own breakfast tray and sat at the table behind me.

"That's a good question," Savage joined in.

"No it isn't. You guys know better than to think like that. To me the question isn't why us, the question I'm curious about is why the US is involved in this mission at all. It should be a solo Israeli operation. All we're doing is complicating things by making it a combined op," I said.

"Don't you know?" Migos seemed genuinely shocked I didn't.

"I was never told. Which means it's a highly classified secret," I said.

"Why do you think?" Savage asked.

"This is just a theory. But I think we're involved because the US requested Israel conduct this operation and Israel insisted on some US participation as a condition to their consent," I said.

"Why would the US want to destroy a Russian S-400 Battalion? That could kick off a war," Migos said.

"China, India and Russia have all fielded the system. Maybe the US wants to see what an S-400 Battalion can really do. They may want to test it for future reference. Another possibility is they may want to discredit the system. Turkey is tearing NATO apart with its plans to buy the S-400 and this may be a chance to make that problem go away, by defeating it," I said.

"You think if the S-400 turns out to be a big nothing burger, Turkey will no longer want to buy one and they'll make nice with NATO again," Migos said.

"Possibly. The government may also want the world to know that the F-35 strike fighter can defeat the S-400," I said.

Savage folded his arms and asked, "Does the US want that or does Lockheed Martin?"

"That's the greed theory. If the Israeli F-35s destroy an S-400 Battalion, then Lockheed wins twice. Every country on the fence about procuring the F-35 is going to buy the two hundred million dollar stealth fighter and all those countries like Turkey who were ditching their Patriot Batteries for S-400s will change their mind and go back and buy more PAC-3s and THAADS."

"There's billions riding on what happens tonight," Migos said.

"I'll bet they'll have recon planes, satellites and sensors

recording the whole thing. We better not screw up or we'll never live it down," I said.

"There's not a lot to screw up. Launch ten birds from Latakia, then shoot down the Syrian coast thirteen miles to the South and launch the second batch. Then we run like hell and let the chaos begin," Migos said.

"I hope it's that easy," I said.

"I don't know why it wouldn't be," Migos said.

The hours before the operation went slowly. The guys were lazy and a little bored except McDonald who worked hard running diagnostic tests on the launch systems from the two ground control stations he'd set up on the dining room table in the yacht salon. By eleven thirty that night, I was seated at the dining room table next to McDonald. We each had a thirty-two-inch computer console from the ground control station in front of us and we were facing toward the triple glass doors leading out to the stern deck where we could see the launcher. Next to each computer console was a joystick controller in case manual control of a drone was needed. I walked out onto the deck and called Mike on a satellite phone. Migos, Savage and Rodriguez followed me out onto the deck.

"I'm calling in to get the final GO – NO GO decision," I said.

"How is everything on your end?" Mike asked.

"No issues, everything is as planned," I said.

"The mission is a GO," Mike said.

"Talk to you later." I hung up.

"The mission is a GO," I said to Migos, Savage and Rodriguez who were all standing close to me waiting for the word.

The four of us unhooked the bungee straps and peeled off the tarp from the two launcher systems. Rodriguez went to the flydeck helm station and took control of the yacht. He was also doing double duty as a watch, scanning the sea from the high point of the yacht with a pair of FLIR Thermal Binoculars. Migos and Savage cranked the launcher legs into position and then locked them. The top launcher system was now aimed upward at a forty-five-degree angle toward the port side of the *Nomad*. Migos did a walk around of the launcher, checking the cable and power connections.

"Everything is good to go," Migos said.

The three of us returned to the salon. McDonald was working on the keyboard of the first launch system's ground control station.

"How much time?" I asked.

"Two minutes."

I walked forward to the wheelhouse and checked the navigation system. The yacht was running dark. The only lights inside the main cabin were from the consoles on the dining table and at the wheelhouse. Our radar was turned off, the only warning system we had was Rodriguez on the flydeck scanning for nearby ships.

"How does it look up there?" I asked Rodriguez over the intercom system.

"I can see four big cargo ships off to our east at the entrance to the Port of Latakia. I don't see anything that looks military," Rodriguez said.

McDonald started to announce a countdown, beginning at ten.

I stared out through the heavily tinted glass of the salon door. The first Mini Harpy launched from its pod and then every two seconds another burst from its resting place. A yellow jet of flame followed each Mini Harpy for the first three seconds out of the pod before it transitioned to propeller propulsion. It took less than thirty seconds to dispense all of the UAV's from the launch system. Once the firing was complete, Migos and Savage ran out to the deck and lifted the empty launcher system up and walked it off the port side of the deck and into the Mediterranean. The two men then cranked the legs on the remaining system that was stored below the first launcher and elevated it into the launch position.

"Hit it, Rodriguez," I said over the intercom system.

The *Nomad*'s speed jumped from ten to fifty knots. The sea was smooth and with the help of two gyro sea stabilizers on board, the launcher system stayed firmly in place. I walked over to the console where McDonald was working.

"How're we doing?" I asked.

"All ten are on course to Khmeimim Air Base. Air speed is thirty knots," McDonald said.

I could see the thermal camera images from all ten on the display. The same as how they were arrayed inside the launcher system, five windows were on the top half of the display and five on the bottom. All of the images were from the downward looking payloads and depicted the dark ocean below. It took us twenty minutes to get to our next launch point. When I felt the yacht decrease speed, I knew we'd arrived.

"Launching the second system," McDonald said after a countdown for all to hear.

Once again, the triple glass back door of the salon was filled with the bright flames of Mini Harpys jettisoning from their pods.

I sat next to McDonald and divided my attention between both display screens. The set of ten Mini Harpys from the first launcher were now over dry land. The second set, which were being controlled from the console I sat behind, were still over the water. Each of the Mini Harpys had been programmed to loiter five hundred feet above ground level at a pre-selected point above the air base. The positions were selected based on satellite imagery of where the targets were located. The Mini Harpys are radiation seekers, the moment they detect a radar signal, they automatically arm and go into attack mode. From the ground control system, we had the ability to abort an attack. Using the thermal cameras in the UAV gimbles, we also had the ability to manually guide an attack. We had two high value targets selected that we would attack with manual guidance if we found them.

An S-400 Battalion has more than ten radars. Each battalion has one 91NGE Big Bird long range panoramic surveillance radar that can detect targets as far away as 350 miles. The Big Bird is used for acquisition and battle management, because although it has fantastic range, it lacks the accuracy to guide munitions to target. For every launcher system or in some cases for every two launcher systems, there's a dedicated targeting radar. The 92NGE Gravestone engagement and fire control radar is a portable truck mounted system. In addition to the standard complement of radars, the battalion we were attacking had a NEBO SVR radar system. The NEBO is a multispectral phased array system, capable of L,C, X and VHF frequencies. The VHF is especially potent against stealth aircraft. The NEBO has a range of 250 kilometers and is effective for both acquisition and target guidance.

An S-400 Battalion has four types of missiles, it has short range 9M96 missiles with a range of 40 kilometers. It has medium range 9M96E2 missiles with a range of 120 kilometers, long range 48NG missiles with a range of 250 kilometers. The battalion we were attacking was also equipped with extra-long range 40NG missiles that have a range of 400 kilometers. The speed of the missiles varies from Mach seven to Mach fourteen.

The S-400 uses a Transporter Erector Launcher (TER) that's mounted on a six by six truck. While moving, the launcher lays flat on the truck and when in the launch position the TER raises itself vertically. Each TER has four firing pods. The number of missiles in each pod varies depending on the type and size of the missile. The long range 40NG has only one missile per pod, while the shorter-range systems have four, which means each launch system has between four and sixteen missiles.

Protecting the S-400 were expected to be eight Pantsir-S1 short range air defense systems. Each Pantsir has six short range 20 kilometer missiles and two 30mm rotary cannons designed to provide rapid fire close-in protection. The S-400 can engage thirty-six targets simultaneously and fire seventy-two missiles in a single salvo. Our twenty Mini Harpys were a small part of a much larger and complex attack scheme. A scheme that had never been tested before and whose success was far from guaranteed.

CHAPTER 12

LATAKIA, SYRIA

MAJOR LEONID DISHKOVITCH sat behind the mission crew controller console of his work station aboard a A50U Early Warning and Control Aircraft that was orbiting at thirty thousand feet above central Syria. Similar to the US AWACs, the A50U is a converted four-engine jet transport with a twenty-seven-foot diameter dome suspended above it. The A50U has the ability to track aircraft within a 250-mile radius and also has surface maritime reconnaissance capabilities. The skies above Syria were a busy place. Major Leonid's role as the mission crew controller was to supervise and coordinate the actions of a team of nineteen personnel manning radar, radio and sensor systems. His was a stressful job.

Major Leonid was tracking seventeen commercial aircraft, each airliner was tagged on his situational awareness screen that consolidated the feeds from each of his sections with the airline and flight number of each civil flight. He had twelve military aircraft that were identified by IFF transponder numbers and tagged by type and country. The Turkish,

American, Russian, French and British all freely exchanged IFF information to avoid mishaps. In addition to the commercial and IFF transponder, Major Leonid was tracking four Syrian Helicopters and three medium UAVs which were not transmitting IFF data but based on radar cross section data and telemetry intercepts, his analysts identified them as American Reaper UAVs. Outside of the Syrian border, the skies above Lebanon, Turkey and Israel were equally busy. Major Leonid focused most of his attention inside the Syrian border, but the crew maintained situational awareness across the full range of the A50U's capabilities.

"What's that off the coast?" he asked Captain Yuri Andopovich, his first officer, who was seated next to him.

"It just popped up," Captain Andopovich replied.

"Looks like ten slow moving aircraft flying low," Major Leonid said.

"They're tiny, they have to be unmanned. They must have been deployed by a ship," Captain Andopovich said.

"There's only one nearby vessel. Put the UAVs and the ship on auto track and pass the vector to the AOC," Major Leonid said.

The A50U passed the location of the ten slow moving UAVs along with the mystery ship position to the Air Operation Center (AOC). The AOC Command Post was located underground in a protected bunker beneath a building at Khmeimim Air Base. As was standard procedure, the AOC scrambled a pair of SU-34 Fullback fighter jets to investigate the threat. The AOC automatically passed the bogie vectors on to the S-400 Battalion Command and Control Center through their digital battle management system.

Major Leonid was watching the second SU-34 join the

first at the air check point when he was alerted to ten more UAVs being launched from the same ship further down the coast.

"I have ten more bogeys launched from that same ship. The first group is on course for Khmeimim Air Base. The second looks like it may be as well," his radar section chief said over the communication system in his headset.

When the information reached the AOC, the Operations Officer alerted the stand-by air crews and prepared to launch the two SU-27 Fencers and two SU-30s they had on the ready line.

A flight of four F-35I Joint Strike Fighters took off from Ramat Air Force base in Israel. It took only twelve minutes for the flight to reach the Lebanon – Syrian border. The F-35Is in the flight were fully loaded with weapons in what F-35 crews call beast mode. The stealth characteristics of the aircraft were compromised by the externally loaded munitions. In addition to the 5,000 pounds of munitions in their weapons bay, each aircraft carried an additional 13,000 pounds of munitions suspended below their wings. At five hundred feet above ground level, while still over Lebanese air space, each of the four aircraft popped up above the border mountains and released a volley of four Rampage guided munitions at Khmeimim Air Base, which was located 150 kilometers to the north. As soon as the Rampages were released, the engine motors kicked in and the fifteen-foot-long, one-thousand-pound munitions rocketed toward their targets at supersonic speed.

"Sixteen vectors, at three hundred feet, speed 1,400 knots, point of impact Khmeimim," Major Leonid reported to the AOC.

"Cruise Missiles? What launched them?"

"Unknown. Possibly stealth aircraft."

Two more sorties of F-35s released Rampage missiles at the S-400 Battalion from different points along the Syria – Lebanon border. Following behind the three flights in beast mode were four F-35Is in full stealth mode. Because of the stealth coverings and characteristics, the F-35s were undetectable to the Russian sensors. The supersonic Rampage radar-seeking missiles took less than five minutes to reach their targets. Arriving at the same time above the Khmeimim Air Force Base were the twenty Mini Harpys launched from the *Nomad*.

Leading the charge behind the Rampage missiles to the target were the twelve F-35s that launched them plus, at a much higher altitude, three of the aircraft from the four-plane stealth mode flight. The first three flights of F-35s were a feint, their job was to get close enough to be acquired by the surveillance radars. But they were careful to stay outside of the thirty-mile radius the targeting radars needed to engage them.

The fourth aircraft from the flight armed in full stealth mode flew directly at the A50U on an intercept course. Minutes before intercepting the big converted four engine transport jet, the F-35I opened its weapons bay doors and deliberately unmasked its position to the Air Defense Battalion below.

"We're under attack," Major Leonid reported after seeing the F-35 on the battle management system with help from the data link with the AOC and the Air Defense Battalion. The two SU-34s that were only minutes away from engaging the ship that discharged the UAVs were instantly re-tasked.

The two SU-34 fighters banked hard and hit their afterburners to race to the defense of the A50U under attack.

"Twelve bogeys, Fighters, Israeli F-35s," reported Major Leonid.

The lone F-35I with the open weapons bay doors remained like a shadow flying at 400 knots, mimicking the bigger aircraft, less than one hundred feet below the A50U. When the incoming missile warning light appeared on the pilot's display screen inside the visor of his DASS helmet, the pilot closed the weapons bay doors and hit the afterburner. Seconds later a surface-to-air missile slammed into the wing of the A50U and the aircraft tumbled from the sky in a ball of flame. A networked bogey location sent from the fleeing F-35I guided sidewinder missiles launched from the beast F-35s charging the S-400 Battalion to ambush the two pursuing SU-34s.

S-400 air defense units rely on their panoramic and multi-spectral radars to find targets. To avoid exposing themselves to suppressing fire, most of the guidance radars needed to engage enemy aircraft are usually not turned on until they're ready to launch. This often gives them the element of surprise when they engage. However in this situation, with twenty UAVs, twelve fighter jets, and forty-eight cruise missiles bearing down on them, all of the radars in the S-400 Battalion were fully lit up. The NEBO SVR radar was tracking the twelve F-35s that launched the Rampage missiles, but because of their tiny radar signature, they were beyond its guidance range. The twelve F-35s were careful to stay out of detection range of the Gravestone radars. The S-400 AOC was in a state of hyperactivity as it tasked the systems to defeat the oncoming threat, at the same time approaching at supersonic speed only thirty miles away, the four F-35s in stealth mode were slipping in unseen by all the Russian systems including the NEBU VHF radar.

I was looking at the 32-inch monitor of my Ground Control Station with Migos hovering over my shoulder. I was trying to puzzle together the picture of ten separate camera feeds from each of the Mini Harpys. I could see tracer rounds coming toward some of the aircraft which I assumed were 30mm rounds from the Pantsirs. Revelations from earlier Israeli encounters with the Russian Pantsirs in Syria were that the Pantsirs capabilities were grossly inflated. I was happy to see the system continue to live up to its reputation for poor radar detection against small UAVs. Even so, my launch group of ten Mini Harpys was down to six. Four had been hit by missiles of some type. I watched one of my UAVs make a dive toward a target. I could tell from the thermal image it was a Pantsir because it was a vehicle with a cannon and six missiles bristling on each side of the turret. It was a direct hit. My five remaining Mini Harpys were flying in a column toward the center of the S-400 Battalion. With that last Pantsir out of the path, I was hoping to get one of my Mini Harpys into the inner ring of the S-400 Battalion to take out either the Big Bird Radar or the NEBO.

The lead Mini Harpy in the column dive bombed at a Gravestone Radar, the window went black, but the Mini Harpy behind it displayed a picture of an exploded radar truck. Two of my Mini Harpy window screens went black, no doubt knocked out by missiles, leaving me with only two. The Mini Harpy on the top of my screen went into attack mode, I aborted it. It was another Pantsir and I couldn't afford to waste it on a low value target. The Mini Harpy on the bottom of my screen was over a radar array that consisted of four trucks. I was certain that was the NEBO, so I took over manual guidance. I gripped the hand control and flew the Mini Harpy directly into a truck parked in the center of the array. I couldn't see the explosion, because as soon as it made contact the screen went black. I shifted my view to my last Mini Harpy just in time to see its final second of flight before it too made contact with a radar system. It looked like it was a Gravestone Radar from one of the firing units.

"I'm Winchester. How're you doing, McDonald?" I asked.

"Same here," McDonald said.

"Did you get anything?"

"I took out the Big Bird, two Pantsirs and a Gravestone. What about you?"

"I got the NEBO, a Pantsir and I think a Gravestone," I said.

"That's pretty good considering I didn't know what a Pantsir, NEBO, Big Bird or Gravestone were a week ago," McDonald said.

"No kidding. Right now, we need to find a way to disappear. That's all that matters," I said.

After the onslaught of the Mini Harpys and Rampage Missiles, the S-400 Battalion was down to seven TER missile launchers and four Gravestone Radars to guide the missiles. The next wave of attacks was performed by a pre-planned salvo of Advanced Anti-Radiation Guided Missile-Extended Range (AARGM-ER), also known as AGM-88G from the beast F-35s. A pair of anti-radiation missiles was launched at coordinates based on satellite imagery from each aircraft. The missiles closed the thirty-mile gap to the S-400 Battalion at 1,400 miles per hour in passive mode, homing in on the Gravestone Radars that were fully lit up to compensate for the loss of the Battalion's surveillance radars and the A50U.

The flight of four stealth loaded F-35Is followed close behind the AGM-88s. With advanced jammer pods engaged, the F-35s prepared for a bombing run on whatever Pantsirs and S-400 firing systems remained. The S-400 needed only two guidance radars to control the remaining launch systems. As a precaution, two Gravestones were shut down to protect them from incoming radar seekers. The AGM-88s found their mark against all five of the remaining Pantsirs. Three of the four Gravestone Radar systems were destroyed including one that, although turned off, remained in the memory of the advanced munition. Before the final remaining radar system could re-activate, a Pavelow II laser guided GBU-82 exploded directly on top of it. A pair of stealth mode F-35s at ten thousand feet made several bombing runs over the TER launch systems and destroyed all of them with Pavelows.

While a flight of F-35Is maintained a close air patrol over the objective area, two of the Beast Flights continued past the air base to a large warehouse located two miles beyond. The warehouse was a converted factory used by the Iranian Revolutionary Guards to manufacture 122mm rockets for Hezbollah, the Iranian terrorist surrogates. The Hezbollah rockets are delivered to Hamas in Gaza by the thousands for frequent attacks against Israel. The first bombing run destroyed the warehouse and all six bunkers that were used to store the completed munitions. Secondary explosions lit up the night sky for the next hour.

CHAPTER 13

MEDITERRANEAN OCEAN

FOLLOWING THE ATTACK on Khmeimim Air Base the *Nomad* continued south at cruising speed. At forty knots we would make it to the Suez in time to join the morning convoy. The plan was to link up with our decoy double in the Andaman Sea and regain possession of our AIS. I went up to the flydeck and spelled Rodriguez at the helm.

"How did it go?" Rodriguez said as he slid out from behind the wheel.

"We did our part, we nailed both of the surveillance radars, but as far as whether or not the Israelis finished the job, I have no idea," I said.

"When will we know?" Rodriguez asked.

"I'm supposed to call Mike once we're in the Red Sea. He'll give me the outcome then."

"Do you think the Russians will escalate?" Rodriguez said.

"I hope not. Protecting Hezbollah missile factories is pretty serious over-reach on the part of the Russians. If I were the Russians, I'd want to keep what happened tonight quiet," I said.

"Is that possible?" Rodriguez asked.

"The story will get out eventually, but the general public will remain ignorant. It's not like it involves the Kardashians or anything most people care about," I said.

It had become a post mission ritual to barbeque and have drinks on the flydeck after operations and tonight we continued the tradition. It was four in the morning and I was into my second bottle of wine and the rest of the guys were feeling pretty good when Migos decided to hold a mock award ceremony.

"It's time to begin the official ceremony. Master Chief Retired McDonald, front and center," Migos announced.

The sheepish McDonald didn't know what was coming, but with Migos he knew he was in for some ribbing. Being a good sport, he played along.

"No major operation is complete without an award ceremony. Back in the old days real men would batter their opponents with swords and shields. This is a new age and the brutal and barbaric behavior of the past has been transformed into a more sophisticated and enlightened approach to warfare."

We were forty miles from the Suez and our speed was down to ten knots which created a gently warm wind in the night air. We were seated around the U-shaped table drinking under the moonlight. McDonald stood at a loose form of attention and Migos was standing next to him holding a pair of plastic kid's pilot wings in his right hand and a furry stuffed penguin in his left.

"Tonight, we witnessed the future of warfare and we found our Braveheart for this new age. We've identified the man best equipped to lead us into this new frontier. Attention to orders."

Migos signaled for all of us to stand, which we all did.

"With complete disregard to his personal safety, we watched McDonald disregard his injuries. We saw him ignore the pain of carpel tunnel syndrome and brilliantly manipulate his keyboard and hand station against superior forces to close with and defeat the enemy. I bore witness to this event and I can verify that he had five confirmed kills. His brilliant Gameboy handset manipulation destroyed three radars, a Toyota Landcruiser and what, after video review, has been determined to be a Russian porta potty. Under the new military rules, McDonald is now recognized as an honest to goodness flying ace. In the future McDonald will be properly addressed by all of you by his fighter pilot call sign and the words Fighter Ace. To recognize this noble maritime aviation achievement conducted from the seat of a La-Z-Boy recliner, I hereby certify McDonald as a member of the order of the non-flying water fowl which is symbolized by this stuffed penguin and I award him this pair of flying wings, which he can wear proudly over either his flight suit or pajamas during future operations."

We all clapped as he handed him the stuffed penguin and pinned the plastic wings on McDonald's polo shirt.

"Speech…. speech. Tell us about how you rebooted your computer under fire," the former Delta Force operator, Savage, said.

McDonald just shook his head, sat down and went back to his beer.

We passed through the Suez without incident, despite using a different registration than the one we used on the passage north. Because we didn't have any contraband, the baksheesh paid to the customs officials was only a fraction of what we paid on the first trip. I waited until we were off the coast of Jeddah, Saudi Arabia before calling Mike.

"Where are you?" Mike asked.

"Off the coast of Saudi, running south in the Red Sea."

"Any problems from your end?"

"We were in and out, undetected. All of the systems worked as advertised."

"You weren't undetected. You came very close to being taken out by an SU-34," Mike said.

"No kidding."

"Yes. At the last second it got diverted to join the air fight, otherwise, you guys would've been toast."

"You shouldn't have told me that."

"Better lucky than good. You guys got the job done. The cousins gave you credit for taking out the Big Bird and the NEBO."

"We did, we also got three Pantsirs and two Gravestones."

"Wait another twenty-four hours and then you can send us the telemetry data."

"Will do. We didn't kick off World War Three did we?" I figured we hadn't, but it never hurts to check.

"Things are pretty tense, but it doesn't look like it."

"What was the final outcome?" I asked.

"The S-400 and the rocket factory were destroyed. The IDF didn't lose any aircraft. It was a complete success."

"My Lockheed stock is going to go through the roof," I said.

"Did you buy because of this mission?" Mike asked.

"No, of course not. I already had some."

"That's good. I think you're right though."

"Are the powers that be sufficiently satisfied that I've

atoned for my sins?" I said in a tone that would've gotten me court marshalled back in the day.

"You're still on a short leash."

CHAPTER 14

ANDAMAN SEA

WE RECOVERED OUR AIS tracking beacon a few miles offshore from Phi Phi Island in Phuket, Thailand. It had taken us four days from the Suez to reach our rendezvous spot. My plan was to spend a few days in Phuket and then take the *Nomad* back to Abu Dhabi. Our communications blackout was lifted, and for the first time in more than a week, I was able to access my email.

When I went through my messages, I found one from Detective Deforest in Nashville. The friendly professional tone found in her previous correspondence was gone, she was angry and hostile. The ruling at the suppression hearing had gone against the Tennessee State Prosecutor's Office. With the video tape excluded as evidence and Becky Anderson medically unfit to testify, the State had no choice but to drop the charges and let the five Somali rapists walk. Detective Deforest minced no words in blaming me for the miscarriage of justice. I considered replying, but instead, I decided to call her.

"Detective, this is Agent McDermott, I just got your email."

"Where have you been?"

"I'm sorry, I couldn't get back to Nashville. It wasn't my decision."

"You keep saying that. Whose decision was it? Who do you work for anyway?"

"You verified my credentials; you know who I work for."

"The local FBI office says you're some kind of spook."

"Do they now?"

"Yes, they do."

"Why would the FBI be talking about me?"

"Because you're a person of interest in a Federal murder investigation and they're looking to bring you in for an interview."

"That murder investigation would be the untimely death of Hodar. Is that who the FBI is all worked up about? The man who arranged the sale of a fifteen-year-old girl from one Somali gang to another."

"That's news to me. How did you learn that?"

"The FBI knows it, just ask them. Why are they spreading rumors about me while withholding case information from you? And why is the death of Hodar, a street punk in Nashville, a Federal case, when the kidnapping and interstate transit of a fifteen-year-old girl wasn't?"

"I have no idea."

"Does the Nashville PD make a habit of handing cases over to the Feds without justification or even a basic understanding of why they would be a federal matter?"

"I'm sure there was justification, it just wasn't shared with me."

"Why didn't you follow my suggestion and produce the video to the court from the sender rather than the recipient?"

"We did. The judge wouldn't allow it. The defense explained that we only knew about the video from the sender, because we first learned of it from the recipient and that makes it fruit of the poisoned tree. The video evidence from the recipient was obtained under duress. The man who supplied it was shot and died of his wounds. His phone was forcibly unlocked with his finger, while he was bleeding to death. That's an illegal act and any evidence that derives from that act isn't admissible. You should know that."

"I know the information on how the video was obtained is highly classified. How did a public defender manage to come by it so easily?"

"The Somalis don't have a public defender. They were well represented, and it didn't take a lot of effort to find the information. It came out the Sunday before the hearing in a *Washington Post* article."

"You're kidding."

"No, I'm not, look it up for yourself."

"A news story isn't evidence. Did the defense counsel have any proof that what was in the WaPo story was true?"

"No, instead the judge asked the DA how they came to know a video existed and when the DA couldn't provide any facts to contradict the WaPo story, the judge ruled against the State. That's why we needed you at the hearing."

"There's a lot about this that isn't making sense," I said.

"Agreed. Too much fishy behavior. Especially from you."

"The newspaper story came out only a few days before the hearing. But the defense requested the suppression hearing weeks in advance. How did they know there was a problem with the video evidence?"

"That doesn't matter," Grace said.

"For a detective, you're strangely incurious. The FBI rolls in and takes over your murder case and you don't know why. Five low-life child rapists arrive in court with top shelf legal representation and you don't know why or how. The origin of the lynch pin evidence, which should never have been known, much less contested, because it's protected by the highest security classification in the US Government, is leaked days before the hearing. The hearing is scheduled weeks before the information is ever in the public domain, so the defense team must have had it before it ever came out in the paper. None of that seems odd to you?" If it didn't, I'd misjudged her skills as a cop.

Grace was quiet for a minute and didn't reply.

"Did you hear what I said?"

"I see your point," Grace replied.

"Get to work, Detective. I'm going to find out if my completely unreasonable boss will allow me to return to Nashville."

After I hung up, I booked a plane ticket to Scotland. I needed information and David Forrest was always a good place to start. I called Mike and asked him to meet me in Edinburgh. As my case officer, he was required to debrief me on the last mission, and I thought Scotland would be a good middle ground between Virginia and Thailand.

We were staying in Karon at the Le Meridien. It was the start of monsoon season and although the skies were unusually cloudless, the winds were high, and the seas were very rough. We anchored the *Nomad* within the sheltered confines of the small bay that formed Le Meridien's private beach. The hotel was kind enough to allow us to tie up the tender at the shallow water dock they used for parasailing and jet skis. With the last-minute change of plans, I was disappointed I wasn't going to get a chance to play tennis and surf at Kata Beach, a well-known surf spot in Thailand and located just two miles south of our hotel. I decided to take the team to dinner and have an early night because I had a flight the next morning.

Two Chefs is on a narrow side street off the beach road on Karon Beach. The no name side street is a busy place, it has a crowded lineup of venders selling souvenirs and street food. Two Chefs is an open-air restaurant with a small stage and a talented musical act made up of two Filipina girls. The food at Two Chefs is a combination of Thai and American. We just happened to be there on barbeque rib night, which was well received by the guys. The restaurant has a hipster ambience and draws a predominantly western crowd. The dining room was full, with a mixture of families, backpackers, couples and rowdy partiers.

"I'm flying out tomorrow morning," I announced to the group.

"Where are you heading, boss?" asked McDonald.

"Edinburgh, I'm going to debrief Mike and hopefully get some help from David on my Nashville problem," I said.

"I thought that was all taken care of," McDonald said.

"I did too. Until a judge set the rapists free. The case against them was based on the video we found on Umar's phone. Apparently, we didn't come about it in a way that was legal enough for the judge," I said.

"Why doesn't the girl testify?" McDonald said.

"She's not able to, they can't even get a written statement out of her," I said.

"That's a shame, she must be pretty messed up," McDonald said.

"I can't imagine," I said.

"What are you going to do?" Migos asked.

"What I'd like to do is return to Nashville and deliver justice, Old Testament style. But according to Mike, I'm on a short leash because of what happened during my last visit to the US of A. So, for the time being, I'm just going to engage David and the Clearwater staff in some intelligence gathering," I said.

"What happened during your last trip that put you in hot water? You didn't mention anything," McDonald said.

"I used a cover that I wasn't supposed to use, and I may have been a bit overzealous in my pursuit of justice," I said.

"So now you have to lay off the Don Coyote act for a while," Rodriguez offered.

"That's Quixote not Coyote. With a name like Rodriguez you should know that, where did you go school?" Migos said.

"I went to Jordan High School in Watts and I might've missed the class on Don Kee-yo-tayy. What does an Arab speaker like you know about Spanglish anyway?" Rodriguez said.

"This situation in Nashville does have a coyote and roadrunner feel to it. I can't believe those gang bangers got away. You might be on to something, Rodriguez," I said.

"That's what I've been trying to explain to professor Migos," Rodriguez said.

"You're going to Scotland and you want us to stay here for how long?" asked McDonald.

"Stick with the plan. Stay four days and then take the boat back to Abu Dhabi. After that you can fly to Cyprus and I'll take care of the *Nomad* later," I said.

"We can do that," Migos said.

"What're your plans tonight, do you want to join us in town, we're going to Patong?" McDonald said.

"No thanks. After dinner, I'm heading back to the hotel," I said.

"Good call, boss, it's *Pirates of Penzanz* night at the hotel. You'll have a blast with the other kids, free hats and plastic swords," Migos said.

"Actually, I was planning on surfing before turning in," I said.

"Seriously?" McDonald said.

"I was looking at that tiny little beach before we came out to dinner, those waves are surfable. Very surfable," I said.

"That's not a good idea, you've had a few drinks. It's dark, when all the night feeders are active in the water. That tiny beach is U-shaped and it's going to have a strong rip current in the center," McDonald said.

"It can't pull me out to sea without taking me right past the *Nomad*. I'll be okay. I'm a big boy," I said.

"If you're going surfing, I'm going with you. It's been a long time since I night surfed," Rodriguez said.

"I'm in. Moons out, conditions are primo," Savage said.

"What about Banglar Road?" Migos said.

"We'll go there after we ride the waves for an hour or two," Rodriguez said.

"I'll go, just to lifeguard you maniacs from the tender," McDonald said.

"That's the spirit," I said.

Breaking through the surf in a twelve-foot tender with four guys in it was an adventure. We all got soaked in the process. The *Nomad* was firmly anchored with two lines. The yacht was one hundred and fifty yards off the beach. We took the surfboards out of the *Nomad's* garage and changed into our bathing suits. McDonald threw each of us a green Chemlite and told us to tie them to the drawstring on our bathing suits. He said it would make it easier for him to rescue us.

I was the first to step off the hydraulic lift, at the tail of the boat, into the water. I was a little excited. The waves were two people high and they were breaking close to the shore onto a sandy floor. The moonlight was just barely bright enough to spot an incoming swell at a distance of twenty yards and the wind was inshore. The conditions were excellent.

The current from the beach to the sea was as strong as predicted and it took a maximum effort to make headway paddling on my board. The rip current was strongest in the center of the mini-harbor. I made my way inshore to the break along the southern side of the inlet. Positioning was a challenge at first, it was an unfamiliar area and we didn't have any reference to find the best place to catch a wave. The next thing I found difficult was situating myself on the wave. I managed to maintain position by using the bioluminescent wake on the top edge of the wave as a reference point. It was real challenge and a lot of fun.

About an hour into our surf session I noticed that we'd drawn a crowd along the hotel restaurant patio. Some of the adult vacationers had left the nightly theme dinner and were cheering and clapping in the outside bar tangent to the restaurant. Wipeouts seemed to be the crowd favorites. After only an hour and a half, we quit. The current made the trip back to the *Nomad* fast and easy. The four of us returned to the dock and decided to have a beer at the outside bar with Migos before they left for Patong.

We found Migos sitting at a table with a group of young Australian Girls.

"These girls are surfing fans. I explained to them that you guys are professionals. Except you, Pat. I came clean and told them you're an eccentric rich guy who's too embarrassed to surf in the daytime, which is why you hired two pros to surf with you at night."

"That makes me sound pathetic."

"I had to be honest. I managed to find two members of the opposite sex that may be interested in Savage and Rodriguez, which is nothing short of a miracle. If I didn't tell the story, that wouldn't have happened. Something like that comes with a price."

"Good work with that. I'm heading to bed; I have an early flight tomorrow. You guys be careful," I said as I walked away.

CHAPTER 15

MUNICH, GERMANY

I WAS TURNING IN for the night when Mike texted me and changed the meeting location from Scotland to Munich. I replied that I'd take care of the hotel. From experience, I know that otherwise, he'd stick me in a per diem compliant Marriott to keep the government happy. I chose the Mandarin Oriental in the old town area.

I booked Qatar Airlines through Doha to reach Munich. It was eighteen hours including the connection. When I arrived in Munich, because of the time zone difference, it was early afternoon the day after I started.

Munich is one of my favorite cities. The architecture, museums, restaurants, beer gardens and greenways make it a fantastic place for a tourist like me who enjoys walking. The Mandarin Oriental is my favorite hotel in the city. It's a boutique hotel with only seventy rooms. The building is a converted mid-nineteenth century opera house located in the old town area near the Glockenspiel and other attractions. The hotel is an ornate seven-story white stone building with a decent Japanese restaurant and one of the best rooftop bars in Europe.

I checked in and hurriedly unpacked. The spring weather was beautiful and after all the travelling, I was anxious to stretch my legs. I met Mike in the lobby.

"Is that bum knee of yours up for a walk?" I asked.

"It could use some work, what did you have in mind?"

"The beer garden next to the Chinese Pagoda in the English Garden."

"It's a nice day to be in the park, let's go."

We threaded our way through some side roads until we reached Maximilianstrasse and headed east along the tree-lined, monument-laden road toward the river. After the road divided, we found the famous statue of King Maximilian II. It's an impressive bronze of him fully robed with a sword in his left hand and a scroll held to his chest with his right. The king stands on a granite pedestal surrounded by four standing children representing the Coat of Arms of Swabia, Bavaria, Palatinate and Franconia. Situated around the broader monument base are four adult bronze figures symbolizing Wisdom, Justice, Love and Strength.

"What's the message here, that the people are children and the government is the adult that has to direct them?" I said.

"If government was supposed to have all of the virtues, I think the artist would've put the adults in the middle with the King," Mike said.

We crossed the river to the entrance of the Maximilanium, which is the home of the Bavarian Parliament. Nearby on a river island is the Alpine Museum, which although lacking the overwhelming majesty of the Maximilanium is still impressive. I made a mental note to check out the Alpine Museum while in town. I'm a climber and I'm interested in the first ascents and the old equipment. The Maximilanium is an awesome sight. The building has a goldish-brown Renaissance façade with lots of round arches, columns and mosaics. It's a spectacular grandiose building that commands the banks of the Isar River.

Mike and I turned north on the walking trail that paralleled the far side of the river and made our way into the English Garden. It was a work day and the traffic on the path was light. After a long winter the seventy-degree temperature was enough to draw out a fair number of sunbathers. I caught Mike doing a double take at a pair of topless German girls bronzing on the grass next to the river. I was a little surprised myself. With the cultural challenges involved with the recent influx of immigrants, I didn't know that kind of thing still went on in Germany.

After a half a mile of walking along the river, we recrossed the river and followed the trail over a couple of streams and into the center of the park. Although still in the woods we knew we were close when we heard the *oompah oompah oompah* from the horns of a traditional German band. In a clearing we found the source of the music and a giant five-story wooden Pagoda that's called the Chinese Tower. The lederhosen-garbed band was playing inside the tower and outside most of the tables were filled with people drinking from liter-sized beer mugs and eating.

Mike and I found a picnic table that was free. I left Mike to save our seats while I went to the self-serve kiosk to find us some food and beer.

I had to make a couple of runs, but eventually, I supplied

us with a couple of liter-sized mugs of Hoffbrau Lager and a good assortment of pork, brats, chicken, fries and spätzle.

"Dig in, buddy, it doesn't get much better than this."

"Do you think we have enough?"

"Don't get too carried away, I made dinner reservations at eight at an Austrian place. You're going to like it a lot."

"Where is it?"

"West of where we're staying, out in the burbs."

I noticed Mike was stretching his left leg out straight in discomfort.

"Are you getting any exercise in?"

"Not much. Unlike you, I ride a desk."

"That stinks."

"I envy you sometimes, the only injuries I get are paper cuts. How'd you get that big old raspberry on your arm?"

"I was surfing with Savage and Rodriguez in Thailand and a wave dumped me hard in the shallows."

"Might be a good idea in the future to bail before running out of water."

"Normally that's the plan, but it was night and on the first run. I had no idea how shallow the water got."

"Who surfs at night?"

"Savage, Rodriguez and I may have been the first at that location, based on the reaction we got. In some overcrowded surf spots, like in Southern California, it's actually kind of popular."

"I wonder about you sometimes," Mike said.

"I wonder about you too. Like why you went to so much trouble to divert me from Scotland and David Forrest."

"You think that's what this detour to Munich is?"

"Of course, I know you too well."

"You may have a future in Intelligence yet."

"I don't think the pay would work for me."

"Lots of hidden hazards, like your recent surfing experience."

"What's going on?" I asked.

"Somebody leaked the details of the Umar operation to the press. There are some political shenanigans going on and I'm under intense scrutiny."

"I heard about the leak."

"It was in the WaPo and then followed up by the other dailies for a few days while you were blacked out. Not front-page stuff, but serious trouble for the Agency. I can't afford to have you make it worse, which is why I can't have David Forrest helping you track down the five psychos who attacked that young girl, so you can end them," Mike said.

"That's an appealing idea, but that's not why I was asking David for help."

"Why then?"

"When I talked with Detective Deforest about the origin of the video, I told her it was recovered from a raid in Somalia, but I never gave her the details. Instead, I notified her that there would be issues with its providence and told her to obtain the same video file from the sender. Even though it was a burner, the Nashville Police wouldn't have any trouble tracking down the rapists cell phone and then pulling the history from the phone company data files."

"Go on."

"Well the Somalis legal team, not a lone public defender mind you, but an expensive legal team, knew all about the origin of that video. They scheduled the suppression hearing before we left for the mission in Syria, before we were blacked out and the news story came out in the WaPo."

"That doesn't mean the Somalis' lawyer knew about the story before it came out. Maybe they were going to make another legal argument against the video and the WaPo story landed on their lap. Being beneficiaries of the leak doesn't mean they were involved in it," Mike said.

"Or the WaPo leak is a smokescreen to cover for giving the Somalis the information. They must know that if they're the only ones with the information, it would be incriminating and easy to trace. But if it's leaked to the news, then it's impossible to connect the two events," I said.

"You think the Somalis have someone inside the Agency?" Mike asked.

"Someone gave that defense team highly classified information. I'll check, but I don't think you can get a suppression hearing scheduled unless you first give the judge a reason. I doubt they got it scheduled for one reason and then argued something different. The circle of people who knew the origins of that video is fairly small. David Forrest will make short work of tracking down who gave it to the Somalis," I said.

"And what were you going to do once David identifies a suspect?" Mike said.

"Talk to them of course."

"That's your plan, huh?" Mike said with a smile.

"Yes, from there I would hope to discover why someone inside our highly professional and patriotic intelligence community wants to keep five sadistic child rapists out of jail."

"We're already looking for the source. You should read the article. It mostly focuses on Umar's cold-blooded killing.

The article accuses the CIA of murdering him in front of his family while he was resting at his home. It said we tracked him to the house from a Mosque where he was praying. The article portrays him as the George Washington of Somalia. The reporter's description of Umar's virtues would've embarrassed Mother Theresa," Mike said.

"Someone from the inside is running an information operation against the Agency," I said.

"Maybe not the entire Agency, maybe just my portion of it," Mike replied.

"They must dislike you more than they dislike Al Shabab."

"That's a rough comparison."

"Let's put David to work on this. He'll keep a low profile."

"I appreciate the offer. It's better if you just stand down for the time being."

"They have a nice bar on top of our hotel that opens at four. I think we should get one more beer here and then take in the view from the top of the Mandarin. What do you think?"

"Lead on, Ranger."

When I got up, the band had escaped the confines of the pagoda and was parading around in their lederhosen with instruments playing in full volume. The weather, the music and food created a festive atmosphere. I don't think there was a person in the crowd without a smile, I thought as I stood in the beer line.

On the way back we detoured to the English Garden surfing area. The clever Germans diverted a stream and created an artificial wave that can be surfed. Mike and I watched for a few minutes. It didn't look like much fun. The cold mountain stream requires a heavy wet suit and there was a long line of surfers waiting their turn on the muddy banks. I crossed Munich out as a surfing destination.

When we returned to the hotel, I slipped the hostess a hundred Euro at the rooftop bar to allow us to sit at a dinner table instead of the crowded cramped bar seats where we could be easily overheard.

We sat facing the gothic spires of Saint Peter's Church, the clock tower of the Glockenspiel and the column of Mary in the center of the Marienplatz. I ordered a bottle of rosé and once it was delivered and poured, we got to work with the debriefing of the S-400 mission. The discussion lasted two hours and we were drinking coffee before it was over.

"How did Migos come up with the Order of the Flightless Water Fowl?" Mike asked.

"How does Migos come up with anything? He's a character, but he has a point. McDonald is a pilot who never leaves the ground, he's always operating aircraft by remote control from the water," I said.

"Migos is a funny guy, but that mission was no cake walk. Did you tell him how close you came to being blown out of the water by a Russian fighter jet?" Mike said.

"I didn't mention that."

"A pair of SU-34s was seconds away from rolling in on an attack of the *Nomad* when they got called back to rescue a Russian AWAC that was under attack by the Israeli F-35s."

"There was a Russian AWAC in the area?" I asked.

"That's how they knew you launched the Mini Harpys and that's why they sent the SU-34s to take you out."

"I didn't know an AWAC could spot surface vessels. You probably should've told me they could see us? I wasn't briefed on an AWAC and I was told the surveillance radar with the S-400 could only find objects in the air," I said.

"The A50U was a problem, at least it was until they shot it down themselves," Mike said.

"You're kidding."

"No, the Israelis got the S-400 Battalion to launch at an F-35 that was shadowing the A50U and then, once the missiles were in the air, they closed the weapons bay doors, disappeared into stealth mode and let the missiles lock onto the A50U," Mike said.

"That was planned?"

"Not only that, it's the second time. They've used that exact same tactic twice against the Russians and it's worked both times."

"Against an S-400?"

"No, the first time it was a Syrian S-300, but we know who really operates the Syrian systems."

"Everything the Russians have is overblown, Potemkin Village is a term that could only have come out of Russia. It's always been that way."

"It's not true about everything."

"It is about a lot of things. I still remember our 25mm rounds cutting through T-72 Tanks during the First Gulf War. These were supposed to be Main Battle Tanks that were a threat to an M1 Abrams and we were destroying them with Bradleys," I said.

"Back then it was in a lot of people's interest to portray the USSR as more powerful than they were. Times are different now."

"Not completely, I still have a hand in the arms biz and the Lockheeds of the world are still leading a chorus on how great the Chinese and Russian equipment is. Look at the hypersonic missiles, there's never been a successful test, but Northrup and Lockheed are spending millions to convince Congress and the public that our adversaries' propaganda is true," I said.

"Russian Hypersonic missiles don't work? I'm in the CIA and that's news to me," Mike said.

"I have it from a reliable source that it's impossible to target accurately at that speed, something to do with lift factors at Mach 5. Has any third party ever attended one of these tests and verified they hit what they're programmed to hit?"

"No, I wouldn't expect that for a secret weapon."

"It's so secret, Mad Vlad promotes it during every speech. Everybody in the industry and government has an interest in the propaganda being true. This S-400 situation is a rare occasion where both wanted to pull the mask off the Russian bear," I said.

"You're way too cynical. The purpose of the mission was never to sell military equipment," Mike said.

"Of course, I forgot, it's a geopolitical thing with NATO and Turkey. I get it."

Later that evening we hired a car to take us to dinner at Broeding. The restaurant was located at the outskirts of Munich in an upscale mixed residential retail area. Broeding is a very unpretentious place. The dress code is relaxed, and the atmosphere is very homey. There was only one item on the menu and that was the six-course tasting menu. The only option was the wine, we chose to take the wine pairing route, which greatly simplified the ordering process. Broeding is an Austrian restaurant and wine shop, I expected they'd do a bang-up job in the wine department. I could tell Mike was enthusiastic about my restaurant choice when he read the menu out loud.

"Marinated Filet, Tomato Soup, Monk Fish, Venison, Cheese and Chocolate Mousse. This is going to be great," Mike said.

"There's a three-star Michelin place by our hotel with higher ratings, but I couldn't even recognize half the items on the menu as food, and the half I did recognize worried me. Who eats duck hearts?" I asked.

"I may have once, but I think that was either at SERE or Ranger School," Mike said.

"Exactly. Why would someone pay for that experience?"

"What are you going to do now that there's no need to visit Scotland?" Mike's real question was, where was I going to go and pretend to stay out of trouble?

"I'm heading back to Eleuthera. I'm gonna clean my weapons and wait for you to call me to bail you out," I said.

"You think I'm going to need to call you?" Mike asked.

"Something big is going down that you don't want me to know about. This leak was targeted. It wasn't just to spring the rapists, it was aimed at you. Somebody in your building has it out for you," I said.

"Is that a guess?" Mike said.

"An educated guess, but I'm right, am I not?" I said.

"Very."

"So, who's out to get you?"

"The Executive Deputy Director," Mike said.

"The number two at the CIA leaked a top-secret mission to the press to get you," I said.

"I'm not ready to say that yet. She's definitely out to get

me, of that there's no doubt. But I'm not sure if she's the one who leaked the story. It might be more complicated than that," Mike said.

"Let's start with motive. Why does the Executive Deputy Director have it out for you? I've heard the Director thought you walked on water," I said.

"Although the Director is a political appointee, she's career Agency. She's a former field operative with lots of gritty experience. She and I worked together in the past and we have a lot of mutual respect. The Executive Deputy Director is also a political appointee with prior CIA experience. But she's a totally different animal, she's political. She worked at the Agency for five years as an analyst and then went to law school. Following law school, she practiced corporate law for one of the bigger DC firms for a dozen years before returning back to public service. She's a compromise; at the Director's confirmation, the Senators who opposed the nomination made a deal, they'd confirm the Director, but only if they got a watchdog in as the number two. The Director's nomination wasn't popular with some in the Senate because of her management of a black site where some terrorists were allegedly tortured. The deal was made, the Director was confirmed, and the Deputy Director was installed as a stooge by those who want to handcuff the Agency," Mike said.

"What's this watchdog's name?"

"Vanessa Bloom."

"What's her beef with you?"

"She's an analyst and a lawyer, she believes the function of the Agency is to study satellite and electronic surveillance data and prognosticate. The operator's view, my view, is that we don't prognosticate about the future, we change it.

Operations is a small and declining part of the Agency. To people like Vanessa, me and my department are an anachronism from a bygone error," Mike said.

"You guys went out of vogue with Mad Men and John Foster Dulles," I said.

"Exactly, and her opposition to me isn't just professional, it's also personal. I was responsible for getting the guy who hired her into the CIA, the same guy who helped her get a job at that swanky law firm, sacked a few years back," Mike said.

"That would be the corrupt deep stater who resigned his position from the opposite end of my nine mil," I said.

"That's the one. She doesn't like you much either, now that you mention it."

"Why fight office politics? Why don't you just retire? You can be the Chairman of Trident and improve your lifestyle ten thousand percent," I said.

"I don't want that. I like what I do."

"What are you going to do?" I asked.

"I'm going to find out if this woman stepped over the line by sabotaging my operations and by leaking classified information to the press," Mike said.

"I know about the leak, what do you mean by sabotage?"

"The woman is smart, really smart, brilliant even. Attacking a Russian S-400 from an unarmed yacht in the Med with a A50U flying cover is suicidal," Mike said.

"You didn't know about the AWAC bird?" I said.

"Of course not. If I had, you wouldn't have been there. You and your team came within minutes of dying," Mike said.

"You mentioned that before. The Israelis must've known. Where do they get off on setting us up like that?" I said.

"What I've learned about the mission after the fact, is that it wasn't the Israelis idea. None of it was," Mike said.

"This woman's dangerous."

Mike nodded. "She is."

"Where does she stand with your management?"

"The Director has to tolerate her. The POTUS likes her. Says she's smart as a whip and believes she's loyal to him," Mike said.

"Is she hot, I heard he has a type," I said.

"She fits it, think Miss March, twenty years later. But she's only loyal to herself and her band of Washington insiders. She's popular at the Agency, except with the agents in the field who view her as an analyst with a chip on her shoulder," Mike said.

"Okay, so she doesn't like you, because you, or more accurately, I took out a former Director who was her mentor. Setting me up to get blown away by the Russians, that kinda makes sense. Leaking information on a classified kill order that she probably signed off on? That doesn't make any sense at all," I said.

"It doesn't. But I still keep going back to the fact that the number of people who knew about the Mogadishu operation in the building can be counted on two hands and she was one of them," Mike said.

"Further study is warranted. I'll give you until Wednesday to look into the matter, then I'll go pay this lovely lady a visit and get some answers," I said.

"No, that's not the plan."

"She set up my team. That can't stand," I said.

"The A50U had been in country for three weeks, I should've known. You can blame me," Mike said.

"The Israelis definitely knew. They had a plan to destroy it, they did destroy it. The Israelis must've shared their plan with the Agency. Why didn't anyone tell you?"

"All of my information came through her. Which is why I suspect she set you up, but I don't know for a fact, because I don't know if she was the person directly liaising with the Israelis," Mike said.

"How did she think you would react if the plan had worked and my guys were dead?" I said.

"That's a tricky one. I don't know, but she obviously wasn't overly worried about it."

"Why don't you let my guy David Forrest hunt for the leaker?" I suggested.

"She'll find out, this woman is sharp, she knows Forrest would be the first call we'd make. We have to be more sophisticated with this woman. Brute force isn't going to cut it," Mike said.

"People who say stuff like that haven't tried brute force. If I hang this lady from her ankles off the roof of the Langley building, she'll tell me everything we need to know and then I can let her go and that will be the end of it, problem solved," I said.

"You need to slow down with the wine; you're starting to hallucinate. The woman's personal security detail will take you out the moment you set foot in Langley," Mike said.

"Austrian Wine is surprisingly good by the way," I said.

"Agreed, but what have we decided about next steps?" Mike said.

"Obviously, we're going to finish this chocolate mousse with fresh cherries and cracked cream which is complemented nicely by this sweet white dessert wine pairing. The combination produces a titillating effect on the palate, don't you think? After that, I suggest we head back into town to Kilian's Irish Bar, near the hotel," I said.

"Is Kilian's any good?"

"Any place where a man can listen to live hard rock and drink proper alcohol is good in my book," I said.

"Our needs are simple."

"Says the man in the Michelin star restaurant with the dainty dessert spoon in his hand."

CHAPTER 16

LANGLEY, VIRGINIA

MIKE GUTHRIE WALKED into the inner sanctum of the Director's Office. Harley Curtis rose from her desk to greet him and escorted him over to a sitting area.

"How was your trip to Germany?" the Director asked

"It was productive. Pat's concerned about our leak. He was a little upset about not being informed of the A50U being on station during the last op," Mike said.

"If that's all that's worrying him, he's a lucky guy. Any chance our leak is really his leak?"

"Do I think Pat, or one of his guys, told a WaPo reporter that they hit Umar in Mogadishu? No. I don't. We can give his team a polygraph if you want," Mike said.

"Do that, just to cover all of the bases. I agree with you though. I don't see the motivation."

"We both know where the leak came from," Mike said.

"She passed her polygraph. It was administered yesterday," the Director said.

"That doesn't mean anything."

"It has meaning. Vanessa is a skilled liar. But she's never had the training to defeat a polygraph," the Director replied.

"We don't know what training she's received, who she's working with or even what her motivations are. It may have been one of her subordinates," Mike said.

"We could be chasing shadows here."

"How do you explain the information on the A50U not passing to the operators?" Mike said.

"Vanessa was never given that information, that's too deep in the weeds for her. She handled the high-level meetings in Tel Aviv. She's a lawyer, not an operator. The operational details were passed by the Israelis to members of her team who travelled with her."

"Who picked that team?" Mike asked.

"She did."

"Have we run down who received the information and the reason why it wasn't passed on?" Mike said.

"No, if I do then it will be open war. I'm not ready to make that accusation just yet. I'm just focusing on the leak at the moment," the Director said.

"This woman is running roughshod over the Agency."

"She's a watchdog. Her power is growing because she's finding genuine abuses and bringing them to light," the Director said.

"There was no abuse in the Mogadishu operation," Mike said.

"No, but what followed certainly was. If word leaks out that one of our assets took highly classified information obtained during a counter-terrorism operation in Africa and used it to go on a vigilante killing spree inside the US, I'm finished. We're both finished," the Director said.

"Does Venessa have that knowledge?" Mike said.

"Not yet, but it's definitely possible she'll eventually get it. That idiot Walsh personally gave the video to the Nashville Police. Vanessa knows that much. In fact, everyone knows that much. The release of the rapists in Nashville is a popular news story. The vigilante killing spree is still a secret, but with the FBI investigating and Walsh or at least his alias already identified as a person of interest, that's not going to stay a secret for very long. He shot a middle school principal in the head when he freed that girl," the Director said.

"That principal wasn't an innocent victim," Mike said.

"Hiring a prostitute is not a death penalty offense. The man was a community leader. He had a wife and kids," the Director said.

"He was a perv, shot in the act of committing statutory rape against a child who'd been kidnapped and enslaved. He got what he deserved," Mike said.

"When the police trace the ballistics on the gun that killed that perv, as you call him, to the gun that killed Hodar in Nashville, what do you think is going to happen?" the Director asked.

"Walsh is going to become a person of interest in the Columbus, Ohio killings too," Mike said.

"Yes, and how confident are you that he wasn't captured on a camera in that Columbus motel?"

"Pat's too smart for that and I think prostitution rings pick sleazy motels without cameras for their own reasons," Mike said.

"He didn't have enough sense to change his weapon, how many other mistakes did he make?" the Director said.

"He's pretty attached to the M1911. He's a sentimental guy," Mike said.

"A weapon that he took from a man in Nashville, who wound up dead the same night the weapon was stolen," the Director said.

"Pat didn't kill the hotel manager," Mike said.

"He only interrogated him and then stole his weapon," the Director added.

"Right."

"All of this was unnecessary. Law enforcement stands a good chance of piecing this together and when they do, it will get out and be used against me and the administration," the Director said.

"It's a scandal. I know."

"You and I have been friends for a long time. For your own good, I'm going to transfer you out of the firing line on this. I'm going to assign a new handler for Walsh. We're going to keep our heads down and hope the FBI doesn't connect the dots," the Director said.

"What about Vanessa? Don't you think she'll know something is up if you transfer me?" Mike asked.

"We'll let her believe you were transferred because a video from your hit team in Mogadishu made its way to Nashville and was used to set five rapists free. The rest of the sordid story isn't needed to justify the transfer. It won't raise suspicion that there's another shoe to drop," the Director said.

"Our assigned watchdog is going to want oversight of Trident and Pat," Mike said.

"She won't get it from me, but that doesn't mean she won't go over my head."

"A meeting between Pat and Vanessa would be worth the

price of admission. Setting up his team by not disclosing the Russian AWAC plane didn't go over well with him," Mike said.

"We've already discussed that. We don't have proof."

"Put Pat in a room with Vanessa and he'll have proof in thirty seconds. Where are you sidelining me to anyway?"

"You're the new head of Research and Development," the Director said.

"You're kidding," Mike said.

"It shouldn't be for too long. They're working on a couple of projects where your insights should be valuable. Tell your man Walsh, he has a new dog trainer. She'll be in touch," the Director said.

"She?"

"In your absence, your Deputy will fill in as the DDO and Emily Quinn will take over as Walsh's handler."

"Is that wise? Emily and Walsh aren't going to get along. She's good, but sometimes heavy handed," Mike said.

"You and Walsh have too much history together, your relationship is too personal and that can affect your judgement. Emily won't have that problem; Walsh needs a heavy hand," the Director said.

"It's your call. Walsh has served us well over the years," Mike said.

"He has, but at the moment, he's our biggest liability and it's Emily's job to rein him in or we're going to have to cut him loose," the Director said.

"People like Walsh can't be cut loose," Mike said.

"I know that. It just sounds better than what would really happen if he were to break off his chain again," the Director said.

"What are you going to do about Vanessa?" Mike asked.

"I have a closed hearing on the Hill tomorrow with Senate Intel. I'm sure she's already fully briefed the opposition. The commie wing of the democrat party will be armed for bear. My plan is to survive the fallout of this debacle and deal with Vanessa later," the Director said.

"I guess this is where I take my leave and find my way to R&D."

"It is, keep your head down and I'll bring you back as soon as I can," the Director said.

Mike left the room and returned to his office downstairs. He called in Brad Steward, his deputy, and let him know that he was going to be running the show while he worked on a special project in R&D. Brad looked surprised and genuinely disappointed. He was a loyal Deputy. He was even more surprised at the news that Emily Quinn was going to be stepping in as Pat Walsh's handler.

Mike's next task was to contact Pat.

"I'm being moved off my desk until this dust storm you created blows over. Emily Quinn will be your contact for the next little while," Mike said.

"Who's Emily Quinn?"

"She's a seasoned agent who works in my department. Very competent, no nonsense type of person. She won't find you amusing. Be nice to her," Mike said.

"Nice it is," I said.

"Stay out of trouble while I'm out of contact. The politicos are not happy with the current situation. They'll throw you to the wolves to save themselves. Don't do anything to make it worse," Mike said.

"I'll just stay in my corner and color inside the lines. You know me," I said.

CHAPTER 17

NASHVILLE, TENNESSEE

D ETECTIVE GRACE DEFOREST parked her Prius in the usual spot and made her way across the parking lot to the precinct building. Her pace was a little faster than usual because she was venting off an excess of nervous energy. She had a meeting with the Precinct Commander. He'd been evasive when he called last night, but she had a pretty good idea of the subject matter. Captain Allison had always treated her well. He was a good boss, he had an unflappable personality, a positive outlook and he always treated Grace with respect.

Grace waved to the desk sergeant and headed down the corridor to the Commander's Office. When she saw that Captain Allison had someone else in the room, she hesitated at the entrance. The Precinct Commander waved her in with his fingers.

"Detective Deforest, this is Detective Bob Lamy from Internal Affairs. He was sent from headquarters. He's here to ask you some questions," Captain Allison said.

A sudden warmth flooded Grace's face and her porcelain

white skin became flushed. She wasn't expecting Internal Affairs.

"About what?" she stammered.

"Don't get defensive, Grace. The local FBI office lodged a complaint. Now its Bob's job to look into the issue and respond back to the Feds."

"What did the FBI complain about?" Grace asked.

"I'm going to let Bob do his interview with you one on one. You and I can talk later. Of all the people working in this precinct, the one I worry least about is you. Just be open and clear with Bob and I'm sure this matter will be behind us soon," Captain Allison said.

Grace clasped her trembling hands behind her back. She was angry at herself for appearing weak. Bob Lamy said something she couldn't comprehend and walked out of the office. Grace sheepishly followed him as he led her into an interrogation room that was already prepared with a video camera and a notepad. As soon as she sat down, the Internal Affairs Officer recited a Miranda Warning, he also informed her that she had a right to having a union representative present.

"Is this necessary?" Grace asked.

"It's procedure. When we're done, I'm going to have a transcript made up and I'm going to ask you to sign it."

"I don't want an attorney or a union representative," Grace said.

"Please state your full name and badge number."

The interview went on for two hours. Grace felt less threatened as the interview progressed. By the end, she'd gone from fear to relaxed to angry.

"That should be all I need to complete my report. You

shouldn't talk to anyone else about this. I'll call you if I have any questions, most likely you'll get an email from me and a request to come in and sign off on the transcript." He retrieved the camera and left the interview room.

After the interview, Grace went into the break room and got a cold Pepsi from the machine. A known vegetarian with a disdain for junk food, her presence in the break room was a noteworthy event. She could feel the eyes of her co-workers staring at her, but wasn't sure if it was because she bought a soda or because they knew about her interview with Internal Affairs. The South Precinct was a small place and she knew that rumors would fly. Instead of satisfying the people's curiosity, she walked out of the break room and headed to Captain Allison's office.

"What was that all about?" Captain Allison asked.

"They didn't tell you?" Grace said with her eyes wide in exasperation.

"Only that the FBI lodged a complaint to the Superintendent. We get millions each year in grants from the Feds, the Superintendent was quick to bend over for them," Captain Allison said.

"I had a meeting with the two Federal Agents who are working the Hodar case. It was originally my case and I still have reasons to meet with them. All I did was ask them why it was a federal case," Grace said.

"What did they tell you?"

"They gave me some bologna about not being able to answer, because I'm not cleared and it's need to know," Grace said.

"What happened then?"

"I got frustrated. The senior agent is a real piece of work.

He's an arrogant misogynist. You know me, I never lose my temper, but I told him that I don't think the problem is my security clearance. I told him I thought the problem was that the Feds were covering their asses because they've made another big mistake," Grace said.

"That's not complaint worthy," Captain Allison said.

"Not yet it isn't. He pushed back and wanted to know what the first mistake was. I told him; the evidence the Federals provided us on the Becky Anderson case was inadmissible. They should've known it was tainted and at a minimum warned us. I told them that it's no coincidence that within days of the Feds ignoring a reported kidnapping and a rape, we have two murders on the same night," Grace said.

"I'll bet they didn't like to hear that," Captain Allison said.

"They didn't, but I didn't stop there. I asked them how it was possible that the defense counsel knew the evidence was inadmissible, when the Federal Government, who gave us the evidence, didn't," Grace said.

"They're a bunch of keystone cops, aren't they?"

"Peterson got in my face. Instead of answering, he went on the offense and tried to intimidate me. I told him to back off," Grace said.

"What happened?"

"He didn't back off, even after I warned him. The guy's six-two and he was towering over me, with his face inches from my face. I could smell the Kentucky Fried Chicken the slob had for lunch."

"What did you do?"

"I kneed him in the family jewels and walked out," she said, smiling just a little.

"He should've been embarrassed; I can't believe he lodged a complaint because you took him down," Captain Allison said.

"The official reason for the complaint was about an unauthorized investigation into a federal case with full knowledge the jurisdiction had already been transferred from the Nashville PD to the FBI," Grace said.

"Did you?"

"No, all I did was ask why the case was transferred to the Feds. I was curious, I didn't talk to anyone about it but the Bureau, it's hardly an investigation," Grace said.

"It's a good question," Captain Allison said.

"I didn't think you knew the answer, or I would've asked you. Who does know?" Grace asked.

"The Superintendent for sure, other than that, maybe no one," Captain Allison said.

"Isn't that suspicious to you?" Grace asked.

"It's unusual. I'll give you that."

"The person who put those questions in my head was Agent McDermott from Homeland. He told me someone had to have leaked the information that was in that news article to the defense counsel, weeks before it came out in the papers. I think he's right. That's why I was asking. How else would the defense know to request a suppression hearing before the story came out in the paper?"

"McDermott is a suspicious character in his own right. Nothing about him rings true as a Homeland Special Agent. When we confirmed his credentials, it took a very long time and the way the call kept getting transferred was odd," Captain Allison said.

"The FBI guys don't like him much. They've insinuated

on a couple of occasions that he's a spook and not a run of the mill Homeland agent," Grace said.

"I'll ask the Superintendent what the reason was for the Bureau to take over the Hodar case. You should make nice with the Fibbies, bring your buddy an ice pack or something," Captain Allison said.

"I'll apologize."

"How did it go with Lamy?" Captain Allison asked.

"He didn't say one way or another. But he's not going to find any evidence of me conducting an unauthorized investigation, because there's no evidence to find. I think the FBI filed the complaint as a warning to keep me from looking into Hodar," Grace said.

"Now I'm curious."

"Tread carefully. Something is definitely off here."

CHAPTER 18

CAPE GOOD HOPE

"**W**HAT DID I get myself into?" McDonald said as we both stared at the weather report on my MacBook. We were onboard the *Nomad*, inside the wheelhouse sitting side by side in the two captain's chairs. We were dividing our attention between the weather report and the churning seas in view through the wheelhouse window.

"Rounding the Cape of Good Hope will be an adventure, he said. The Suez Canal is for sissies, he said. This is a bucket list item, you should come, he said," McDonald slowly intoned with the maximum amount of regret emphasized in his voice.

"The *Wayward Nomad* was built to withstand a typhoon. We'll be fine," I said.

"We're looking at fifty-foot seas. Twenty years in the Navy and I experienced that once and that was on an Aircraft Carrier. It was scary on an aircraft carrier," McDonald said.

"These will be more like thirty-foot seas, don't exaggerate," I said.

"Where the Indian Ocean and Atlantic meet, the current

produces freak waves. That's where we're going to be when the storm hits. I promise you we have a chance of having to deal with fifty footers," McDonald said.

"I've done it before and you're a better captain than me," I said.

"You have?" His skepticism was clear.

"Yeah, I drove the *Sam Houston* through a hurricane once. *Nomad* is twice the boat. I'm not worried," I said.

"You don't want to turn and run?"

"It'll cost us at least a week and even at forty knots we can't outrun what's bearing down on us," I said.

"But we can make contact at someplace other than the Agulhas Bank," McDonald said.

"Is the Agulhas that bad?" I asked.

"It's the point where the currents collide, even in perfect conditions the seas are fifteen feet with the threat of rogue waves," McDonald said.

"How about this. We cut our speed. Deal with the storm tomorrow and then deal with the Agulhas Bank the following day," I said.

"That makes more sense. Meaning it's not suicidal," McDonald said.

"We'll putter towards Port Elizabeth at five knots. Deal with the storm and then go back to cruising speed to get around the Horn."

McDonald shrugged. "That's as good a plan as any."

"Your lack of faith in the Italian craftsmanship that went into the *Nomad* is an insult to the descendants of Michelangelo and Davinci who designed and built it," I said.

"*Nomad* is solid, but much bigger ships have been lost in the Cape," McDonald said.

"Since we now have a day of leisure before two days of roller coaster rides, I'm going to check all the tie downs and grill some steaks on the flydeck," I said.

"It's raining."

"Pre-hurricane traditions must be followed. The sea gods are very unforgiving when they're not."

I was on shift when the heavy seas reached storm levels in the pre-dawn hours the next morning. The sleek ninety-ton yacht was unsurprisingly nimble as I worked to keep the bow into the cascading waves. Three 1,900 horsepower Man Engines married to a waterjet propulsion system allowed for forward speed even when the *Nomad* was in a forty-five degree climb up a fifty-foot oncoming swell. At times the downward momentum submersed the *Nomad* up to the main deck as it plunged downward into the trough of a big wave. The composite hull with Kevlar and carbon reinforcements withstood the immense pressures with ease.

I was standing between the twin captain's chairs in the wheelhouse with my left hand on the wheel and my right on the thrust controls. The rain was driving hard and I could barely make out the small pennant mounted on the bow of the yacht. I relied on the thermal FLIR display on the left console for visibility. The 360-degree camera system in the center console reassured me of the structural integrity of the yacht. The Cape of Good Hope is a frequently trafficked shipping lane, but not on this day. I had the radar limited to twenty-five miles and we were the only craft in the area according to the navigation and radar display picture I kept on in the third computer console.

McDonald slid into the seat behind me to the right. I saw

him move into position in the reflection of the windshield glass. The two huge windshield wipers moved hypnotically.

"Do you mind if I turn on the stabilizers?" McDonald said.

"I shut 'em off, because they didn't seem to be doing any good."

McDonald switched on the two Seakeeper gyro stabilizers. "It should stem the roll some."

"You want to take the wheel, while I go make some coffee?"

"Is that even possible?"

"Yeah. Of course," I said as the sleek black hull of the *Nomad* surfed down a giant swell and knifed into the ocean below. A cascade of rushing water impacted against the angled windshield with a thud and I pushed on the thrusters to propel the *Nomad* through the pressing sea.

"Switch," I said while moving to my left and allowing McDonald to take the wheel.

"Got it," he said.

"Do you want milk and sugar?"

"I'm gonna need both hands," McDonald said as he turned and powered the boat up the next huge swell.

"All right, I'll get you a Thermos," I said.

"Black's good."

"I'll fix you some breakfast too, something you can eat with one hand."

I pinballed myself downstairs to the galley. Midship and inside the stairwell, the pitches and rolls felt more pronounced for some reason. I have a gimbled pan holder that I attached over a stove burner; it allowed the pan to stay level while the stove surface tilted constantly. Coffee was even easier. The stainless-steel galley was built for rough seas and in thirty minutes I had a stack of bacon and egg English muffins for McDonald and myself.

When I returned to the wheelhouse with breakfast, the sky was noticeably brighter, the cloud cover gave the morning sky an ominous grey appearance and the South Indian Ocean was almost black. It was light enough to spot the incoming swells without the aid of the FLIR and McDonald had retasked the console dedicated to the FLIR to display the weather report.

"We have I'd say two to three more hours of this before we get a break."

"I'm going to do a walk around and make sure we still have everything and then I'm going to get some sleep," I said.

"I'll be up on the comms, keep me updated."

I staggered back through the dining area to the salon. Through the windows, I could see we had lost a few of the fenders. Watching the water wash over the stern deck was enough to dissuade me from venturing out and checking the garage. I could see the uninflated extreme weather life raft McDonald had secured on top of the garage in case of an emergency. The bucking movement of the boat made climbing the outside staircase to the flydeck too dangerous. I wound up doing the survey from inside the main cabin. I'd been up most of the night and decided that survival was the better part of valor and called it quits and went to bed.

Three hours later, I awoke to darkness. The nightlights in my cabin were off. I reached down into my side table and retrieved a flashlight. I put my headset on and called McDonald.

"What's going on? Power's out on the lower deck."

"Main generator shut down. I'm using the second one to run the wheelhouse."

"Any idea what's wrong?"

"I was going to wait for it to calm a little more before checking."

"It seems to have calmed a lot."

"It has, but I still need to be at the wheel."

"I'll check it."

I entered the engine room through the door next to my walk-in closet in the owner's state room. The *Nomad* has twin 28KW Kohler Generators. With all of the electrical systems on, both generators usually operate at seventy percent capacity. If one of the generators drops off the power network, the computer automatically turns off non-essential power users and keeps the more critical areas like the wheelhouse, sensor systems, galley, anchor chain, hydraulic lift, HVAC and main deck powered. The generator system has a digital control panel and I cycled through the reset. When that didn't work, I went through the troubleshooting menu. It took forty minutes, but I eventually found the issue and restarted the generator. After that I went to the wheelhouse.

"You don't look the worse for wear," I said to McDonald.

"All's well. The weather is clearing. I've brought us up to forty knots, so we can reach the Agulhas Bank while we still have a few hours of light."

"So, I'll take this shift and you get the excitement," I said.

"We should both be up in the wheelhouse when we reach Agulhas Bank. One to control and the other to watch. The waves can come from any direction," McDonald said.

"How will we know the exact spot where the warm

Agulhas current meets with the cold south Atlantic current? Is it always in the same point on the chart?" I said.

"The location varies, we'll know because the waters will become wild," McDonald said.

Contrary to the expectations set by McDonald, the churning tumultuous waters of Agulhas Bank were fairly tame compared to the previous day's storm. The seas were under fifteen feet and we were fortunate not to experience any of the rogue waves the area is famous for. We rounded the southern tip of Africa and set out for St. Helena Island which is located about a third of the way to the Caribbean across the Atlantic. The remainder of the trip to Eleuthera was uneventful. Having McDonald along on the trip made it far more comfortable than my original plans to solo. McDonald was the consummate master chief. He was always inspecting, fixing and upgrading his surroundings. A quiet unpretentious guy who's never idle. Over the years, he'd emerged as a reliable and solid leader who kept the team together during my frequent absences. He's a great second in command and I enjoyed his company.

CHAPTER 19

ELEUTHERA, BAHAMAS

AFTER SECURING THE *Nomad* at the marina, McDonald and I were driven to the house by Jonah. After twenty days at sea, working a minimum of eighteen hours a day, I was tired. McDonald had an arm-long list of tasks we worked our way through every day. We returned with a yacht that was in better shape than when I bought it. The *Nomad* was cleaned and serviced from top to bottom. McDonald and I were both sporting beards from the trip and we were looking forward to one of Maria's homecooked meals and a drink. When we drove through the gate and down the long driveway, there was a car I didn't recognize parked near the house.

"Who's the visitor?" I asked Jonah.

"I don't know. That car wasn't there when I left to pick you up."

I grabbed my bag of dirty clothes from the back of the Tahoe and headed up the stairs to the main entry. I wasn't two steps inside the hallway before a woman stepped in front of my path and stuck her hand out.

"Hi, I'm Emily Quinn."

"Did I get the days mixed up? I thought our meeting wasn't for another two days," I said.

"No mix up. I saw you were going to arrive early, so I adjusted my schedule."

"This is Roger McDonald." I gestured to McDonald.

They shook hands.

"Do you mind if I have a word alone with Pat?" Emily said to McDonald.

"No problem," McDonald said while giving me the hand and arm signal for danger area behind Emily's back.

I walked Emily down the corridor to the living room. I sat on a chair and Emily took the couch across from it. Maria entered and took our drink orders. Emily asked for green tea. I asked for a tall Scotch on the rocks. Emily waited for Maria to leave the room before starting the conversation.

"Is there someplace more private?"

"I have an office on the third floor. I thought this was a social visit," I said.

"It's not."

"Do you make unscheduled business meetings a habit?" I asked.

"Yes, when it suits me."

"What about me. Do I get a vote?" I said.

"No, you don't," Emily said.

"If the price of my continued relationship with your organization is to be tracked and intruded upon, then I think it's time we parted ways," I said.

Maria entered the room wheeling a drink trolley. She removed a tea service and placed it in front of Emily. She had three bottles of Scotch arrayed on the top shelf and I stood up to review my options. I poured myself an inch of Talisker 18 over a single ice cube.

"Thanks, Maria," I said with a smile. I could tell by her facial expression that she was concerned with the visitor. Maria is a very perceptive person and the tension between Emily and myself wasn't difficult for her to sense.

I returned to my lounge chair and put my feet up on the ottoman. I tasted the Scotch. It had a citrusy smell and a smoky finish. It was pleasant and warm, unlike the stone-faced woman sitting across from me.

"Why are you still here?" I asked.

"There seems to be a misunderstanding, Mr. Walsh. I don't believe I've properly introduced myself."

"By all means."

"I was sent by the Director to meet with you at the earliest possible opportunity."

"That's all well and fine. It still doesn't explain why you arrived unannounced. You must have been tracking our voyage. I have phone, internet, satellite and radio. We'd already scheduled a meeting by email. I'm not that hard to get a hold of," I said.

"I don't believe I need to explain myself. Like you, I follow orders," Emily said.

"Well that's just the thing. At no time did I ever agree to follow orders from you."

"We both work for the same agency. We follow the chain of command and like it or not, I'm your new handler," Emily said.

"That's where we disagree. Trident contracts with the Agency. The Agency is under no obligation to contract with Trident and Trident is under no obligation to accept work from the Agency. I'm not at your beck and call and you're not my plantation owner," I said.

"You make it sound like you have a choice," Emily said.

"I do have a choice. I don't need the Agency any more than the Agency needs me. Because I trust Mike, I was willing to take risks that come with Agency assignments. With you, I'm not. You should return to Langley and go back to whatever it is that you do," I said.

"Mike has given you too much leeway. Your ties to the Agency are not breakable. If you try to break those ties it will be done on the Agency's terms or you're going to find yourself in serious jeopardy," Emily said.

"I've had the Agency turn on me before. That didn't turn out all that well for the people involved. You should've known that if you're my dog trainer or whatever you call yourself," I said.

Emily's face was ashen white. This meeting was obviously not going the way she expected it to. I'd been leaning forward in my seat. I sat back and sipped my drink.

"What are you saying, Mr. Walsh? Are you stopping work on all of Trident's activities?" Emily asked.

"I'll of course finish the deliveries on the orders we're contracted for. If you want to send Trident more logistics work, then we'll be happy to support. But on the operational side, I'm only going to accept assignments from Mike," I said.

"And why is that again?" Emily said.

"I trust Mike. I don't trust anyone else at Langley. I never have. I've had enough of bureaucrats endangering my team for reasons that are political and have nothing to do with the mission," I said.

"Such as?"

"Such as not being notified of a Russian AWAC plane in the area of operations during our last mission," I said.

"You know about that?"

"Yes, you seem surprised that Mike shared that information with me. That's what I mean by trust. With Mike, Trident is a partner. To most DC bottom dwellers, Trident is a disposable collection of guys whose lives can be traded for their personal aims," I said.

"I assure you that is not the case with me," Emily said.

"Sure, you think so highly of me that you didn't even give me the consideration of advanced notice. I'm sure you'll be very respectful of the lives of my team."

"The two are hardly equivalent."

"It's the little things."

I got up and fixed myself another drink. I returned to my chair and we both sat in silence. I stroked my beard and waited for the tiresome woman to excuse herself and leave. The color had returned to her face, but she wasn't showing any signs of departing. Emily looked to be in her mid to late thirties. She was wearing a black pants suit that was loose fitting and disguised her figure. Her only jewelry was a simple silver watch and she wore no make-up. Her brunette hair was tied in a bun. Despite the obvious attempts to hide it, Emily was a green-eyed beauty of the Catherine Zeta-Jones variety.

"I've worked for Mike for the better part of seven years. He's been removed from his desk because of you. It was your actions that put him in the trouble he now finds himself in. You've made it clear that you don't have any loyalty towards the Agency, but you should at least consider him," Emily said.

"Bravo, Emily. You're a quick learner. I've heard it said that the job of an agent is to get people to betray their country and you definitely have the requisite persuasive skill set. Since I'm sure you wouldn't have come down here without first reading my considerable personnel file, was it your plan all along to deke me with the frontal attack and then hook me with the 'let's save Mike together' meme?" I said.

"I would never do that. I just want you to understand that we have a mutual interest. Mike's been my mentor and boss for my entire career at the Agency," Emily said.

"I've known him for decades and I can tell you that if given the choice between allowing that poor girl from Orono, Maine to remain in the hands of those Somali savages or to suffer whatever humiliation and exile the Agency has punished him with, he'd choose the punishment every time," I said.

"I'm sure that makes you feel a lot less guilty," Emily said.

"I don't feel guilty at all. What's the purpose of this meeting anyway?" I asked.

"Since we're going to be working together, I wanted to introduce myself and get some ground rules established."

"Talk to Mike and he'll brief you on the routine. I get a call once or twice a month. Requisitions get sent to the Trident main office by email and get handled by my Office Manager, Jessica. We face to face only if we're planning a covert op and until Mike's back there'll be none of those," I said.

"That was Mike. He's a Deputy Director with many other important obligations. Me, I'm just a humble agent. I've been assigned to you and only you," Emily said.

"What does that mean?" I said.

"It means we're joined at the hip until Mike gets back at his desk," Emily said.

I looked across to the woman. Her stubbornness was exhausting, and I was already tired from my journey. I decided to take the path of least resistance and give in to the inevitability of it. I was too tired, and this was not what I had planned for the evening.

"Whatever you say, Emily."

"Where should I unpack my stuff?"

"Maria will show you to a room," I said as I stood up and walked out.

CHAPTER 20

WASHINGTON, DC

ABDULWALI MUSE DROVE his black Mercedes S550 down New Jersey Avenue past the Congressional Black Caucus Institute and turned right into the parking lot IAIR shared with the Democratic National Committee. He found an open space on the opposite side of the lot and with the help of a cane, shuffled the hundred yards to the IAIR Headquarters. He pressed the doorbell and looked up at the camera. He heard the buzz of the lock release and he opened the door and entered.

It was Saturday morning and except for a lone security guard, the building was empty. Had they been in, Abdulwali would not have been recognized by any of the IAIR staff. He walked under a banner above the reception desk pronouncing IAIR as America's largest Muslim Civil Rights organization. Abdulwali was at the IAIR Headquarters to meet with the other two leaders of the American Muslim Brotherhood.

The Ikhwan, or Muslim Brotherhood in the US, was organized with a simple mission statement. The words were known by the members as the explanatory memorandum.

"The Ikhwan must understand that their work in America is a kind of grand Jihad in eliminating and destroying the Western civilization from within and 'sabotaging' its miserable house by their hands and the hands of the believers so that it is eliminated and God's religion is made victorious over all other religions."

To achieve the mission, or the Project as they liked to call it, they formed three support organizations in 1994 with complementary purposes. The Institute on American Islamic Relations (IAIR) was formed to serve as the propaganda arm of the movement. IAIR was created to carry out information operations and to weaken the American culture through the application of soft power. The North American Islamic Group (NAIG) was created to serve as the operational arm of the triad. The serious work of the NAIG wouldn't begin until IAIR had properly weakened the enemy and set the conditions for a successful open confrontation. NAIG was constantly being renamed, reinvented and reorganized. Exercising the application of hard power, even planning for the use of force, was a serious crime and as such, NAIG was constantly under threat from American Counter-Terrorism activities. The Safa Group was the financial arm of the Project and like NAIR, it could only exist as a covert organization.

Of the three organizations, IAIR was by far the most successful. In just a short twenty-five years, IAIR had achieved such a high level of acceptance in American society that it was considered to be part of the civil rights fabric of the nation. IAIR was a sacrosanct institution. For any politician or government official to question IAIR's activities or motivations was to automatically trigger an outcry of Islamophobia and the inevitable social and political death that follows such a serious betrayal of the cherished twin values of diversity and inclusiveness.

Unlike IAIR, which was nourished in the warm embrace of the Washington establishment, NAIG and Safa were feral, hunted organizations that lived underground under the constant threat of discovery by American Intelligence and Law Enforcement. NAIG and Safa were organized in small independent cells and employed hundreds of cutouts and shell organizations to protect themselves.

The three founders of the Project were as different as the organizations they managed. Abdulwali managed NAIG, he was a Palestinian who fought beside Yasser Arafat in the seventies and endured ten years of torture in an Israeli prison. His outwardly frail physique and prematurely aged features could cause one to let down their guard and overlook a brilliant tactical mind and the fire of a true zealot. Akrim, who managed IAIR, was perfectly suited for the public spotlight. A charming affable man with a warm smile and calm pleasant demeanor, Akrim truly was a wolf in sheep's clothing. In contrast to Akrim, the dapper, slightly overweight Egyptian propagandist, the leader of the financial organization had the physique of an elite long-distance runner. Siyam, the head of Safa, was also from Egypt. He had black eyes, a big nose and hawkish features. All three men were the same age and, although different in looks and demeanor, were equally unified when it came to the purpose and resolve to see the Project through to success.

Abdulwali walked into the Director's Office and sat on the couch at the corner farthest from the door. The IAIR HQ was the one place where they could be sure the authorities would never dare to electronically monitor their meetings and communications. He was early as was his habit and he always took the same seat during meetings because it gave him a view of the door and the exterior windows. He removed a pack of French cigarettes and with a gold lighter bearing the image of Yasser Arafat, he lit it.

Akrim and Siyam arrived before he finished his cigarette. Abdulwali rose to greet each of the two men with a kiss on both cheeks.

"You're looking well, my friend," Akrim said to Abdulwali.

"You lie so well, Akrim. I look like hell frozen over and you know it," Abdulwali said showing his gaunt arm with an IV starter bandaged to the crook of his elbow.

"How do you feel, Abdulwali?" asked Siyam.

"I'm going to beat this. I have only one more chemo session to go and I've decided I look better without hair."

"That's the fighting spirit, Wal," Akrim said.

"Where are we on this situation with the Somalis?" Siyam asked.

"It's contained," said Abdulwali.

"The Somalis are behaving like raving maniacs; they're jeopardizing years of work," Akrim said.

"In the current political climate our immigration efforts are hard enough without the Somali gangs confirming people's worst stereotypes," Siyam said.

"We need to ask them to temper themselves," Akrim said.

"How do we do that? They only listen to their gang leaders. Does anyone know a Somali gang leader?" Abdulwali said.

"I know a relative of a Somali gang leader," Akrim said.

"Who's that?" Abdulwali said.

"Our very own Congresswoman Noor Qalanjo," Akrim said.

"What's her connection?" Abdulwali said.

"Her ex-husband, who's also her brother, runs the largest Somali gang in the country," Akrim said.

"She married her brother?" Siyam said.

"It was a marriage of convenience to expedite his immigration application," Akrim said.

"Oh, makes sense, but you never know with the Somalis," Siyam said.

"Will the Congresswoman help?" Abdulwali asked.

"Definitely. She worked for us at the IAIR Minneapolis Office for several years and it was our organization that got her to where she is today. She's depending on our funding for her re-election. She'll help," Akrim said.

"Then you should meet with her, Akrim. Ask her to speak to her brother and calm things down for a while. We can't have any more negative publicity," Abdulwali said.

"I thought you said the negative publicity was contained," Siyam said.

"On the major news networks it is, but the internet is less easy to control," Abdulwali said.

"I'll talk to Noor. She's a good girl and she'll listen to me," Akrim said.

"Will her brother listen, that's the question," Abdulwali said.

"The Somalis remit billions of dollars each year. Much of it for Jihad. And it's not just money. From Minnesota alone they sent many jihadi warriors to the levant and even more back to Somalia recently to pursue Jihad with Al Shabab. Noor's brother is of a like mind. Of course, he'll understand, he just needs to be given the message," Akrim said.

"The gangs need to alter their business behavior. Kidnapping American girls and prostituting them is to invite retaliation," Siyam said.

"I don't see any retaliation, only submission. The stories on the release of the Nashville Rapists on the major news outlets are careful not to mention the nationality or religion of the assailants," Akrim said.

"Not all of the networks and certainly not on all of the social media services," Abdulwali said.

"This is not Rotherham, the American people will not accept the widespread exploitation of young innocent girls," Akrim said.

"American girls are never innocent, look at the way they dress and how they behave. The gangs are merely putting them to work doing what they've been bred to do," Siyam said.

"Agreed. But not now, not while we're fighting in the courts to block this Administration's ban on Muslim immigration. We need public support and the Somalis must not be allowed to jeopardize public sentiment," Abdulwali said.

"I'll have Congresswoman Noor in here first thing next week to discuss her next campaign fundraiser," Akrim said.

*

Two days later Akrim greeted Congresswoman Noor and the two sat around the very same coffee table.

"You look very happy, Noor, Washington, DC is agreeing with you," Akrim said.

"I like it very much, Akrim. I love what I do."

"You've had your share of bad press lately," Akrim said.

"A small group of haters out to destroy me. My poll numbers in the district are through the roof," Noor said.

"Even with your recent comments about the Jews buying support with the Benjamins as you call them," Akrim said.

"My poll numbers are rising because of that remark, not despite it." The two laughed.

"Do you and your brother stay in contact, Congresswoman?" Akrim asked.

"Yes, we talk, not every week, but we're in contact," Noor said.

"The Nashville Rape case has been bad for us. Many leading supporters of IAIR have voiced concern. The story plays to the worst stereotypes and we believe it's important that we not have another like it," Akrim said.

"What can I do?" Noor asked.

"Can you talk to your brother? We know he has influence with the gangs. Ask him to tell the people to tone it down for a while. We're fighting the ban on Muslim immigration and many other initiatives designed to erode our rights. We must have popular support. This story and others like it will cause that support to disappear," Akrim said.

"I'll return to Minneapolis this weekend and give him the message in person," Noor said.

"Will he listen to you?" Akrim asked.

"I don't know. My brother is not one to take advice from a woman, even from his own sister," Noor said.

"Do your best. Tell him that if he's willing to tone things down, I can make it worth his while," Akrim said.

"How?"

"It's best I not tell you. You're a Congresswoman and a

member of the Foreign Affairs Committee. Suffice it to say, that I know of an organization that moves large sums of money out of the US by courier and they would benefit from someone like your brother who could provide the labor," Akrim said.

"That's the kind of advice my brother understands, regardless of the gender that supplies it," Noor said.

The subject of the meeting switched to fundraising and then to IAIR. Noor smiled deferentially while Akrim pontificated. When Akrim's gaze went to his phone, she checked her watch, careful to hide her anxiety. She had dinner plans and Akrim didn't seem to want to stop talking. Having finished extolling her about his brilliant leadership, he switched over to an analysis of the Jewish problem in American politics. Noor half listened to Akrim, she'd heard it all before and she nodded dutifully at all of the right points. Akrim's face flushed and grew even more impassioned on the subject than when talking about himself. She was always careful to throw red meat to her donors and constituents on this red button topic that was guaranteed to energize her base. Even the non-Somali leftists living in her district reacted positively to Jewish bashing. She believed none of it, she hadn't for years, but she recognized her political future was married to the subject and was always careful to send out an anti-Semitic tweet or two every month to remind her voters that she was still down with the struggle.

Finally, Akrim ran out of steam and finished his lecture. As with most of her meetings with Arab men, she spent almost all of the time listening and deferentially agreeing. Playing the role of the quiet and demure supplicant was a behavior she'd learned from her brother who was not afraid to take off his leather belt and beat her if she disagreed. She dreaded visiting him in Minneapolis. But recognizing that she had no choice, she sent a text to her Chief of Staff to make the travel arrangements before starting her Volkswagen Passat and leaving the parking lot.

CHAPTER 21

ELEUTHERA, BAHAMAS

I DROVE EMILY QUINN to Governor's Harbor and escorted her over to the Trident Headquarters. The building was a restored mansion that was constructed by a wealthy trader in the early nineteenth century. It was a pastel-colored three-story stucco house with white storm shutters and a widow's peak offering an amazing view of the Harbor on the Caribbean side of the narrow island.

After a quick meet and greet, I handed Emily over to Jessica's charge to familiarize her with the Trident operation. Jessica joined my team while I was still in the construction business in North Carolina. Her dad was a legend in the special mission unit I'd once served in and at his request, I hired her when she graduated from the University of North Carolina. The years had been good to Jessica. She was a successful businesswoman in her mid-thirties with two great kids and a devoted husband. A five-foot-nothing Korean American, Jessica barely tipped the scale at one hundred pounds. She was an attractive woman with a happy outgoing demeanor, but when the situation called for it, Jessica could be as tough as her dad who was a Son Tay Raider, which is as hard as woodpecker lips. Jessica kept the global operations of Trident running with great efficiency.

I didn't stay around long once we reached the office. After a brief introduction, I got out as fast as I could, anxious to lose my shadow. I was on Banks Road driving back to my house thinking of ways to extend my separation from Emily when an idea hit me. I should take advantage of this pause in operations and go climbing.

My first duty assignment as a young second lieutenant was at Fort Lewis, Washington. I grew up in South Boston and went to school all the way through college in the city. The only grass I ever saw as a kid was on either a baseball or a football field. I had absolutely no experience in the wilderness until I joined the Army. As a poor kid from the city, coming to the great Northwest with its forests, mountains, rivers and oceans, it was impossible not to fall in love with the outdoors. On sunny days, the snowy peak of Mount Rainier was always visible on the eastern horizon and to the West across the Puget sound was the Olympic Mountain Range.

Armed only with two weeks of basic climbing skills I picked up at Ranger school, I wasted little time before venturing out and exploring the peaks of the nearby mountains. I climbed Mount Rainier three times in my first year, each time taking a progressively more difficult route. A popular climbing book at the time was titled *Fifty Classic Climbs of North America*. I found the book in the REI store in Seattle and decided right then and there to complete the list. The first climb I ticked off on the checklist was the Liberty Ridge route on Mount Rainier. What makes bagging the climbs so challenging is that it's not enough to just ascend the peaks, you have to follow the prescribed route from the book to claim credit. There are more people in the world who've climbed the Seven Summits, which are the highest mountains on each continent, than there are people who've completed the *Fifty Classic Climbs of North America*. The last time I checked, only three people had completed all fifty. I was three climbs short of the finish line and had been for years. I've attempted all fifty, but there are three where the mountain gods have denied me success.

The first is Mount Logan, Hummingbird Ridge in the Yukon. The second is Mount Alberta, Japanese Route in the Canadian Rockies and the third is Mount Waddington, South Face in British Columbia. The Hummingbird Ridge route on Mount Logan has only been climbed once, that was in 1965. I've tried it twice and both times I was forced to abandon the climb after being nearly killed in an avalanche. At 19,850 feet it's not the highest peak I've ever attempted, but it's by far the scariest. The mountain is unstable with frequent rock falls and avalanches.

On my first attempt at Mount Alberta, I encountered a freak blizzard in June. I'm confident I can make the climb if the weather conditions are good. But since late spring has already demonstrated itself as not a good time to climb Mount Alberta, I crossed that off the list, which by process of elimination left me with Mount Waddington as my reprieve from Emily.

I went back to the house and began preparing. I contacted my mountain guide friend Bill Walk and arranged to meet him in Vancouver. I lost myself for the next five hours while I hunted around the house gathering my climbing gear. I had the maps and my kit assembled in my office on the third floor when I received a call from Jessica.

"I'd rather not," I said to her request to meet at the Buccaneer for lunch.

"You need to, Emily has questions that I can't answer and I'm hungry," Jessica said.

I reluctantly agreed and thirty minutes later, I was at the outside dining area of the Buccaneer club, sitting at a table with Jessica and Emily. The Buccaneer is on a hill, a quarter mile up the street from the Trident Headquarters. It's a terrific lunch spot, with a pirate themed motif, a big beautiful oak tree throwing shade over the entire dining area and an innovative menu that is always well executed.

Seeing the two girls together, it was apparent they were getting along very well. Jessica is a friendly girl. I wasn't expecting hostility between the two, but I didn't expect them to be finishing each other's sentences either. Both of them began to pepper me with questions as soon as I sat down. I asked for a reprieve until our orders were taken. I ordered the broiled grouper and a beer, resigning myself to the fact that the food was going to be excellent even if the conversation wasn't.

About half of the supplies we procure are manufactured in Asia and Eastern Europe. I shield Jessica from the shady characters we deal with in those territories, which is all of them and the reason why she couldn't answer Emily's questions on the subject. Most of the questions Emily had were about the government officials and arms brokers we work with in Ukraine, Russia, Serbia and China. I soldiered on through the lunch and at the end, Jessica and Emily agreed that I would take Emily back to the house and return her to the headquarters the next day.

After lunch, Jessica returned to the office and I drove back to the house with Emily. She continued the interrogation for the entire drive. It was about as pleasant as having sandpaper rubbed on my face. The arms business outside of North America and Western Europe is dominated by kleptocrats and criminals. The business rules are different in those countries, there are no morals, but there are ethics. The Chinese government has tried to kill me more than once, but they've never refused an export permit to Trident and I've never refused a payment to a Chinese Defense Manufacturer, which are all state controlled. Once we got back to the house, I left Emily and took the elevator to my third-floor office where I was in full prep mode for the Mount Waddington attempt.

I was packing my equipment bags in my office when I spotted Maria in the doorway. She looked flustered. A few seconds later I saw Emily's head poking up over the stairs behind Maria. I looked at Maria and she looked at me. I had given Maria specific instructions to keep Emily off of the third floor. Her facial expression made it clear that she'd communicated my message and that Emily refused to listen. I waved off Maria and decided to deal with Emily myself.

"Being my controller or handler doesn't give you free rein. This office is my refuge, if I wanted to see you up here, I would've let you know," I said.

"I didn't mean to barge in, I was just curious. What are you up to?" she asked picking up an ice axe.

"I'm prepping for a climb," I said

"Where are you going?" Emily said.

"Mount Waddington, South Face," I said.

"*Fifty Classic Climbs*?"

"Yes."

"Where are you?"

"This will be forty-eight," I said.

"I'm going with you."

"Do you know what this climb involves?" I said with a sneer.

"Yes."

"The last time I attempted it, I turned back after a nasty fall. This may be my last opportunity; I'm not interested in taking on a new member of my team," I said.

"I'm qualified," she said.

"Explain."

"McKinley, K2, Annapurna."

I looked at her. For the first time, I gave her body a serious study. Most serious climbers have outsized lower bodies, off the rack clothes big enough to fit over their thighs and calves are usually baggy at the waist. Emily had an alpinist's body.

"When?" I asked.

"Different times within the last five years."

"What do you know about the South Face route up Waddington?" I said.

"Five thousand feet of technical ice climbing. Not many have made it. Bentley made the first accent in the forties," she said.

"I don't know much more than that," I said.

"So, can I come?" she asked.

"I have a guide, who I've been climbing with for years.

I don't really want to introduce another variable into the equation. Maybe next time," I said.

"That's okay, I'll put my own team together. Maybe we'll see each other at the base camp."

I looked at Emily searching for a tell. If she was bluffing, I couldn't read it.

"We leave for the airport at 5 a.m., be ready," I said.

"My equipment is at home," she said.

"We'll gear up in Vancouver. We'll take a day to get what we need and then chopper to the base camp," I said.

We flew to Vancouver in a private charter from the tiny airport in Governor's Harbor. Bill Walk met us in the lobby of the Fairmont Hotel. The flight was productive. Emily and I spent it studying maps and making supply lists. She had a flair for logistics. A very detailed person who took the time to figure out the cubic space and the weight of everything we needed. We were planning an assault climb, which meant we were not going to stockpile supplies. We were going to carry everything we needed on our backs in one trip. We would set up a base camp and then leave our tents and heavy gear and ascend to the summit in a single leg.

After check-in, the three of us jumped into Bill's SUV and headed to Valhalla Outfitters. Bill and Emily compared equipment lists. Bill and I already had most of the common equipment like ropes, tents and stoves. We were just filling gaps with clothing, personal equipment and food.

Vancouver is a nice city with a lot of terrific restaurants. We had dinner on the rooftop of Joe Fortes. I've known Bill for a long time. When I was in the Army, my unit used to contract with his company for advanced mountaineering training. It was with Bill that I first ascended Mt. McKinley.

Bill knew I could hang with him. It was amusing watching Bill and Emily interact. Bill, the consummate mountain guide, was constantly probing Emily to figure out how much of a liability or asset she was going to be on the attempt. Like most military endeavors, climbing is a combination of technical and physical skills. Simple things like the ease with which someone ties a knot can be a useful indicator. Throughout the day of shopping, Bill was testing Emily. By the evening as we sat down to dinner, it was obvious that Emily had passed Bill's evaluation, because she had him eating out of the palm of her hand.

The next morning, we jumped in a Bell 412 Helicopter and headed to our drop off spot. Three hours later, the helicopter set us down on Bravo Glacier on Mount Waddington. We hiked to the base camp at 8,000 feet, pitched our tent and prepared the ropes and equipment to strike out the next morning at three. I cooked a freeze-dried four cheese tortellini and the three of us were in the rack by nine with the glare of the northern sun still shining through the yellow nylon fabric of our tent. I was encouraged by the clear sky; the forecast for the next twenty-four hours was good.

I led out the next morning. All of the pitches of the Southern Route up Mount Waddington were technical ice climbs requiring an ice axe in each hand and a lot of crampon work. The early pitches were relatively easy compared to what was ahead. I led because we needed to save Bill for the more complex reads that were still to come. The wall of snow and ice I started up was a seventy-degree slope. I was wearing stiff crampons under my hiking boots with sharp prongs in the toe that bit into the firm ice wall with each kick. It was a routine that I had repeated thousands of times. Plant the ice axe in my right hand, then the one in my left. Shifting some of my weight to my arms, pulling out of my right foothold and kicking in at a higher point, then doing the same with the left. Every thirty feet, I removed an ice screw from my harness, screwed it into the ice wall, attached a carabiner and then snapped the rope into the carabiner for protection against a fall. It was slow deliberate work that allowed for steady progress. The headlamp fixed to my lightweight helmet illuminated the white ice in front of me.

The three of us were all tied to a single one-hundred-and-fifty-foot rope. Bill and I alternated in the lead for most of the day while Emily remained in the center of the rope. My GPS/altimeter had us at eleven thousand feet with only twelve hundred feet to go by five in the afternoon. We'd been climbing for fourteen hours and the fatigue was starting to show. Bill was leading us up a couloir, which is a narrow gully on the mountain face. The couloir can act as a chute for falling rocks and ice, but the advantage of climbing it was the uninterrupted ice surface that offered firm placement. As the last climber, I periodically had to hug the ice to avoid a deluge of ice and small rocks kicked loose by either Emily or Bill. I tried to stay as close to the wall as possible, while my small backpack bore the brunt of the impacts.

We were less than five hundred feet from the 13,190-foot peak at eight. We were all carrying assault packs with water, food and warm gear. The slope was nearly vertical, and it was difficult for us to communicate. We were at the point in the climb where the combination of fatigue, altitude and stress had reduced our activity to only the bare essentials, which was driving the spikes of our crampons into the icy wall and swinging our ice axes.

"Falling!" I heard Emily yell.

I looked up and saw Bill fly past Emily. He must have blown through at least one ice screw otherwise he'd have arrested much earlier. He jerked for a second, ten feet above me and then continued to fall.

"Falling!" Emily yelled again, this time referring to herself.

I braced myself as Bill flew past. I felt the hard tug of the rope, my body was pulled up toward Emily, but my feet and arms held me in place. I looked up and watched Emily spin and reattach herself to the mountain with the axes in her hands and then her cramponed feet. I looked below and could see Bill doing the same thing. The tension from the rope slackened as Bill began to climb.

"Anybody hurt?" I yelled.

"I'm good," Emily replied.

"I'm good," Bill said.

At this point in the climb, my lips were cracked. My face was sunburnt from the sun's reflection on the snow. The temperature was dropping, giving me a chill from the sweat running down my back.

"I'll take the lead. You could use a break," I said to Bill.

"Be careful, it's crumbly up ahead and the rocks under the ice are loose," he said.

I started to climb. A few minutes later, Emily and I were shoulder to shoulder in the narrow couloir.

"How are you doing?" I asked.

Emily smiled. She was wearing a red helmet, climbing sunglasses with side flaps, a purple fleece pullover and black yoga pants. She looked a lot less drained than I felt. She looked like she was actually having fun. I could see the dried sweat on her face and the lines of exhaustion on her forehead, but there was no mistaking the fact that Emily was in the zone.

"Good, only another four hundred feet. Last push," she said.

"Bill's worn out from pulling me up this hill. I'm going to lead the rest of the way."

"I'm right behind you. Watch the cornice," she said.

"I'm going to have to hack through it, prepare yourself for a snow shower."

"I could use a little hygiene about now," she said with a smile.

Emily's attitude buoyed me. I ate a candy bar, finished off a water bottle and pushed myself to reach the summit before the sun set. A while later the three of us were standing on the summit of Mount Waddington, the peak barely big enough for three people to stand on it at the same time. We took the obligatory photos. We were on the Coastal Range and from the summit we had an amazing view of the mastiff of neighboring mountain peaks that were almost as high as Mount Waddington. We watched the sun set while we were on the summit and it was like a fire was extinguished and all the heat and light left the world.

We were tired when we started the descent. We'd been going steady for over twenty hours. Rappelling five thousand feet on a one-hundred-and-fifty-foot rope means a lot of rappels. When we finally reached our base camp, it was two in the afternoon. We'd been climbing for thirty-five hours straight and we'd all reached that point of fatigue and sleep deprivation where it's difficult to think clearly. Upon reaching our tent, we tossed off our harnesses and helmets, disrobed down to our thermal underwear and climbed into our sleeping bags. I was asleep as soon as my head hit the ground.

When I woke at three the next morning, I was sore, hungry and thirsty. I got the stove running and melted some snow to make coffee. Then I decided to cook breakfast. Emily crawled out of the tent an hour later at dawn.

"Something smells good," Emily said as stood erect and began to stretch.

"Bacon, steak and eggs," I said.

"You lugged all that out here?" She gestured to the food.

"Oh yeah. Carrying heavy objects long distances is my special gift. Would you like a breakfast beer to go with it?" I offered gesturing to the six cans of Heineken cooling in the snow.

"Beer?"

"It's tradition. The mountain gods demand it, I always pour the first one out on the ground as a sacrifice."

Emily laughed. I was wearing sunglasses, a black watch cap, a purple Furman University sweat shirt, white thermal underwear bottoms and black snow slippers. She was wearing thermal underwear and a watch cap. A few seconds later Bill followed behind equally disheveled.

Three hours later, we'd hiked down to our original drop off point and were waiting for the helicopter. I sat on my backpack and drank a Heineken. It was a good climb. Nobody was injured and we reached the summit. Emily was animated, funny and bursting with joy. She sipped on a beer and told story after story of her previous climbing adventures. Eventually, the helicopter arrived, kicking up a storm of blown snow. We boarded and headed back to Vancouver.

We parted ways with Bill at the Vancouver Airport.

Emily and I returned to our rooms at the Fairmont that we'd left open. Our flight back to Eleuthera wasn't booked until the next day. We decided to go to dinner. I found us a table at Miku on the waterfront at the Burrand Inlet. The view of Vancouver harbor at Miku is spectacular. The flame-seared sushi concept they have at Miku is really nice. I spotted a Montrachet and it reminded me of Migos, so I ordered it. It was a great complement to the seemingly endless stream of seabass, lobster, salmon and monkfish brought to us by the wait staff. We had a window seat and the view, the food and the company made for an amazing meal.

"What do you have left on the list?" Emily asked me.

"Logan and Alberta."

"If you have an opening on your team, I'd like to go with you."

"Alberta would be okay. Not Logan," I said.

"Why not Logan?" Emily asked.

"I tried Alberta already and was turned away by the weather. If the weather was good, I would've made it. Hummingbird Ridge is a different story," I said.

"In what way?"

"The climb we did today has been repeated at least six times. The Hummingbird Ridge route has never been repeated. When I tried it the last time, an avalanche almost swept me off the mountain. I was almost killed, there must have been three other avalanches near me that day. The Ridge is unstable. I don't know if it can be climbed, the first team must have been extremely lucky," I said.

Emily pointed her chopsticks at me. "So, you're going to give up?"

"No, I'm just not going to make the next attempt with you. I'd kinda like to keep you around," I said.

Emily looked at me with a puzzled expression on her face that turned to a blush. I gulped the last of my glass of wine to distract from my awkwardness.

"Do you want to go back to the hotel?" she said in a soft voice.

I nodded.

CHAPTER 22

MINNEAPOLIS, MINNESOTA

NOOR PICKED UP her rental car from the airport counter and drove to the Westin Hotel in downtown Minneapolis. She rented a small house in her district, which was in the Cedar-Riverside part of Minneapolis, but avoided staying there whenever possible. An unescorted woman in her neighborhood was never safe from harassment, even when properly covered. She yearned to be free of a culture that she felt suffocated women. In her district, two thirds of the Somali men stayed home while their wives went to work each day to support the family. Jobs were available, but most of the men chose to be unemployed, demanding their wives support them. Somali women led difficult lives, they worked long hours, often doing menial labor for low wages under adverse conditions such as those at the nearby Amazon Fulfillment Center and the chicken processing plant. When they were done toiling away at their day job, they were expected to return home and care for their family.

In her view, the only thing Somali men worked hard at was graft. Welfare fraud was their specialty. Imaginary schemes to bilk the welfare system were forever being created by the idle hands of Somali men. Many of their abuses came back to harm Somali women who relied on those very same systems for support. A good example was the latest scam being carried in the papers about a day care center for the underprivileged. The criminals were arrested for accepting millions of dollars in day care subsidies for the care of children who registered, but who never actually attended the center. Did those men not realize how abusing that system made those children ineligible for support elsewhere and how it would affect Somali working women in the future when such programs were eliminated because of the bad press? Did they even care?

Noor was only a little girl when she and her brother moved to the refugee camp in Kenya. Her brother was in his late teens and was an aspiring warlord. When her parents died in the civil war, months earlier, he became her caregiver. Inside the *Lord of the Flies* environment of the camp, Bashir was a natural. He rose to a position of influence and arranged for Noor to be one of the lucky ones selected by the corrupt UN officials for relocation to the US. She arrived in Minneapolis in 1993 at the age of eleven. Assigned to a foster family, Noor worked hard to become an excellent student and thrived in her new environment. Seven years later, while a freshman at the University of Minnesota, her brother sent her a Marriage Certificate and gave her instructions on what to do. Noor presented the document to the US immigration authorities and requested a resident visa for her husband slash brother, who now called himself Bashir Asad.

Bashir had changed his name but remained on the same career path as when they were both in the refugee camp.

During her sophomore year in college, he lived with her in their one room student apartment. By her senior year, Bashir had advanced in the Somali Mafia gang and the two moved into a small two-bedroom house in Cedar-Riverside, a neighborhood often referred to as Little Mogadishu.

Having tasted freedom for seven years, living under the control of Bashir was a difficult adjustment. Noor suffered under the quick fists and leather belt of Bashir for five years following his arrival to the US. Thankfully, once Bashir received his citizenship, he moved away. At the time of their divorce, Noor was working as an outreach coordinator with the Minnesota IAIR office. Having survived a civil war, a UN-run refugee camp and her brother, Noor was committed to improving the lives of her people. Although dedicated to the protection of her people from outside discrimination, Noor was convinced the greatest threat came from within. Females were little more than property in her community, most having less value than a healthy cow. Many young girls were forced to marry men who were much older in arranged marriages created to profit their fathers. Genital mutilation, physical abuse and endless labor was the life of the female Somali refugee. Helping her people, especially the women and children, was her cause and a dynamic and articulate Noor quickly became the best advocate in the region. It wasn't long before she caught the attention of the IAIR National office, and the decision was made to groom Noor for political office.

Noor's first elected office was as a Minneapolis City Council member. She thrived in local city politics and her constituents were grateful for the efforts she made to improve the community. Most of her campaign funding came from IAIR and it came with a price. It wasn't long before she realized that in addition to her brother, she now had a second master in her life demanding obedience. That second man was Akrim, the head of IAIR and like Bashir, Noor was determined to escape his yoke.

Noor checked into her room and unpacked. She called Bashir.

"I've arrived, I just checked in at the Westin," Noor said.

"Come over, I'm at the club," Bashir said.

"I shouldn't go into the district, I'll be recognized. What I have to tell you is sensitive and our meeting should be secret," Noor said, hoping to avoid meeting her brother in a private place.

"It will be all right."

"No, it won't."

"I'm not asking," Bashir said in a menacing tone.

An hour later Noor walked into the Red Sea Bar and Restaurant. She found her brother sitting alone in a booth. Noor walked over to the table and Bashir gestured for her to sit.

"You should come around more," Bashir said.

"I have many obligations," Noor replied.

"You think you're so big, you don't need to listen to me no more," Bashir said.

"That's not true," Noor said.

"Yeah, it's true, but it's something that I can fix," Bashir said.

"Please, Bashir. Be reasonable."

"I am, it's you who think you're too good," Bashir said.

"I came here to deliver a message from Akrim. He's requesting your help," Noor said.

"You mentioned something about him utilizing my Hawala service," Bashir said.

"Yes, he said it will be very lucrative for you, he moves a lot of money," Noor said.

"What does he want in return?"

"He wants you to put an end to the investigation in Nashville," Noor said.

"Why?"

"The police are following up on the release of the accused rapists; they want to know how the defense team knew the evidence was tainted two weeks before the information was leaked to the newspaper," Noor said.

"They find that out, it could be bad," Bashir said.

"Exactly, which is why Akrim wants you to end the inquiry," Noor said.

"How does he expect me to do that?"

"Nashville police is small, give them something else to investigate," Noor said.

"A distraction," Bashir said.

"Yes, a distraction. Make some noise," Noor said.

"I have a good relationship with the authorities in Nashville. Especially the Federal. I don't want to jeopardize that. It's not good for business," Bashir said.

"You're the one always bragging that you have the Nashville FBI office on your payroll. If you take the local police off the case, you'll be doing them a favor. It will be good for business," Noor said.

"Maybe. They're looking into the murder of Hodar. They're not happy with the Nashville PD doing the same," Bashir said.

"You see, that's what I mean. It's to your own benefit," Noor said.

"You were missed at Hodar's by the way. Your own uncle and you didn't even visit to extend your condolences to his son, your own cousin," Bashir said.

"I'm a nationally recognized figure now. I couldn't go," Noor said.

"Why not?"

"Hodar was a gangster, he was your top lieutenant in Nashville. If I went to Nashville, it would've raised suspicion and that would've been bad for you," Noor said.

"He was family and he was a big earner. You should've gone." A lightning-quick strike, so fast his hand was a blur as it whipped across the table and landed with a thunderous crack across Noor's right cheek. The force of the blow knocked Noor from the booth and onto the grimy dining room floor. Dazed, Noor slowly got to her knees and then unsteadily stood and pulled herself back into the booth. She kept her head down and stared at the table as she sat.

"I'll consider this distraction you're asking about," Bashir said.

"Thank you, it's the right move to make," Noor said.

"It's your own fault, you shouldn't make me discipline you," Bashir said.

"I'll do better," Noor said.

"I'm trying to find you a husband. You make it hard with your behavior. Who would want you?"

"I don't know, thank you for trying."

"You may take your leave. Have Akrim contact me directly and we'll make the arrangements for his Hawala service," Bashir said.

Noor pulled her hijab forward on her face to cover the beet-red slap mark that was throbbing as she left the club. She was still trembling when she reached her car, parked on the street at the end of the block. She both feared and hated her brother. Every dreaded visit with Bashir and Akrim convinced her further that the world would be a better place without men. The risk she was taking kept her up some nights, but she knew that if she didn't escape her madman brother soon, he would eventually kill her.

CHAPTER 23

NASHVILLE, TENNESSEE

ABDI ABDULLAH CIRCLED around the block two times before stopping in the strip mall parking lot. Always a careful man, Abdi had become obsessively cautious since the death of his father, Hodar. Since assuming his father's position as regional boss of both the Somali Boyz and Somali Mafia gangs, staying alive had become even more of a focus. The two brother gangs had shared the same leadership since Hodar unified them more than a decade earlier and it now fell to Abdi to keep the organizations together and running.

Hodar had been a coalition builder and a peacemaker. He'd been Abdi's teacher for over a decade, showing his son how to keep a low profile and how to profit from their many enterprises while accepting only a minimum amount of risk. Hodar was generous with his payroll to government officials, large and small. He was raised in the Somali culture of corruption. Paying baksheesh was a way of life, as natural as breathing, and Hodar was always more than happy to trade coin for assistance and information. Hodar preferred to avoid violence. Not because he had an aversion to hurting people, but because violence generated hostility from law enforcement and the local population, the two groups who could destroy his business if they turned against him.

Because he subscribed to the business philosophy of his mentor and father, Abdi was especially ill prepared for his upcoming meeting.

"Salam Alakum," he said to the man in the black t-shirt sitting in a chair in the outside seating area of the Costa Coffee Shop.

"Alakum Al Salam," the man replied.

"I'll get you a coffee, what would you like?" Abdi asked.

"Double espresso," the man replied.

"Coming right up, we can't very well sit here and not order anything can we," Abdi said nervously.

Abdi returned minutes later with two espressos. The man seated across the table smoked a cigarette and chose his words carefully, while his eyes constantly studied his surroundings.

"This USB contains all the information we have on the target," Abdi said as he slid the thumb drive across the table.

"I was hoping you would have something larger than this," the man said picking up the USB drive.

Abdi withdrew a thick envelope from the waistband inside his shirt. "You can count it, but there's fifty thousand dollars in there."

"I'll expect the other half when the job is finished."

"And you'll receive it then, but only when the job is finished."

Abdi studied the man. He didn't look anything like what he thought an assassin should look like. He was a thin, slightly balding, middle-aged man with glasses. But even without the physically intimidating characteristics of a fighter, there was something about the man that made Abdi nervous, a mendacity that couldn't be explained.

"Keep your men clear of the target. I don't want anyone tipped off and I don't want any evidence that will come back to me. That would be very bad."

"Understood. When are you going to do it?" Abdi asked.

"I don't know yet. Are you in a hurry?"

"What did Bashir tell you about the timetable?"

"I don't know a Bashir. Don't ever use names around me."

"Okay."

"I'll be in touch when it's time to collect the other half," the man said as he stood up and faded into the sidewalk foot traffic.

Abdi was left alone at the table. The process seemed unusual, but he preferred it to doing it himself. The men in his gang were unskilled, they lacked the sophistication to commit a murder and get away with it. During the rare conflict between gangs, his men were quick enough to draw weapons and certainly willing to use them, but that was a far cry from getting away with killing a police officer. The last thing Abdi wanted was for the killing to come back on him.

*

Greg Allison sat in the visiting team's bleachers at the high school baseball field. His son's team was in the second round of the high school baseball playoffs and they were about to close out the series and head to the next round. They were up 7-2 and it was the opposing team's last at bat. His son was playing third base and was having a good game, having gone two for three at the plate with a solo home run. With the game well at hand he decided to grab a hot dog from the concession stand.

The concession stand was next to the home team seating area and the fans were loud as they exhorted their players to deliver a miracle with only three outs left in their season. The concession line was short, and because the workers were trying to close up the stand for the season, the line moved slowly. When Captain Allison was second in line from reaching the counter, he heard a man slip into line behind him. Three shots from a pistol were fired into Captain Allison's back in rapid succession. After he fell forward to the ground, the man stepped over him and fired a fourth bullet into his temple.

The entire South Precinct was shocked when the news reached the station house. Even though the murder was outside her precinct, Grace went to the crime scene. By the time she arrived, the area had been cordoned off with police tape and the body was gone. Grace recognized the detectives handling the case and walked over to them.

"Can I help out in any way?" she asked.

"We have it, Grace," one of the detectives said.

"Were there any witnesses?" Grace said.

"Middle-aged black man shot him in the back with a snub nosed .38 while he was in line at the hot dog stand. Thin, about five-eight with glasses. Wearing jeans and a blue jacket. We found the weapon; we're still looking for the man," the detective said.

"Was he driving?"

"Grace, let us handle this. I know he was your Captain, but we have a job to do." The men returned to their discussion.

Furious, Grace turned and walked back to her car then drove back to the office. On the way, she mentally listed the people who would want to kill Captain Allison. She couldn't think of a single one. It could have been a perpetrator in an old case, but that seemed unlikely. He hadn't arrested anyone in years.

The only recent conflict the Captain was involved in was the explosive response from the Superintendent when he inquired about the Hodar investigation. Captain Allison asked the Superintendent why the case was taken over by the FBI. Nothing about the FBI taking over the investigation smelled right. The FBI had framed and intimidated her when she asked about it and in a rare display of temper, the Superintendent had yelled at Captain Allison when he inquired about it. Making a false charge against Grace was a long way from killing Captain Allison, but still it nagged at her.

Her gut told her it was more than a random killing and that it was tied to Hodar and the FBI in some way. The Nashville PD wasn't going to allow her to do anything and she certainly couldn't go to the FBI. The one Federal Agent the FBI appeared to hate as much as her seemed to be Agent McDermott. On a whim, she decided to call. The call was forwarded to my regular phone.

"Agent McDermott?" Grace said.

"This must be Detective Deforest," I said.

"It is."

"How can I help you?" I asked.

"Captain Allison was shot and killed this afternoon at his son's baseball game."

"That's terrible. I'm sorry to hear that."

"I did what you asked. I looked into why the FBI took over the Hodar murder investigation. Doing that really stirred up a bee's nest. I was physically intimidated by the FBI when I asked. I almost got suspended after the FBI registered a complaint and Internal Affairs was called in. I was accused of breaking procedure for jumping jurisdiction by investigating a Federal Case. I asked Captain Allison to look into it at his level. The Superintendent went ballistic on him and now only a few days later he's been killed," Grace said.

"You think it's because he asked about Hodar," I said.

"What else could it be? Captain Allison was respected by everyone. Criminals thanked him after he arrested them, he had no enemies."

"It could've been random. There are crazy people in the world."

"Not in that neighborhood. I need your help, Agent, and this time I won't accept no for an answer," Grace said.

"I'll be there tomorrow. Don't tell anyone that I'm coming. That's my only condition," I said.

"Accepted."

CHAPTER 24

SAVANNAH, GEORGIA

ARRIVED IN SAVANNAH late in the afternoon. The cruise from Eleuthera to Savannah took nine hours over calm seas. I left the marina in Eleuthera while it was still dark. I didn't tell Emily where I was going. I'm pretty sure she would've tried to stop me if she knew what I was up to. It would be even worse if she wanted to come along. Either way was a losing proposition, so I took the cowardly route and slunk out of the house in the middle of the night. There would be hell to pay when I got back, but that was a worry for the future.

I couldn't fly, because things were probably going to get ugly and for that I need weapons. My preferred method of bringing guns and gear into the US is with the *Nomad* and its hidden armory. The customs folks in Savannah Port were professional and efficient, they brought the dogs through the yacht to search for drugs and had me in and out in less than two hours. After leaving customs, I docked at a slip I booked at the Isle of Hope Marina inside the Intercoastal Waterway. I had an early dinner and a quick nap while waiting for my car rental to be delivered from Enterprise. The next leg of the trip was an eight-hour drive from Savannah to Nashville. I texted Detective Deforest and gave her a new contact phone number for me. She agreed to meet me for breakfast the next morning.

My Homeland Security credentials with the Agent McDermott identity were a government issue alias supplied by the CIA. I have a few other alias packages with passports and credit cards that the Agency doesn't know about; they don't have badges, but they're still useful. It was early morning when I checked into the JW Marriott under the same alias as my car rental. I immediately hit the rack. After a few hours of sleep, I met Grace at the hotel breakfast restaurant, a place called Stompin' Grounds. The dining room was almost empty, I requested a booth in the corner away from the window and the entrance. I watched Grace as she entered. She looked a little weary as she scanned the dining room for me. I waved an arm and she headed to my table. I got up to greet her. We shook hands. She was even less personable than the first time we met, which I didn't think was possible.

"Where have you been?" she demanded before even sitting down.

"Would you mind if we ordered first? I'm really hungry, it was a long trip."

"A trip from where, that's my question."

"It can wait."

The waitress came over and took my order. I got the cowboy hash with bacon and cage free eggs.

"What's the difference between free range and cage free?" I asked the waitress.

"They mean the same thing."

"Are you sure, it could mean they're in a box or behind glass, not in a cage, but still cooped up."

"No, it means they run free."

"Can we stop this?" Grace said.

"I'm just making sure the mother of my chicken embryos is being treated humanely," I said while the waitress poured our coffee.

Grace waited until we were alone before continued her tirade.

"You disappear. Nobody from Homeland or the FBI knows where you are."

"That's not true, the people I work for knew where I was, they're the ones who sent me," I said.

"The local office doesn't know who you are you or anything about you," Grace said.

"I work for the US Government. My work is undercover. I've told you all I'm authorized to disclose. I'd like to tell you more, but I can't. I'm here to offer my help if you want it, but there's no point in asking me questions I can't answer, you're just wasting time."

"I've worked with undercover federal agents before, they're a lot more forthcoming than you are," Grace said.

"In my agency and in my assignment, the rules are obviously very different," I said.

"And what agency is that? Because it sure as hell isn't Homeland Security."

I just smiled and took a drink from my coffee mug.

"I'm here because you said you have a problem with the FBI. I hope you don't think I'm bragging here, but I'm particularly good at sorting out problems with the Feds.

How about we focus on the problem at hand and table the classified stuff until later?" I said.

Grace was red faced. Her eyes were a little bloodshot, and she had small puffy bags under them. She was going through a tough time with the loss of her Captain and it showed.

"I don't know if I can trust you. That's why I'm asking these questions," Grace said.

"Why? My track record's pretty good. Last time I said I'd rescue Becky Anderson and I did. This time I'm telling you I'm going to find Captain Allison's killer and I will," I said.

"How?"

"I need more information to say exactly, but in general, it'll be the same as last time. I have access to assets that you don't," I said.

"Is that how you did it last time?" Grace asked.

"Yes, that's how I found the girl and ID'd her attackers. I won't make the mistake of stopping at a mere identification this time," I said.

"What do you mean by that?"

"It means I'll take care of the follow through myself. Nobody is going to walk free this time."

"You think it's my fault the evidence was contaminated, and the rapists walked?" Grace asked.

"No, I don't, I think it's your fault that the only evidence you had was what I gave you. Five guys in a hotel room, that should leave a lot of evidence," I said.

"You should've told me your evidence was tainted," Grace said.

"I had no idea the damn government was going to leak the source of the video."

"You're awfully confident for a screw up," Grace said.

"That's why I came back, to fix this mess. I like to keep a perfect win-loss record and this game isn't over yet," I said.

"It is for Captain Allison," Grace said.

"If you let me, I promise you, I'll get him justice."

Grace's facial expression became decidedly less pained at my words. It was such a contrast to her earlier disposition that I found it uplifting.

"I don't know who you are, 'Agent McDermott', and I use that name in quotes, because I don't believe I know who you are or who you work for. I don't understand your methods and I don't know when you'll disappear again. The sad truth is, I'm so desperate that I'm willing to take a chance with you," Grace said.

"I hear variations of those words from most of the women I meet." That brought a chuckle from Grace.

"I can believe that," she said.

"Now that we're done with the preliminaries, it's time to buckle up, Pat's crimefighting express is ready to leave the station," I said.

We ate our breakfast, although I'm not sure if Grace's yogurt and sparkling water qualifies, and then Grace spent the next two hours explaining the situation.

"Thanks for catching me up. I'm going to need the afternoon to put some things in motion with my back office. Let's get together again, how about tomorrow night for dinner?" I said.

"What are you going to do exactly?" Grace asked.

"I haven't fully decided yet. I'm definitely going to request electronic surveillance on your two FBI agents," I said.

"You think the Agents are dirty?" Grace said.

"It would explain a lot, wouldn't it?" I said.

"We don't have any evidence to support it. How are you going to get a warrant without evidence?"

"This case involves terrorism, and for terrorism, the standards are different. I'll get the surveillance approved in a FISA court," I lied.

"You can do that?" Grace said.

"I can."

"That's a long shot and it may not be worth the trouble," she said.

"I grew up in Boston when we had a gang leader named Whitey Bulger who ran all the organized crime in the area. He lasted a long time because he had a big chunk of the local FBI office on his payroll covering for him. The behavior of the FBI in this case doesn't make sense unless they're working for the other team," I said.

"It doesn't make sense. I got serious pushback from them when I asked about the Hodar investigation. Captain Allison was killed right after he went to the Superintendent with the same question," Grace said.

"We need to see if there's an FBI – Somali gang connection," I said.

"You think the Somalis may have killed Captain Allison?"

"All I know is that the description of the killer could apply to a Somali. You seem to think that there's a Somali connection and that's good enough for me. I'm going to have a talk with the gang leaders. If you could get me an outline of who's who in the Somali gang hierarchy that will be helpful," I said.

"We don't have any idea of who's who when it comes to the Somali gangs. They're a closed society," Grace said.

"You must have biographical information on our five rapists, give me what you have, and I'll start with them and work my way up. Once I know who's who in the chain of command, I'll open up a dialogue with the gang leaders," I said.

"Nobody is going to tell you anything."

"You'd be surprised, I can be very persuasive," I replied in the most confident of tones.

"We'll see about that. Where do we meet tomorrow?" Grace asked.

"I'll make reservations and get back to you. Do you have any preferences?"

"This is not a date."

"I didn't say it was, but if we're going to have dinner, it might as well be at a place where you'll enjoy it."

"Anywhere is fine. I'm a vegetarian by the way. I'm going back to the precinct. Keep me informed."

"I will, please do the same and send me the info on those rapists as soon as you can."

Grace nodded and got up and left. I paid the bill and went upstairs to my room. It was early morning in Scotland. Too early to call David Forrest. I powered up my other phone and saw that I had five missed calls from Emily. Rather than call her back, I changed clothes and went to the gym. All of the goodwill the hotel created with the fast check-in and at the Stompin' Grounds breakfast was lost at the gym. They had a weight bench, but barely any weights to go with it. I used the Nautilus machines and went for a run on the treadmill. I was the only one in the gym except for the lady at the spa counter who kept staring at me.

I called David at noon and told him what I needed. I

gave him the names and phone numbers of the two agents that confronted Grace and asked him to do a deep dive into their financial records and for anything else that may indicate they had a source of income outside of the FBI. Grace gave me what she had for contact information on the five attackers who raped Becky. Since they were gangsters who used burner phones, I had little faith the numbers were still in use. But she did have numbers and addresses of the next of kin, which is how they arrested them the first time. Armed with photos and a place to start, I picked the first name on the list and went to work.

Before I left, I made sure to bring my black Under Armour backpack containing my firepower. Inside the bag I had two weapons: an AAC Honey Badger .300 blackout carbine with a nine inch barrel, attached suppresser and an ACOG sight. My sidearm was a HK45 Tactical with a threaded barrel in case I wanted to use a suppressor and a red dot laser sight. I also had a set of PVS-31 night vision goggles, four flashbangs, six frag grenades and a lot of extra ammunition. The bag weighed about thirty pounds and the covered collapsible stock of the Honey Badger stuck up out of the top of the pack.

The drive to Mohammed Juma's parents' house took twenty minutes. It was in the same part of Nashville as where Hodar lived. I was definitely not going to blend. I parked my Chevy Suburban across the street from Juma's house and waited. I'd driven through a McDonald's on the way to the stakeout and I ate lunch as I waited for Juma to show. According to Grace's info, Juma lived at home with his parents and two younger brothers. The house was a one-story ranch design. There was a car in the driveway, it was a tricked out red Cutlass Supreme with rims that looked like they were worth more than the car.

By three in the afternoon, I became impatient. I twisted the suppressor can onto the HK45 and slipped on a thin sweatshirt with a front zipper. I tucked the long pistol into the waistband of my pants and headed to Juma's front door. I could hear a television behind the door, it sounded like cartoons. I rang the bell. A man who looked to be in his forties opened the door.

"I'm here to see Juma," I said.

"He's not here," the man said.

I swung my right fist down, hard and fast at the shorter man. My knuckles stung after they connected with the point of his left cheekbone. He tumbled backward into the front hallway winding up flat on his back, unconscious. I stepped into the hallway and saw a man jump off the living room couch. He was a step away from the dining room entry when my .45 round caught him in the side of his chest. I lost sight of him, but I heard the thud as he hit the floor.

"Are you Juma?" I asked while standing above the man, who was lying on his back, holding his right side with both hands. He just stared up at me. I compared the photo on my phone with the anguished face in front of me. It was Juma.

"Who do you work for?"

He just stared. I returned the phone in my left hand to my pocket and raised the pistol.

"I'm not going to ask you again," I said. The defiance in the twenty-year-old man didn't change.

"Suit yourself." The pistol issued a suppressed cough. I walked over and picked up the ejected round and went back into the living room and found the other expended cartridge.

Juma's father was still in the hallway on his hands and knees attempting to stand. I put the red laser dot onto the side of his head and pulled the trigger. I retrieved my final brass casing and left the house.

As I pulled the SUV away from the curb, a yellow school bus approached in the opposite direction. The police were going to be on the scene quickly once Juma's school-aged brothers got to the house. I sped up and headed to my next destination.

The next day, I woke up at one in the afternoon and remembered to make a reservation for dinner and notify Grace. I'd changed hotels, partly for security reasons and partially because of my disappointment with the gym. I booked a table at The Chef and I, the reviews looked good and it was within walking distance of the Omni where I was staying. I checked in with David Forrest, but he didn't have anything to report beyond a call he received from Emily. I told him to keep looking into the two FBI agents that confronted Grace and I gave him the name of two Somali men in Nashville to search out as well. I had been up all night, crashed mid-morning and then slept until the early afternoon. I was moving pretty slow. I decided to check out the gym and then maybe hit the rooftop pool and do a swim workout.

The walk to the restaurant took a little longer than expected and Grace was already seated at the bar when I arrived. The Chef and I was about half a mile from the hotel. The weather was warm, and I was a little sweaty from the exertion. The room was crowded. I didn't do a very good job of reconnaissance, because the dining room was crowded, and the seating was communal. It was an edgy kind of place with a chef operating from an open kitchen in the center. The set-up made it impossible to talk shop, but the food more than made up for it. It was fantastic. I could tell that even the vegetarian Grace loved it. I had the Elk Tenderloin with a three-cheese hash and made a mental note to come back the next night.

With the wine bottle empty and my crème Brûlée a memory, it was time to get down to business.

"There's a bar down the road at the Omni. Feel like a walk?" I said.

"After that meal, I need one, but I'll drive, my car's in the lot," Grace said.

I folded myself into her Prius and then we left it with the valet while we went into Barlines, which is a sports bar in the hotel. We sat at an outside table where we could talk without anyone in earshot. I had a Jackalope IPA while Grace had sparkling water with lemon.

"Where were you last night?" she asked.

"I was all over, looking for answers. I even found a couple. What about you?"

"I was investigating too. We had more murders in Nashville last night than we've had in more than a decade," Grace said.

"No kidding."

"Eight dead at five different crime scenes," Grace said.

"Were they related?"

"You don't know? Where were you last night, Pat? Several witnesses described a tall white man," Grace said.

"A tall white man, is that all?" I said.

"Five of the eight who were killed were our rapists. The ones I helped you to find," Grace said.

"Vigilante justice it would seem," I said.

"That's the current theory."

"Given the amount of press the story of the rapists' release received, I can't imagine how many people wanted those five men dead. Must be thousands. That's a lot of suspects, you're going to have your hands full," I said.

"Thousands, huh?"

"Yup."

"Why are you laughing?" Grace said.

"The irony of it just struck me as funny."

"What irony is that?"

"It was the press that got the five rapists released and it was the press that motivated the person who killed them. You should arrest Jeff Bezos, he owns the paper that ran the article," I said.

"Where were you last night, Agent McDermott?" Grace asked.

"I told you, I was investigating. Doing my job, fighting crime. That's all I'm going to tell you. Do I need a lawyer?"

"It's like you said, even if we narrowed it down to just tall white men, we'd still have tens of thousands of suspects. I can't arrest you without more than that," Grace said.

"Good to know," I said.

"You said you learned something, what did you learn?"

"I have two names. Abdi Abdullah and Salam Saeed. They're supposed to be two of the top Somali gang leaders in town. Of the Somali Boyz and the Somali Mafia, or so I'm told," I said.

"I've never heard of them. How'd you get the names?" Grace said.

"Detective work. What I need to know now is how do I find them. Can you help?" I asked.

"I'll ask around. What are you going to do once you find them?"

"I'm going to ask if they know anything about Captain Allison's death," I said.

I finished my beer and signaled the waitress. The girl was very attentive, which is important in a waitress, she was also beautiful to the point of distraction. She had to be an aspiring country music star. The hotel is adjacent to the Country Music Hall of Fame and probably patronized by the big names in the business.

"I don't believe in coincidences, Pat. Both times you've been in town, we've had multiple murders. The deaths are all professional. Never any useful evidence. Last night we had eight victims, all killed with a coup de grace through the forehead, twenty-one shots were fired, all .45 caliber, most likely from the same pistol, not a single bullet missed a target, nobody heard a single round fired, nobody saw the shooter, the description of the tall white guy came from a witness who saw a man fitting that description in the general area before one of the murders. There wasn't even a single shell casing found. We have nothing," Grace said.

"That's quite the mystery you have there, Nancy Drew. I'm sure that'll keep you busy for a while. In the meantime, I'm going to find the person or people who killed the only good guy to drop in this mess," I said.

"I hope you find him, Pat. I'm going to talk to our gang unit and see what they know about these two names. I'll get back to you as soon as I can. Eight murders from the same gun is enough to allow the FBI to play the serial killer card and get involved in the investigation. You need to be careful, Agent," Grace said.

"If I don't get anything on the Somali angle, I'm going to talk to your two G-men. I'll give it another day, to see if anything develops with these two gang leaders first," I said.

"Do you need a ride back to the Marriott?" Grace asked.

"I'm good. Drive safe."

I drained my glass and signaled for the waitress to come over. I told her I was hoping to satisfy my curiosity as well as my thirst for a top-quality cognac. A few minutes later she brought back a Louis XIII and a CD with her name on it. We were both laughing as I paid her the same amount for the CD as I did for the cognac.

CHAPTER 25

WASHINGTON, DC

ABDULWALI SHUFFLED WITH the help of his cane into Akrim's office at the IAIR headquarters. It was after hours and as usual, the security guard was the only other person in the building who was not a principal in the Project.

"Did you talk to Noor?" Abdulwali said.

"Yes, she confirmed that Bashir received the message," Akrim said.

"We told him to tone things down. He responded by killing a Police Captain in Nashville?" Abdulwali said.

"Yes," Akrim said.

"Why would he do that?" Abdulwali said.

"I've asked Noor to talk to him and find out. She said he refuses to answer her questions," Akrim said.

"The man's a liability," Abdulwali said.

"He's bad for the cause. After the murder of the Police Captain by what is being reported as a Somali suspect, they had eight more murders in Nashville, all Somalis. The newspapers are speculating it's Somali gang violence," Akrim said.

"Reports of rampant Muslim violence are not helpful to our agenda," Abdulwali said.

"What do you recommend we do?" Akrim asked.

"Bashir is uncontrollable, he must be killed," Abdulwali said.

"I agree, but I think we should wait. There's too much Muslim violence in the news already," Akrim said.

"That's why I think we do it now. We take advantage of the negative press. We'll hang Bashir's murder on a white supremacist. Then we raise Bashir up as a martyr and use his death as evidence of Islamophobia," Abdulwali said.

"How will we do that?" Akrim asked.

"Leave that to me. I have a few ideas," Abdulwali said.

A few nights later it was the weekend in Minneapolis. Bashir was seated at the bar at his club on Cedar Street, the Red Sea Bar and Restaurant. Originally an Ethiopian establishment, the previous proprietor had signed the brick building over to Bashir when he finally came to grips with what it meant to be three months behind on payments to a shark loan. The old proprietor exchanged the deed for the life of his eldest son and forgiveness of the loan. He left Minneapolis forever and never looked back.

The restaurant bar was popular. It only seated forty, but on the far side of the room near the stage and dance floor, there was sufficient room for another seventy to stand. The band was African, and they played an eclectic mix of rap, reggae and Somali Folk music. The patrons were almost all Somali, except for a handful of culture seekers from the nearby University who were behaving adventurously.

From Bashir's vantage point, seated at the bar, he could see most of the restaurant. He relied on the bar mirror in front of him to view the front door. The mirror also allowed him to keep an eye on the other people seated around the bar. Over his left shoulder he could see the line of dining tables against the outer wall all the way to the far side of the room where the dance floor was. He could see the people dancing and behind them the band up on the elevated stage. Encircling the dance floor was a crowd of people standing. The only empty chair in the building was the stool next to him. He kept it empty for visitors. Throughout most evenings, his people would drop by and supply updates on his business activities.

Bashir saw the front door open and two young men enter. They were college-aged and both had backpacks slung over their jackets with the local University logo. The two went directly to the bar, ordered drinks and then joined the rowdy crowd in the back of the room. Bashir's attention went back to his phone and his que of unanswered messages.

A short while later, Bashir watched the door open again through the reflection of the mirror. From the back, it looked to be the same two college kids leaving, only they no longer had their backpacks. He looked down the length of the bar and saw behind one of the stools, the straps of a backpack. The pack was unattended at the base of the bar where the students had ordered their drinks. He couldn't spot the second pack.

Bashir jumped off his stool and sprinted the ten steps to the front door. He crashed against the door at a dead run, but it only opened a few inches before stopping. He spotted a chain in the narrow gap between the door and the frame at the same time the room erupted into flame. Almost immediately, a crush of people pressed Bashir against the door as they tried to get out of the fiery restaurant. He dropped down to the floor, beneath the smoke, and fought his way back to the bar on his hands and knees. He climbed over the bar and continued crawling through the swinging door into the kitchen. He could hear screams and yelling behind him as he entered the kitchen area. He heard other people following behind him. He had no idea how many, because the smoke was too thick.

The smoke thinned when he passed the kitchen area and he reached the loading entrance. A group of kitchen staff were crowded around the closed door. Bashir stood and diverted left into a storage room. On one of the shelves, he found the tool kit he loaned out occasionally for breaking and entering jobs. He returned to the kitchen with a heavy set of bolt cutters. The smoke had grown thicker and adding to uniformed kitchen staff were panicked patrons escaping the hot flames in the dining room. He swung the bolt cutters from side to side like a bat. He cracked skulls as he fought his way to the door. When he reached his objective, he found the narrow gap between the door and the jam and slipped the bolt cutters through the gap and onto the chain. His biceps flexed as he pressed the handles together with all of his might. He felt the chain break as the knuckles from both hands came together. The door exploded open from the pressure of the crowd. Bashir was trampled to the ground as people raced over him. He used his knees and elbows to crawl over the asphalt parking lot until he had enough room to stand.

He sprang up from the ground and ran around to the front of the building. He cut the chain around the main entrance. The door opened, but behind it were only flames.

He ran to the emergency exit at the other end of the build-ing where the dance floor was located. He could see flames escaping from the shoulder-height windows as he ran. He cut the chain blocking the emergency exit. This time, he had to jump to the side as a throng of people burst from the opening and fled to safety.

Bashir walked across the street and sat on the curb. He watched as the fire department arrived and went to work extinguishing the flames. A steady stream of ambulances came and went as they ferried people to nearby hospitals. After the flames were extinguished and the smoke receded, he watched as the fire department worked to recover the bodies of victims. At dawn a detective came over, handed him a water bottle and asked to talk. He refused. The detec-tive placed him in handcuffs and took him to the station for questioning.

Bashir and his lawyer left the police station twelve hours later. He learned from the police that thirty-seven people had died in his restaurant and twenty-three were still in the hospital. Before they released him, the police told him that were it not for his actions, the death toll would have been much higher. A few hours before he left the station, it went into a frenzy of activity. They'd received a tip on the arson-ists. A raid was conducted at a farmhouse outside the city. A man with ties to right-wing organizations was the owner of the farm. The farmer's pickup truck was seen in the area at the time of the attack. Security footage of the parking lot showed the pickup enter the lot. The footage recorded two men in ski masks exit the pickup and chain the rear exit door. Incendiary bomb materials were found inside the man's workshop. The case against him was strong and it would have been a quick trial had the man and his brother survived the police raid.

Bashir didn't share with the police that he saw the two men who planted the incendiary devices. The local and national news tried repeatedly to interview him, but he refused. He was made a hero anyway. Cries of Islamophobia and demands to censor and shut down the civil liberties of right-wing hate groups dominated the news cycle.

Bashir conducted his own investigation, he started by identifying the two men who planted the incendiary devices. The men turned out to be Egyptian exchange students attending the nearby University. Before dying in great pain, the two chemical engineering majors revealed their membership in the Muslim Brotherhood and how their orders and payment came from an organization in Washington, DC. Bashir wasn't absolutely sure, he couldn't prove it, but he had a feeling and that was good enough for him. Akrim would be held responsible for attacking him. The same Akrim that had been on every news channel for the past week chastising the American public about their bigotry and intolerance while the IAIR donation coffers overfilled.

Although he was tempted to do the job himself, Bashir called on his specialist. He had a brief meeting and paid a hefty deposit to the thin, slightly balding, middle-aged man with glasses. A few days later, Akrim died in a tragic hit and run automobile accident. The President ordered the flags flown at half-mast as the nation mourned the death of a civil rights legend.

CHAPTER 26

NASHVILLE, TENNESSEE

I WOKE UP AT dawn feeling good. Cognac agrees with me. I went downstairs to the gym and had it mostly to myself. I punished myself for the excessive calorie consumption the night before. When I was done lifting, I went to the rooftop pool and swam 1,500 meters. Still feeling healthy and virtuous, I went downstairs and had a light breakfast at the hotel restaurant. Not an easy achievement in a place that has a buffet section dedicated just to southern biscuits.

I returned to my room and considered what to do. I wanted to call Emily and give her an update, but couldn't imagine a scenario where that phone call went well, so I didn't. It was too early to expect anything from Grace's gang expert, and based on what Grace had mentioned before, the police knew precious little about the Somali gangs anyway. The way Grace looked at me last night definitely showed that her view of me had changed. I could see it in her eyes, it was fear. She thought I killed those eight gangsters and she was scared of me. My downward slide with women never ceases to amaze me. Grace is afraid of me and I'm hiding from

Emily. The only happy relationship I have at the moment with a member of the opposite sex is the nice waitress at the bar. While I was waiting for it to be a reasonable hour in Scotland, I put Lindsay Ashton's country CD into my room's entertainment center.

My call to David began with a report on Emily's inquiries. She'd threatened to close down Clearwater, the company David and I co-own. Most of Clearwater's revenue is paid by shipping and insurance companies that have a need to track cargo ships. I told David that at her worst, Emily could pull the CIA contract, which is not nearly enough to close down the company. David already knew this, but he was still wary of Emily's wrath and begged me to make peace with her. I told him I would when the time was right.

"Did you find anything on Abdi Abdullah and Salam Saeed?" I asked.

"I have a phone number and location on Salam Saeed. I have a photo I'm going to send you."

"Where is he now?"

"At a motel in Nashville. A place called the Drake, it's south of the river next to the highway."

"Can you pinpoint a room?" I asked.

"No, the best I can do is the section of the building. I can't determine what floor he's on," he said.

"Send me his image and the best you have on the location," I said.

I grabbed my backpack, checked out of the hotel and headed out to my SUV. At the Drake, I backed into a spot facing the motel. Only four rooms met the criteria of being within fifty yards of the GPS location David gave me. I regretted eating a light breakfast, because I didn't know how long I was going to wait.

After three hours, I still hadn't seen Salam, but I was beginning to pick up a pattern. Every thirty to forty-five minutes a person showed up at the door of room 217, went in and then after ten to fifteen minutes left. My guess is the person in room 217 is dealing drugs and what are the odds two gangs were operating out of the same motel? The man in 217 had to be Salam.

The curtain was pulled closed in the room, but I could occasionally see it move. It would make sense that if there were people in the room dealing drugs, they'd have some surveillance. Maybe an adjacent room with a lookout or even someone looking out from the same room. The windows of my SUV were tinted and given the distance to the room in question, I didn't think they knew I was out here.

I pulled the Honey Badger carbine from the back pack and loaded it. I took two extra magazines and put them into the cargo pocket of my pants. I pulled off my polo shirt and slipped on an armored t-shirt with level II ballistic protection before covering it again with the polo. I waited until the next courier showed up at the door of the first-story motel room. The parking lot was two thirds filled with cars, but when I stepped out and approached the hotel, there was no one else in the lot except me. As I walked forward, a door on the second floor opened. I dropped the man before he could squeeze a round off with his pistol. At seventy-five yards with a three-power sight, the man's face filled my optic view when I hit him with the second bullet.

The door on the first floor flew open. Even suppressed, the sound of my gunfire behind him spooked the courier and he raced into the room as soon as he had a chance. An arm with a pistol poked through and I put three rounds next to the door where I knew the man would be standing. I sped up my approach into the room. Five yards from the open doorway, I threw a flash bang inside. I waited for it to go off and then followed it in.

I shot a man using the twin bed as cover in the face. I dropped the courier as he raced for the bathroom. A man in the corner of the room to my right got off a single shot with his pistol. I shot him once in each shoulder, he was Salam. I grabbed him by the shirt and threw him over my left shoulder and headed to the door. I was halfway to my Suburban when gunfire erupted behind me. The bullet impact against my back caused me to do a face plant. Free of Salam, I rolled left and sat up into a crouch facing the motel. Two men were on the railing changing magazines in their machine pistols. I shot the first one in the chest. The second man got off one more burst before I dropped him with two shots to the chest. I took Salam by the back collar and dragged him to the SUV and threw him in the back, on top of the tarp I'd covered the back seat with.

When I pulled out of the parking lot, I could hear sirens. I drove the speed limit and got onto the highway and headed out of town. I drove north on Interstate 65 and then turned off to I-24. It took thirty minutes, but eventually, I found myself on a dirt road surrounded by hills and forest. I pulled a semiconscious Salam out of the back seat.

"I didn't bring you here to kill you. I came for information," I said.

Salam looked up at me. He was in a lot of pain.

"I have a shot of morphine I can give you for the pain."

I showed him the syrette from my medic kit. "Just tell me who killed Captain Greg Allison."

"Hodar's," he said.

"Hodar's who?" I asked.

"Hodar's son."

"Who's that?"

"Abdi, Abdi Abdullah," he said.

I leaned over and stuck the syrette into the side of his neck. I waited a minute for it to have an effect. I went to the truck and retrieved two water bottles. I opened one and poured it into Salam's mouth. He drank thirstily.

"Where do I find Abdi?" I asked.

"He moves around a lot. Doesn't sleep in the same place two nights in a row. He does his business out of coffee shops. You can't find him," he said.

"Do you have his phone number?" I asked.

"Yeah."

I went through his pockets and found his phone. I used his finger to unlock the phone and scrolled through the contacts. There were only four contacts, one of them was Abdi.

"Is this the number?"

He nodded.

I walked away, out of earshot, and called David. I gave him the number and asked him to track it. He gave me an address. When I went back to Salam, he was dead. I rolled him in the tarpaulin and dragged him into the forest. I removed my polo shirt with the hole in the back and replaced it with a black Under Armour t-shirt, then I headed back to Nashville.

I parked the Suburban at a mall and rented a Blue Chevy Malibu from a nearby Avis. I drove back to the Suburban and retrieved my backpack and supplies. I called David and got an update on Abdi; he was on the move. David vectored me to his direction and then told me he was at a Starbucks on Charlotte Ave. I tucked the HK45 into my waistband as I walked into the coffee shop. I no sooner had the Grande Latte in my hand when a younger version of Hodar walked past me to the door. I hurried after him. As soon as he got through the doors, he went into a run. I pulled the pistol from my waistband and shot him. I was aiming for his legs, but I wound up putting a round into his buttocks. The bullet collapsed him. I was next to my vehicle so I started it up and drove to Abdi in the center of the parking lot. I helped him into the tarp on the back seat and drove off.

I returned to the same forestry road in the hills where Salam drew his last breath. I pulled Abdi out of the back seat and leaned him against a tree. I gave him a shot of morphine, because his shattered pelvis was causing him so much pain, he was blacking out. I started an IV of ringer's lactate, stuffed some Celox clotting gauze into the wound to slow the bleeding and bandaged it tight. Eventually, he regained consciousness.

Abdi and I talked for a long time. He told me about Bashir and about the thin man with glasses who carried out the hit. He told me how to make contact with the hit man who executed the Captain. He told me about the two Federal Agents on his payroll. He said it was Bashir who notified the Defense Attorneys that the video evidence was tainted, before it came out in the newspaper. He talked until he passed out. It was almost six in the afternoon when I left him. I returned the car to Avis and walked the half mile to my SUV in the parking lot. I got back on Highway 65 and headed south to Savannah. Once I crossed into Georgia, I called Grace.

"Do you know anything about a gunfight at the Drake Motel? The FBI has taken over the case," Grace said.

"The person who paid for the hit on Captain Allison was Abdi Abdullah. He's the top Somali gang leader in Nashville. He has two FBI agents on his payroll. I just sent you a pin with a location, bring an ambulance. You need to hurry if you want to keep him alive. He'll testify against your two Federal Agents. Abdi's father was Hodar, the previous head of the Somali Mafia and Boyz," I said.

"Where are you going?" she asked.

"I'm going to meet up with the trigger man that killed your boss."

"This has gone way too far. Pat, you need to stop and turn yourself in," Grace said.

"I'm not done yet. Get a statement signed by Abdi on the Captain's murder and on the two FBI agents. The Feds might as well have killed him themselves. Abdi will cooperate," I said.

"Is that it?"

"Yes, you won't be hearing from me again."

"Don't be so sure about that. The FBI and the Tennessee State Police are both looking for you," she said, right before I hung up.

CHAPTER 27

SAVANNAH, GEORGIA

I T WAS TWO in the morning when the taxi dropped me off outside the marina in Savannah. I returned the rental at the airport Enterprise counter and settled my bill. I was tired and my back was killing me from the long drive and huge bruise caused by the gunfight in the motel parking lot. I walked through the security gate with my backpack and a small suitcase with some clothes. The *Nomad* was right where I'd left her. I found the key and unlocked the salon door. I turned on the salon interior light and who did I find sitting on my cream-colored custom Italian leather couch but Emily. She looked beautiful, she had sleep in her eyes and a 9mm Beretta in her right hand.

"I'm too tired for this right now. Can we talk in the morning?" I asked.

"It is morning. And we'll talk when I say we'll talk."

"On account of you're the person holding the gun."

"Exactly."

"Can I at least shower first? I'm filthy," I said.

I returned upstairs after a refreshing shower, wearing

a bathrobe. I opened a bottle of Chateau Saint Michelle Cabernet and set it on the coffee table along with two glasses. Emily still had the pistol in her hand. I poured two glasses. I took mine and sat back in the recliner. Emily held the pistol in both hands with the weapon pointed at the ground.

"Explain yourself," she said.

"Where should I begin?"

"Start with walking out in the middle of the night without telling me."

I told Emily everything I'd been up to. About halfway through the story she put the weapon down on the coffee table and exchanged it for a wine glass. The sun was rising when I finished my tale.

"What do you plan on doing next?" Emily asked.

"Mike's problem stems from a leak. I've traced the leak to Bashir. Now I'm going to find out how Bashir got the classified information. I'm guessing Bashir is only one or two points in the network from the original source. I'm getting close," I said.

"What do you plan on doing to Bashir once you've interrogated him?"

"I'm going to kill Bashir and then I'm going to kill his trigger man. Then I'm going to work my way up the chain to whoever is leaking highly classified CIA information for political reasons," I said.

"And you think Mike would want you to do this?"

"Same as you, he'd quote the book to me, but yeah, when he learns of it after the fact, all would be forgiven," I said.

"And that's what I'm supposed to do?" Emily said.

"You're his stand in, aren't you?" I said. She put her glass down and picked up the pistol. She leaned back in her chair.

"You're the most frustrating man I've ever met. You're insubordinate, inconsiderate, sneaky, sadistic and stupid."

I leaned forward and poured the last of the wine. "I never claimed to be anything more than I am. I'm not a saint, I fix problems and I don't care about the CIA rule book or the FBI rule book or anyone else's book for that matter."

"What am I going to do with you?"

"You can shoot me, or you can get out of my way. I've already been shot once today, so if I get a vote, I'm for getting out of the way," I said.

"Where did you get shot?" she asked with a hint of concern.

"In the back. I was wearing protection, but I think I may have broken something."

"You're going to take on a psychotic Somali gang leader, a professional hit man and a shadow leaker in the CIA with a broken something in your back and absolutely no plan. This is why I said stupid," Emily said.

I finished my wine and put the glass down. "Thanks for the kind words and encouragement. I'm going to bed, I have a busy day tomorrow, we sail north in eight hours." I got up and walked down the stairs to my cabin. I tossed the robe on a chair and was asleep within seconds.

When I woke up, I felt someone next to me. I was sleeping on my stomach to lessen the pain and I had to lift my head to turn in her direction. Emily was asleep, she had both hands wrapped around my right bicep and was curled up like a koala bear. I rolled onto my side and she woke up. I brought her in close and put my arms around her. Neither one of us said anything, we'd talked enough the night before.

CHAPTER 28

WASHINGTON, DC

EMILY AND I motored up the Potomac to the Wharf Marina in DC. It was late in the afternoon when we finally tied down. The *Nomad* was built for speed and spending an hour on the river at six knots in a no wake zone wasn't something I'd factored into the trip planner. I wasn't in a big rush, the charter wasn't booked into Minneapolis until the next morning. David needed the time to get me some usable inteI and I needed the break to allow my body to heal. Nothing was broken, but I had a deep bruise on my upper back near the spine.

Emily wasn't good company during the trip. She was distracted and on edge, worried about what story she was going to tell her bosses.

"If you throw in with me, you'll have to leave the Agency. There's no going back from what I'm doing, especially without approval," I said to her.

"I'm not the one operating domestically. What I'm doing is recovering a runaway asset and preventing him from making the situation worse," she said.

"Nobody is going to believe that."

"We'll see," Emily said.

"What you should do is return to your desk and find out what you can on Bashir. David only has access to open source intelligence. If you could get David access to the refugee databases and the classified stuff, he'd be a lot more successful figuring out who Bashir really is, not to mention finding him," I said.

"How are you planning to find him?" Emily asked.

"I'm relying on David. But I don't have a lot to go on. I don't even have a usable family name, Bashir Asad tells me nothing and I don't have a phone number. It's not going to be easy."

"Will David be able to do anything with the Dark Web URL for the assassin?" Emily asked.

"That may be our best bet. David's not the best at deception. One thing you could do for the cause would be help us catfish the killer for hire on that Serbian message board. At the same time, you could help David do a deep dive on Bashir. I'll set up a base of operations in Minneapolis and if things get hairy you can join me," I said.

"What do I tell my boss?" Emily asked.

"Everything."

"Seriously?"

"Can you lie your way through a poly?"

"No."

"Tell him the truth. Explain that you tracked me down, but you couldn't convince me to stop. Make sure he knows about our rogue FBI agents and why relying on federal law enforcement wasn't an option. Let him take it to the Director and get you some top cover," I said.

"If I do that, they might put me on suspension or just outright fire me," Emily said.

"What they won't do is arrest you, which is what might happen if you help me without approval," I said.

"I'll give it some thought."

"Tomorrow morning, you go to Langley and I'll head to Minneapolis. Tonight, we relax," I said.

"Feeling better, I see."

"Painkillers are kicking in nicely," I said.

"What are you taking, you travel with a pharmacy?" Emily asked.

"Just ibuprofen. I have to keep my detective skills sharp."

"Why don't you put those deductive skills to use and find us a place for an early dinner, I'm starving," Emily said.

After we tied down the boat and connected the power and water, we got dressed and headed out to dinner. La Vie was only a quarter mile away from our slip. We walked along the waterfront, past the Capital Yacht Club and into the restaurant that had floor to ceiling windows and an excellent view of the river below. La Vie is a trendy place with a relaxed atmosphere. It had an open Mediterranean design and I liked it immediately. The menu was small, but it was creative. It was happy hour, but the waiter was kind enough to allow us to order from the full menu.

When I ordered both scallops and lamb chops for a main course, Emily looked at me with a disapproving glare.

"I haven't eaten a decent meal since breakfast yesterday and the appetizers don't appeal," I said.

"Don't let me hold you back," she said.

I also ordered a bottle of Duckhorn Cabernet and a Devils Head draft.

"I'm trying to properly pair my main courses," I said.

"Don't bother to explain," she said.

The restaurant was fantastic. By the time we finished the wine and asked for the bill the place was packed.

"What now?" Emily asked.

"I thought we'd go back to the *Nomad*; we both have busy days tomorrow," I said.

She smiled, because she knew I had something else entirely on my mind. On the way out, we passed a sign for an event scheduled at the restaurant the next week called Newszines. It's a venue for people to meet celebrity reporters covering the DC beat. It gave me an idea.

"I may need to attend that event. If we don't get anywhere with the other two avenues, maybe I'll take the direct approach and just ask the reporter who wrote the story who leaked it to him."

"You'll never get him to divulge his source," Emily said.

"I'm pretty sure I will, but I think we'll stick to the plan for now," I said.

The next morning, I made Emily breakfast in bed. Then I took a taxi to Dulles and flew a charter to Minneapolis. Prior to leaving the *Nomad*, I replenished the magazines for my HK45 and my trusty Honey Badger. Because of the time difference, I made it to my hotel in Minneapolis by noon. I took a room at the Hilton in the Mill District which is adjacent to the Cedar-Riverside area. I checked in with David, but he didn't have any progress to report. I tucked the HK45 into my holster, covered it with a light workout jacket and left the hotel for what we used to call in the Army "Local Area Orientation".

The Cedar-Riverside train station was half a mile from the Hilton. It was easy to find the neighborhood, because it's bordered by the Mississippi River on one side and I-35 on the other. It's a diverse neighborhood with lots of small stores, restaurants and bars catering to multiple demographics. There's a Medical School and a Law School in the area and during the day, nothing in the neighborhood appeared particularly threatening.

When I got back to the room, I took out my laptop with the intent to familiarize myself with the local news. Particularly the crime reports, especially those that were gang related. The biggest story over the past month was a fire that killed thirty-seven patrons at a Cedar-Riverside bar owned by none other than Bashir Asad. None of the stories had a photo of Bashir, but they were all effusive in their praise for the man who arranged for the murder of Captain Allison. Subsequent articles delved into the ubiquity of racism and the white supremist arsonist who set the blaze and was later killed in a shootout with police.

Bashir was a lot higher profile than I expected. I found this to be an encouraging sign. David's artificial intelligence powered computer system that he called ALICE was remarkably adept at tracking down people that didn't want to get found. A high-profile gang leader like Bashir would eventually surface and be discovered. I was sure of it.

While I had my computer open, on a whim I decided to check to see if I could get tickets for the night's baseball game. Target Field is only a twenty-minute walk from the Hilton and the red-hot Twins were hosting the Red Sox. As luck would have it, I managed to find a seat close to the field on the first base line on one of the resale sites. Emily called me during the bottom of the sixth.

"How are you doing?" she asked.

"Not so good at the moment. Game's tied. Sale's in a jam. Men on first and third, one out."

"Where are you?"

"I'm at the game, the Sox are in town, I had the night free and I found a ticket."

"Is that why you didn't want me to come?"

"I wish you were here. It's a good game."

"Do you want me to call back later?"

"No, you're more important. How are things with the company?"

"I've been advised that I did the right thing. Management understands that you're uncontrollable, so they don't blame me. They've decided that since you're not working for us and the work you're doing is in our interest, to leave you alone for the time being."

"That's encouraging."

"Yes, but we can't help David, he's on his own."

"That's a fair trade," I said as the crowd around me erupted in a cheer drowning out whatever Emily said next.

"What was that?" she asked

"A two RBI double. Sale's about to get the hook. It hasn't been his best season."

"Hang in there, be strong, don't cry."

"I'm trying. Good news about you still having a career and all."

"Yeah, I'll let you get back to the game, keep in touch."

"I will."

On the way back, I overshot the hotel and stopped at the Republic Brewpub. It was a half mile from the hotel and on the Cedar-Riverside side of I-35. I sat at the bar, hoping to strike up a conversation with somebody from the neighborhood who could help me with finding Bashir. It was eleven thirty, midweek and the bar only had four patrons. I ordered a Grand Cru Ale and the Cajun Walleye from the bartender. The bar may have better crowds during the school year, but on this night, it was fairly dead.

I finished my plate and signaled the bartender. I asked the bartender for suggestions, but she told me she didn't drink beer. Which was believable, she was a dead ringer for the African singer Sade, no extra calories on this girl. I don't think she was a Somali; she wouldn't be working in a bar if she was religious and she wouldn't be allowed to not be religious if she was a Somali. I guessed she was from either Kenya or Ethiopia. She asked me what I was doing in town and I told her I was a reporter doing an exposé on local hate groups. I told her I was trying to interview the owner of the Red Sea Bar but was having trouble locating him. The girl offered to ask around. The Republic Brewpub didn't look like a place patronized by the local gang leaders, but I had nothing to lose. She asked me for a business card; I fumbled around and told her I left them in my room. I gave her my phone number and left a little while later.

I returned to my room and crashed for the night. It was five in the morning when my phone woke me up. It was David.

"I have a meeting arranged with our assassin," David said.

"Does he have a name?"

"No."

"Not even an alias?" I said.

"No names are his policy."

"Where…. When?" I asked.

"This afternoon. He'll send me the location thirty minutes before the meeting, which is at 2 p.m. I told him I was in

Downtown Minneapolis; the meeting will be somewhere in the city," David said.

"This was all with messages; he's not expecting a Scottish accent, is he?" I asked.

"He's expecting an American man that fits your description."

"Who's he bumping off for me?" I said.

"A hostile business partner. I emailed you the message traffic, so you can familiarize yourself. He's expecting a deposit of fifty thousand dollars in cash, payable at the meeting."

"Any idea of the venue?" I asked.

"No, only that it will be public," David said.

"How's he going to send you the location?"

"On the same message board."

"Did he give you a description? How am I going to recognize him?"

"He said he'll supply that info when he provides the location."

"Anything else I should know?"

"That's the all of it."

"Good work, stay in touch."

At one thirty, I was ready and waiting for Dave to message me the location. I'd debated back and forth whether or not to go to the meeting armed. I eventually decided against it. The man was very cautious and I'm sure he would be making certain I had the cash and didn't have a weapon before revealing himself.

I put the money in a small white plastic bag I found in the closet of the hotel. Five stacks of hundred-dollar bills was about the size of a standard brick. I was using real cash I'd brought with me for the operation. I was wearing a tight t-shirt to emphasize my not being armed and a pair of jeans. I don't know how the man was going to check that I wasn't wearing a wire, but I imagine he had a system for that.

I got the message at thirty-five minutes after one and headed to the Starbucks on Fifth and Marquette. I had planned to take a taxi, but it was only a ten-minute walk from the hotel according to the Google Maps app on my phone.

I arrived at the Starbucks ten minutes early. The coffee shop had six tables on the way to the counter and a bunch of couches and lounge chairs on the far side of the counter. I ordered a Venti Coffee and took a seat facing the doorway in one of the three open tables. The restaurant was on a corner and had windows facing both streets. After I surveyed the crowd and didn't see any thin black men with glasses who were going bald, I concentrated on the outside traffic.

A man fitting the description walked to the entry door on Marquette Street and entered the cafe. The identifier he had passed to David was a green Vikings ball cap. The man's condition for the meeting included my name, phone number, age and home address. The man knew what I looked like. David had set all of that up prior to the contact. He spoofed the phone and he even created a website of the engineering consulting company I fictitiously co-owned with the man I was going to have killed.

I made eye contact and the man approached my table and sat down across from me with his back to the door.

"Do you have something for me?" he said.

I slid the rolled-up bag over to him. He opened it and looked inside. I scanned outside and didn't see any back up.

"Did you drive or walk here?" he asked.

"I drove, I parked over by the Stadium."

"Do you mind if I get a tea?"

"Not at all."

The man stood up with the money in his left hand. He took two steps toward the counter and then I saw his right hand disappear from his side. My Venti Coffee was halfway to his face and I was on my way to the floor by the time his hand reappeared with a small pistol in it. He ducked away from the scalding coffee and I pounced. I hit the man with a straight right in the face at the same time he fired off an errant shot. He backed up to free his weapon and I stayed with him. I knocked his left arm away and he fired a second shot, this time into the ceiling. He hit me in the throat with a knife strike from his left hand and took another step back.

I continued to thrust forward, backed him against the side of the coffee counter. I slammed the side of my right fist down hard onto his right shoulder and heard the snap of his clavicle breaking. I released his right wrist and with an open palm I pounded the side of his right shoulder with a brutal strike. I drove his splintered clavicle deep into his lungs. Despite the agony he must've been in, the man raised the pistol. I spun counterclockwise, pivoting away from the pistol, and used the momentum of the spin to drive my left elbow into the man's face. I connected perfectly and his head hit the glass counter so hard, it made a thunderous crack before it crashed through. The man sank to a sitting position with his back sliding against the counter. I checked for a pulse on his neck to be sure, but I already knew he was dead.

The people in the coffee shop streamed to the exits. One of the baristas was behind the counter on his cell phone, I saw the second one run into the back room. I picked up the white bag with the money and hopped over the counter. I took the phone away from the barista and pulled him by the collar into the back room. The second barista stared up at me terrified.

"Give me your phone," I said.

"What do you want?" he stammered.

I pulled the cash out of the bag and tossed two bundles to each of them. They caught the bundles in the air.

"That money is for your phones, I'm keeping them," I said

"Where's the security camera footage stored?" I asked. Neither looked at me like they wanted to answer. I didn't hear any sirens, so I figured I had time. There was only one door in the back room that wasn't an exit and I gave it a try. It was a small office and I found the CCTV data storage box bolted to a wall. I opened it up and removed the hard drive. I left the two terrified baristas in the office while I left out the loading door in the back of the coffee shop.

The door exited to a small driveway. I got onto the sidewalk and walked along 5th Street in the opposite direction of my hotel. The tree-lined sidewalks afforded some concealment from the street. I didn't hear sirens approach until I was a good three hundred yards away from the Starbucks. I crushed the cell phones and kicked them into a storm drain, then I ducked into Nicolette Mall. Inside the mall, I bought a blue short sleeve button down to go over my black t-shirt. I also picked up a pair of sunglasses and a blue Patagonia baseball hat.

I was close to Target Field. Game two of a three game series between the Twins and Red Sox was scheduled in four hours. I decided to go to Kieran's Irish Pub which is adjacent to the ball park and have a late lunch and hang out until the baseball crowd arrived. My plan was to eat, watch batting practice and then the game. I could return to my hotel room later, hidden by the darkness and security of a crowd. The pub was fairly empty when I arrived. It was the dead period between lunch and the pre-game dinner rush. I found a corner booth and ordered a Reuben Sandwich and a Summit IPA. I managed to buy another baseball ticket at a resale site using my iPhone. This time I got one behind the plate.

By five, the pub was packed. Half looked like the after-work crowd and the other half were baseball fans. I called David.

"Do you have anything yet on Bashir?"

"Not yet. I'm still working it."

"We really need to make some progress; I didn't get anything from Mr. Nameless."

"How did it go, or should I not ask?"

"His murder for hire business is closed, I can tell you that much."

"I suppose that's a good thing."

"It was never going to be pretty; I had no control over the timing or the location. He arranged for circumstances that made it very difficult for a capture and interrogation. A daylight meeting in a public place, with me unarmed and no vehicle nearby. Two minutes into the meeting he stepped away from the table and drew on me. I was lucky to survive."

"And you didn't get any information?"

"I didn't even remember to take his phone. It was a mess."

"What are you going to do if I can't find Bashir?"

"Introduce myself to the local gangsters and work my way up."

"That seems as perilous as your last plan."

"Exactly, which is why I need you to perform a miracle."

CHAPTER 29

MINNEAPOLIS, MINNESOTA

W HEN I AWOKE the next morning, it was to the sound of my cell ringing. It was Emily. I gave her an update on the search for Bashir, which didn't take long, because I'd made very little progress. I let her know the assassin was no longer converting oxygen to carbon dioxide. She wanted details, but I was evasive. The way the Starbucks scenario played out wouldn't instill much confidence in my fieldcraft, the less said the better. I told her I was going to hit the streets today and let people in Bashir's network know I was looking for him. I told her about my cover as a reporter.

"That's kinda thin."

"It'll do the job. Gives me an excuse to ask questions and spread money around."

"It's going to make you a target."

"I can take care of myself."

"You have a bruise the size of a basketball on your back that says otherwise."

"Thanks for the confidence."

"You should bring out the rest of your team."

"That's a reversal. What made you change your mind?"

"Upper management is distracted by some other very serious issues that have been in the headlines. The fallout from Nashville was nil, I don't think a few more rogue contractors is going to upset the balance of things."

"I could use the backup; I'm getting nowhere alone. I've been to two ballgames at Target Field and seen fewer strikeouts than what I'm experiencing."

"I'll fix that when I see you again," she said. That made me laugh.

I called McDonald and asked him to fly the team to Washington, DC. They were going to need weapons which meant they had to stop off at the *Nomad* before coming to Minneapolis.

I planned to stay in the hotel, I didn't see any advantage to walking around town in daylight. I hadn't checked the news yet but was sure the police were looking for me. Given the amount of witnesses at the coffee shop, they probably had a decent description. I held onto the CCTV footage; if I was arrested, it would at least exonerate me for murder by showing it was self-defense.

By mid-morning, I was getting a little stir crazy. I was tempted to call David, but I saw no point in badgering him. The bruise on my back kept me away from the gym and that left me with nothing to do but watch TV in the room. I was mindlessly channel surfing when my phone rang. Salafa, the bartender who I met my first night at the Republic Brewpub, asked me to come by at lunch. She said she had a tip on Bashir's location. She refused to give me the information over the phone. I'd given her a big tip the night I met her and told her I'd pay for any information. It made sense she wouldn't want to supply the info without being paid first.

When I arrived at the Republic Brewpub it looked much different than the empty dark place of my last visit. It was bright and they had a big lunchtime crowd. The tables on the front patio were filled and inside there were only a couple of seats available on the long twenty-five seat bar. I found an open table on the bar side of the restaurant. It was in the back where I could see the length of the bar and the front entrance. The table was probably empty because it was under the air conditioning vent, but I was sweating from my walk from the hotel. I was wearing a light jacket to cover my holster and because I had an armor-protected t-shirt under my shirt, the cool breeze felt great.

Salafa was behind the bar with two other guys working at a steady pace. The bar area had five tables and occasionally, she would move from behind the bar to attend to a guest seated at one of the tables. When Salafa came to my table, she was all smiles. We said hello and I gave her my order, which was the blackened Walleye and an Alaskan Ale. I slipped her two one-hundred-dollar bills in advance for the information and she returned behind the bar counter to submit my order. When she came back a few minutes later, she took a seat across from me at the table. I was surprised she sat down.

"It's okay, I'm on break. Bashir sees a girl who comes in here sometimes. She's a student who escorts on the side, I think that's how she met him. She's scared of him."

"How did you come to learn this?"

"Since you told me you were looking for him, I've been asking about him to our regulars."

"Did she tell you where he is?"

"No, she wants to talk to you first."

"Why does she want to talk to a reporter?"

"I didn't tell her you were a reporter. I've never seen a reporter with arms like yours and I don't think that bulge under your jacket is a notepad."

"Not the best cover, was it?"

"No, plus reporters are cheap."

"When are you going to introduce me to your friend?"

"Stay here and enjoy your meal, she'll be along shortly." She then got up and went back to work.

I was on my second cup of coffee when a tall girl with long dark hair came through the door alone. She went over to the bar and Salafa led her to my table. I stood up and shook her hand.

"Hi, I'm Pat," I said.

"I'm Marianna."

"Are you hungry, can I get you something?" She ordered only a Diet Coke.

"Why do you want to find Bashir?" she asked.

"I'm going to kill him," I said.

"Why?"

"He had a friend of mine executed. He had a young girl kidnapped and raped. He needs to be put down."

"Do you think you can do it?"

"We'll have to find that out won't we."

"What I mean is, do you have any experience with this? If I send you to Bashir and he makes you talk, he'll come after me next."

"That's a risk."

"This is his home; he's surrounded by his crew. He smart, big and strong. I need to know if you're up to it," she said with a look of concern on her face. I waited a couple of seconds thinking of what to say.

"I do this professionally. I've hunted and killed some of the worst terrorists in the world. I can't guarantee anything, but if I don't get him, it will only be because I'm dead. There's no chance any of this is going to blow back against you."

Marianna spent a minute thinking about her options. She wouldn't have gone this far if she wasn't serious. I could see the lines of worry on her face. She seemed intelligent and street smart; I was curious about why she ever got involved with Bashir but thought it best not to ask.

"He's been staying at a condo he owns near the University. It's nearby on 1st Street, the name is Riverside Tower. His apartment is on the top floor, it's number 2106. The apartment has a security guard at the entryway, but the guard won't stop you as long as you look like you know where you're going," she said.

"Is Bashir there now?" I asked.

"I don't know. I only see him a few times a month. Always after midnight."

"Always in the same place?"

"Not always. Usually it's at his place at Riverside. When I was there last week, it looked like he's been staying there every night," she said.

"And before that it didn't?"

"Before it was like a hotel, now the place looks lived in with food and clothes and all."

"Okay. Does he keep weapons in the apartment?" I asked.

"Yes, pistols."

"Is he alone, or does he have security inside the apartment?"

"He's usually alone, but sometimes he has others. He doesn't introduce me, but they don't look like bodyguards," she said.

"Do they look armed?"

"They're gangsters, I think they're always armed," she said.

I shrugged at her comment. "Any idea of his work routine?"

"No."

"When does he wake up?"

"Late, usually noon. He stays up late."

"Do you work for him?" I asked.

"No."

"Why see him if he hurts you?"

"I didn't say he hurt me."

"Answer the question."

"He told me that if he calls and I don't come, he'll kill me."

"And you believed him."

"I have no doubt."

"Do you have his phone number?"

"Yes."

"How often does he change his number?"

"At least once a month."

"Can I have it?"

After she left, I called David and gave him Bashir's telephone number. The damage David could do armed with only a cell number was amazing. I walked over to Riverside Tower, which was only half a mile from the restaurant and had a look around. Bashir's apartment had underground parking and minimal security. School was out for the year and the parking area was mostly empty. Like the area around it, the Tower had seen better years. It was sandwiched between the University of Minnesota campus and the Mississippi River. Looking at the apartments from the outside, they all had that destitute look of student housing, where acceptable window covering options included bed sheets and aluminum foil. Having a predator like Bashir living in the midst of their college-aged children is definitely not what the good people of Minnesota had in mind when they generously opened their arms and green-lighted the development of Little Mogadishu around the school.

I returned to my hotel room and waited for David to contact me with the fruits of his electronic surveillance. Several hours later, David called.

"What do you have?" I asked.

"He's been on the move all day. At the moment, he's at a car wash," David said.

"Has he been there long?"

"About an hour. He seems to be visiting businesses he has an interest in. He's been to a number of laundries, car washes and restaurants today," David said.

"That makes sense, those are good cash businesses to launder drug and prostitution money. Who's he been talking to?"

"Mostly text messages. Only two phone calls. One to Washington, DC and one local."

"Were you able to record the calls?"

"No, I'm having some software challenges. He has an old phone, probably a Nokia. Pegasus was developed with smartphones in mind, it misses a lot on the older phones," David said.

"What do you know about the people he's been communicating with?"

"They're all criminals. The message traffic is all about money, deliveries and meetings. The only interesting contact is the person in DC," David said.

"Why?"

"The number he called is the main office number of his Congresswoman," David said.

"Any way to find out who he spoke to in the office?"

"No, but his Congresswoman is a Somali. And when I researched her, what I discovered was that Bashir is her ex-husband," David said.

"You should've led with that. When did they divorce?"

"Five years ago."

"He must have been calling her, but why on the office number and not direct to her cell," I said.

"I think the main office forwards to her cell. He's likely trying to obfuscate, between having a burner phone and not calling her direct," David said.

"Can you pierce it?"

"I've already gained access to her office exchange. I have the date stamp when Bashir called her. It won't be long before I have Congresswoman Noor's private cell," David said.

"We'll look into her later, once we finish with Bashir. What else can you tell me about him?" I asked.

"He's being driven around town, but not by the same car. Several people have the task of taking him from business to business. I have a good location on him, but there are no records of him owning anything, not even the condo at Riverside is in his name," David said.

"He's an economic ghost," I said.

"At least when it comes to property. I can't get into his banking records, but it stands to reason some of them will have to be in his name."

"I want to get him somewhere in private. Either where he sleeps or at an office. I'll need him to remain in place for at least three hours. Let me know when that condition exists," I said.

"Have you been to his apartment at Riverside Tower?" David asked.

"I have, it's suitable, but I'm not positive that's where he sleeps most nights; he might just use it to rendezvous with his playthings," I said.

"I'm tracking him and even if he gets rid of his cell phone, I have the contact information for his drivers and his network, I'll be able to find him again," David said.

"Perfect. I'm going to check out of my hotel room and then rent a car. Keep me posted," I said.

"I will."

"And one more thing. The team should've landed at Dulles by now. Pass McDonald the info you have on Congresswoman Noor. I'll have them begin surveillance on her, I don't think I'm going to need them to come out here after all," I said.

"Do you think she's the source of the leak?"

"Maybe not the original source, but the info came from DC and so far, she's the only contact he has in DC," I said.

Seven hours later, I was parked in a Blue Honda Pilot along the side of Cedar Avenue. I was listening to the Twins give the Red Sox a trouncing and watching the traffic go by. It was the ninth inning and the game was mercifully almost over.

David called me.

"Bashir is at a night club. It looks like he's going to be there a while."

"How do you know?"

"He just sent a text to a woman telling her to come over."

"What's the name of the place?"

"Medusa."

"What can you tell me about it?"

"Uptown Posh. Tonight's theme is seduction. It's a popular place."

"Will I get in if I show up?" I asked.

"No, but I can get into their system and get you a table. When do you expect to arrive?"

"Thirty minutes, I'm going to have to change my clothes first."

"Good enough then. I'll keep you abreast of any developments."

David was starting to enjoy the hunt, I could tell. I went to the back of the SUV and opened my suitcase and found a sports jacket, jeans, an Oxford shirt and shoes. I drove to a dark parking lot, did a contortionist routine of changing inside the vehicle and then drove to North 1st Ave. to go clubbing.

I cut the line at the velvet rope and made it past the bouncers with the help of David and Benjamin, two Benjamins actually. As I entered, I went through a metal detector and a bouncer gave me a pat down. I advanced through a corridor that led to another door. I was stopped by a hostess who checked my name against a list and then had someone take me to a table. A middle-aged man sitting alone on a couch at the Medusa was an odd sight. I felt awkward and was grateful when two party girls came by and introduced themselves. I asked them to join me and they did. I ordered a couple of bottles of champagne and some appetizers. Seeing the largess, the girls asked to bring over two more of their girlfriends. I said fine, happy for the cover, and then I excused myself.

Visibility in the club was difficult. It was a big club with hundreds of guests. The décor was purple and blue with a hideous Medusa snake head image placed anywhere it would fit. The lighting was dim, with the liberal use of black lights. The dance floor was a writhing throng of humanity in the center of the room. The cordoned VIP area where I had a table sat adjacent to the dance floor. The common area consisted of tall tables arranged in an elliptical pattern where people could stand. The outer walls had a single row of couches lining them. It was a weekend crowd and I found it difficult to weave through the throng of people. Overhead were disco balls and lasers and in some places clouds of smoke from smoke generators. A deejay was on an elevated stage playing a mix of salsa and electronic dance music at a deafening volume that shook the room. I walked a full circuit of the club to get a feel for the security, exits and flow of the place. I had an image of Bashir sent to me by David. I scanned the crowd for him but thought it more likely I'd find him in the VIP section.

When I returned to the VIP section, which consisted of about thirty coffee tables with highbacked blue couches arranged around them in a U shape, I noticed one table at the far edge of the section had a man blocking access. He appeared to be on a security detail. I said hello to my friendly new guests, ordered more food and another bottle of champagne. I refilled my glass and headed out again.

Because of the lighting, I had to get within ten feet before I could distinguish who was sitting at each table in the VIP area. As I approached the table at the far edge, the guard I spotted earlier stepped in front of me. He was a compact, muscular looking guy. He may have been a Somali, but he didn't have the stereotypical build. He was wearing dark pants and a tight black button-down shirt that showed off his physique and more importantly the absence of a weapon. I looked behind him and spotted Bashir sitting with two men on either side. The coffee table in front was loaded with bottles, glasses, ice buckets and a fruit tray. Two girls sat on an adjacent couch to Bashir's.

"I'm here to see Bashir," I said to the guard.

"Who are you?" he said.

"I just want to offer my condolences for his man who died in the Starbucks yesterday."

"Stay here," the guard told me.

I slowly trailed behind the man as he walked to Bashir. I was halfway to the table when they signaled me to come over. I sat down on an ottoman across from Bashir who remained seated on the couch flanked by the other two men.

Because of the music volume, we both had to lean forward with our heads practically touching over the coffee table to communicate.

"You're a very stupid man," Bashir said.

"Just doing my job," I said.

"And what job is that?"

"I work for the government. I need you to tell me how you learned the evidence was tainted against your five rapists in Nashville. The ones who tragically died this week," I said with a grin.

Bashir leaned back away from me. He had a temper and I could see the rage building on his face. I leaned forward further to close the gap, so he could hear me when I spoke. I put both of my hands on the table. In my right hand I palmed a steel drink stirrer that was laying on the table.

"I just want the information. There's no need for you to wind up like your fixer or your guys in Nashville," I said.

I saw the arms of the short strong man coming around my neck before I felt them. In a short chopping motion with my right arm I drove the steel point of the drink stirrer through the interior side of the man's right knee. Bashir reacted brutally fast and hit me square with an uppercut to the jaw on his way up to a standing position. The man could punch, the blow knocked me back and the bells were ringing as he dove over the table and landed on me. I went with the momentum and rolled backward off the ottoman, bucking him off in the process. As I was getting up, in my peripheral vision I saw one of the men come around the table with a bottle in his hand in mid-swing. I stepped toward the man and hit him with the knife edge of my right hand in the throat. I crushed his thorax and he went down.

Bashir had regained his footing and was attacking. I pivoted to my left to face him and was hit with a flurry of stinging fists. He was fast and skilled. I jabbed with my left hand to put some distance between us. When Bashir stepped forward with a right hook, I uncoiled. He hit me hard in my already badly bruised jaw, but a half a second later the fight was over. I landed a bone crushing right straight into his nose. He was already limp when I followed through with a left while he was starting on his way down. I grabbed him with my left hand and was getting ready to hit him one more time when my back exploded in fiery agony. The sound of the first gunshot registered in my brain as the second bullet hit me and knocked me forward. As I fell forward with Bashir in my grip, I rotated him over me and hit the ground with Bashir on top, shielding me as the man continued to empty his pistol. I could feel the impacts through Bashir's body.

When the firing stopped, I rolled Bashir to the side and sprang back to my feet. The man swung at me with the butt of his empty revolver. I blocked the blow with my left arm and hit him hard in the ribs with my right. Unlike Bashir, he was no fighter. I slipped a lazy left hook and slid behind him and wrapped my right arm around the Somali's neck. I locked the choke hold with my left hand as I faced him to the table and tripped him. He fell forward toward the coffee table and with my arms still around his neck I sank his face into the corner of the glass table. I felt the man's neck break as it snapped backwards on impact.

I sat up and surveyed the scene. The guests within earshot of the gunshots were hurrying away, the bouncers were nowhere to be seen. They either didn't notice the fight or chose to keep their distance from an active shooter. I joined the swell of people and exited the VIP area. The clubbers in the common area were blithely unaware that anything had happened. I made my way to the front exit. The lights came on in the club as I stepped into the corridor leading to the exit. I walked the length of the corridor, past the bouncers and onto the street.

I was a hundred yards from the club walking to my rental when the adrenaline wore off. Every breath brought a stinging pain to my back. I found my SUV where I'd left it on a side street and headed East on I-94.

CHAPTER 30

WASHINGTON, DC

'D BEEN DRIVING for the better part of two days, surviving on painkillers and fast food when I dropped the SUV off at the rental center in the Ronald Reagan Airport. I called McDonald from the taxi and let him know I was on the way. The team was waiting for me on the *Nomad* when the taxi dropped me off at the Wharf Marina.

I wheeled my suitcase and attached backpack through the marina security gate and down the long slipway to the *Nomad*. Emily met me as I stepped on board.

"Are you okay?" Emily asked.

"My back's a lot better, just a little tired is all," I said.

"We have news; it's been a big day," she said gleefully.

The gang was gathered in the main salon.

"The weary traveler returns," McDonald said.

I dropped my bags at the entryway and sat on the couch closest to the sliding glass door.

"I don't know what you've been up to, but we've been out busting our hump solving the case," Migos said.

Emily handed me a bottle of Sam Adams and joined me on the couch.

"You're going to want to hear this," Emily said.

"Let me tell it," Migos said as he got up and stood in front of the television and addressed the assembled audience arrayed around him.

"Don't keep me in suspense, Migos, the floor is all yours," I said.

"Please set your cell phones to vibrate. I don't want any interruptions." He paused for effect.

"As you know, acting on a tip from David, we began around-the-clock surveillance of Congresswoman Noor. The representative from Minnesota keeps a full schedule. Most of her workday is spent at her office in the Rayburn House Building next to the Capital. After work she spends her evenings at a small studio apartment near Lafayette Square.

"Our first day surveilling her was last Friday. She left for work at seven that day and went straight to the Rayburn building. She walked to her office. At six-thirty that night, she left her office and walked straight home, where she remained for the evening. The second day we followed her was Saturday. She spent the day and the night inside her apartment, except for one short trip on foot to pick up groceries at a local store around the corner. If you haven't figured out by now, Congresswoman Noor is a homebody. That Sunday, the third day of our surveillance, she spent another full day in her apartment. I was on watch when she changed things up on us and pulled out of her apartment garage at seven that night. I followed her to Falls Church. She parked at Tysons Corner Mall and when she got out of her car, I noticed she'd removed her hijab.

"I parked and watched her walk into Eddie V's restaurant. I gave it a few minutes and then I went in thinking I could find a seat at the bar, which I did. I ordered a beer and after it arrived, I took a stroll through the dining room in such a way as to make people think I was looking for the men's room. That's when I spotted Noor seated at a table with another woman. I walked past both of them and snapped a burst of pictures with my cell as I did. They didn't know I was taking photos, because I held my phone to the side. Then I went back to my place at the bar, sorted through the images and sent the best ones to David, who didn't do anything with them because he was asleep, on account of it being past his bedtime in Scotland. I finished my beer and then I went back to my car and waited for Noor to leave. At a little after eleven, Noor walked out of the restaurant and returned to her car. She was alone and I thought she was driving home, when she surprised me again and turned north on the highway, away from DC.

"I followed Noor to a gated community in Langley. I knew I wouldn't be able to gain access, so I parked outside the main gate and waited. We have a tracking device on Noor's car and when she parked, I sent the address to David. Then it was midnight and my shift was over, and Rodriguez took over. Go ahead, Rodriguez," Migos said.

"Not much happened, I took over for McDonald at six this morning. She drove out of the gated community at around noon and returned to her apartment. She hasn't left her apartment since getting back. She's now being covered by Savage," Rodriguez said.

"Who was she with at the restaurant?" I asked.

"Let me finish," Migos said. "When David got up this

morning, he ran the address and the photo image. The woman Noor had dinner with last night was Vanessa Bloom, she's a Deputy Director at the CIA. The house she parked at last night belongs to Vanessa Bloom."

"How would those two know each other?" I asked.

"Vanessa's a political appointee; they could've met at a political event," Emily said.

"Is she gay? Last night sounded like date night, no hijabs allowed," I said.

"Vanessa isn't married. But if she's gay, it's a well kept secret," Emily said.

"What about Noor? She's America's most vocal Israel basher and a practicing Muslim, how could she be gay and dating a Jewish woman?" I asked.

"Hard to believe, but if the two were having an affair that would explain a lot. Noor could've learned how the rape video was obtained from Vanessa, maybe through pillow talk. Then she could've passed the information on to her brother, who used it," Emily said.

"Does Mike know about this?" I asked.

"No, we just got the information ourselves," Emily said.

I called Mike and asked him to come over to the marina. I used the time waiting for his arrival to clean up. When I looked at myself in the mirror before jumping into the shower I looked pretty rough. I had a black eye, the left side of my jaw was swollen. My back was mostly purple and my eyes were bloodshot. It had been a difficult ordeal, but at least I was alive.

Mike arrived by the time I returned to the main deck. He had a soda in his hand and was fully engrossed as Migos retold his tale. When Migos got to the part where David reveals who was seated with Noor at the restaurant and who owns the house in the gated community, Mike burst out laughing. Before long everyone else was laughing too. That brought on a game of who could come up with the funniest headline for when the story broke in the media.

We had a good thirty-minute joke fest at the expense of Vanessa and Noor.

"This can't get out. None of it can," Mike said.

"Why not?" Migos asked.

"If it remains a secret, it gives the Agency the leverage we need to keep our appointed watchdog from sabotaging future operations," Mike said.

"What about Noor, are we going to let her get away with the hypocrisy?" McDonald asked.

"I don't think we have any choice if we want to control Vanessa. Besides, from the look of things, Noor's story is kind of heroic. She's just trying to survive. Noor may say the things she says to pander to her constituents, but from the looks of it, she's not a true believer at all. If anything, I see her as something of a victim," Mike said.

"Her brother was a woman beating psychopath, I can tell you that much," I said.

"I wonder if she didn't have a hand in his demise?" Mike mused.

"You think Noor leaked details of the Mogadishu operation to Bashir, to put him in our gunsights," I said.

"What other motivation would she have? It was a secret; Bashir couldn't have known to ask for it. What other possible incentive could she have for freeing five rapists?" Mike said. "When Emily talks with Noor, she'll ask that question, but I doubt she'll get a straight answer."

"Emily is going to talk with Noor?" I asked.

"We'll have a sit down with both of them to explain their new reality. Noor will respond better to a woman. It'll have to be cleared by the Director, but I'll recommend Emily. It will be good to have a friend on the Foreign Affairs Committee," Mike said.

"They'll just deny it and claim the photos are a fake," I said.

"It won't be hard to get security footage at Eddie V's of the two entering and leaving the restaurant. Same with Noor driving into and leaving the gated community, you know they keep track of what cars come and go. But the photo of the two together at the restaurant is enough. Imagine how her constituents would react to a photo of Noor sitting close to the Jewish Executive Deputy Director of the CIA, with her face and head completely uncovered in a romantic restaurant," Mike said.

"That should be pretty damning," I said.

"Good work, everyone. I'm looking forward to getting my old job back," Mike said.

"Does this mean Emily isn't my Agency contact anymore?" I said.

"Why, do you like her better?" he asked.

"Much," I said. Mike furrowed his brow.

"Did I miss something?" Mike asked. Emily looked down.

"She's a lot prettier than you and she smells nice," I said. Emily turned red.

"I didn't expect you two to get along," Mike said.

"We get along fine, we even climbed Mount Waddington together. It was a bonding experience," I said.

"I see," Mike said.

"Is she in or out?" I asked.

"I don't know, let me think about it," he said. "I'm going to the Director with this information. If she approves, Emily and I will hopefully talk with the two paramours this week and then we can discuss what Emily's role will be with this mob of yours later."

CHAPTER 31

ELEUTHERA, BAHAMAS

THE DAY AFTER I arrived in DC, I headed out again. This time I was alone in the *Nomad*. The team flew back to Cyprus and Mike and Emily made plans to confront Noor and Vanessa. I was bruised and battered and feeling a little sorry for myself. I needed time to heal, so I took the slow route down the Intercoastal, through North Carolina, South Carolina and Florida as far as Jacksonville. Then I went open water direct to Eleuthera on a straight line.

I spent some of the cruise planning a climbing trip to Mount Alberta in the Canadian Rockies. I felt good enough by the time I docked in Governor's Harbor to handle the exertions of an attempt to bag number forty-nine of the big fifty. I was surprised when Mike called and asked me to pick him up at the airport.

I found him waiting under the sun shade in front of the tiny terminal building. He was wearing shorts and a polo shirt and was carrying a bag of luggage.

"It wasn't hard to find you. Those white legs of yours are blinding," I said.

"Not a lot of opportunity to bronze in the sun this summer. I thought I'd relax for a day or two before returning back to Virginia if that's all right with you," Mike said.

"That's excellent. We can go fishing while you're here. Catch a Marlin or something you can mount on a wall."

"I'd like that."

We returned to the house and Mike settled in. It was live band night next door at Tippy's Restaurant and after dinner we wandered over and found a seat in the bar. Tippy's has open walls and a spectacular location right on the pink sands of the most famous beach in Eleuthera. The construction is little more than a connected series of thatched huts. We'd already eaten, but it was a nice night to drink mojitos and listen to Jimmy Buffet songs with the smell of the ocean and the sound of the surf in the background.

"What's the purpose of your trip? By now I've normally received the full mission brief and gone into prep mode," I said.

"Not this time, there's no mission. I thought I owed you an explanation for a few things and this seemed like a good time for both of us to catch up," Mike said.

"It is for me. Go on."

"Emily told me you two haven't spoken since you left DC," Mike said.

"That's true. What of it?"

"You shouldn't be mad at her for something I did."

"I'm not mad at her. What did you do anyway?"

"I declined her request to continue to work as your handler," Mike said.

"If she wanted to be with me and be part of Trident, she

could easily quit. I don't blame you for making her choose," I said.

"You don't?"

"Of course not. You have a lot invested in her, why would you want to lose her?"

"I'm not afraid of her spending time away from her desk. I'm more worried about the risks involved with working with you," Mike said.

"That's another reason why I don't fault you. We can drop the subject now if that's all right with you. As I said, I don't blame you."

"Are you curious to know what happened when we talked with Vanessa and Noor?"

"Just a bit."

"The Director and I met with Vanessa in the Director's office. I laid it all out for her. I explained that it was an open and shut case of mishandling classified information."

"How'd she respond?"

"She's a lawyer, she wanted to argue her way out of it. I explained every bit of evidence we had on her relationship with Congresswoman Noor and the connection between Noor and Bashir and Bashir and the five attackers. It's black and white and we had her dead to rights."

"Did she confess?"

"She's no quitter, she switched from defense to offense. She accused the Director of breaking the law and using the CIA for spying domestically on political opponents etcetera... etcetera... I explained that the Agency didn't surveil her, that it was the group of contractors she tried to get killed during the S-400 take down in Syria paying back the favor."

"She's lucky nobody got hurt or she'd have had to deal with more than just a little surveillance," I said.

"I made her aware of what's happened to others who've crossed you."

"Is she going to play ball?" I asked.

"She is. Partly to save her own skin, but I think also to protect Noor. Those two mean a lot to each other."

"What about the Congressional Representative of Little Mogadishu?"

"That's a different story. I met her with Emily in her Congressional Office, the day after meeting with Vanessa. That meeting was completely different than what we'd prepared for."

"In what way?"

"We expected the seven steps of grief, like we had with Vanessa, denial, anger and the rest. Instead, what we got was complete cooperation from the get go."

"I hope you weren't being played. The girl's clever, I think it's possible that from behind the scenes, she was the one pulling strings on everything that happened."

"She said as much. She not only managed to get the CIA to kill her abusive brother, but she got her brother to sever her connection to the Muslim Brotherhood."

"Where does the Muslim Brotherhood come into this?"

"Noor tells a tragic story of her parents getting killed and her escaping Somalia. Then of her brother's abuse and joining IAIR to put distance between her and her brother. She claims to have run into the mouth of a lion, because IAIR is a cover for a radical Muslim Brotherhood organization that has designs on destroying America," Mike said.

"Did you believe any of what she told you? The woman's a gifted manipulator," I said.

"She admits as much. But her story resonates as true. She's not a conservative religious Muslim, she's an agnostic gay woman. She disguised her beliefs in order to survive in the radical Islamic environment she grew up in. She didn't choose to grow up in her environment, it was through no fault of her own. That environment was further complicated by the curse of having an abusive organized crime leader as a brother."

"Her life was hell. She saw an opportunity to get out of it and she took it," I said.

"Exactly."

"How did she get away from the Muslim Brotherhood? I wasn't even aware they were involved," I said.

"The Brotherhood requested she intercede with her brother to get him to tamp down on the violent behavior of his gang members. IAIR was incensed because the media coverage of the Somali gang activities was hurting their public relations efforts at a time when they needed public support on a couple of key issues. Noor, instead of passing a message of peace, prodded her brother into more violence. The Muslim Brotherhood reacted to Bashir's perceived defiance by attempting to kill him. Bashir survived the attempt on his life, which was the firebombing attack on his club, and he retaliated by killing Akrim, the head of IAIR."

"If she's the one who triggered the killing of Captain Allison and she's the one who instigated a firebombing that killed dozens of people, how does that make her a hero?" I asked.

"It doesn't. I never said she was a hero, but you have to give her some credit. She's a woman born into a culture that values women less than livestock. She grew up in poverty in the middle of a brutal civil war in the poorest country on the planet. She's used her brains to overcome her circumstances. Now she's a member of Congress in the most powerful country in the world. When she was threatened by her brother and the Muslim Brotherhood, she pitted her enemies against each other. And if that wasn't enough, she suckered the CIA or at least you into going after her brother. In the end, her foes are dead and she's earned the freedom to live the lifestyle she wants."

"You can save the fawning adoration for the next rainbow parade. As far as I'm concerned, the woman's a Machiavellian sociopath who'll do anything to achieve her goals, including killing innocent people."

"She may be a sociopath, but she's our sociopath, and she's going to be our ticket to taking down whatever it is the IAIR is up to with this 'Project'."

"That I understand, for a minute there I thought you were smitten with her."

"Not even a little bit."

"Well then I guess it was a happy ending."

"Not completely, I know you're not happy and neither is Emily with the way things turned out."

"She's a big girl, she can dump your team and join mine in a heartbeat, if that's what she wants. You forced her to make a choice and she did."

"I did."

"You won't hear me complain, I know first hand how dangerous it is to be around me."

The End.

AUTHOR NOTES

DEAR READER, I hope you enjoyed The Somali Affair. I'm currently hard at work on the next one. Pat Walsh novels don't need to be read in order, because they're not a true series in the sense that there's not a story arc spanning across all of the books. If you do choose to read them in order, the reader order is below from left to right.

Links to James Lawrence's other adventure thrillers:

Be among the first to learn about future releases of Pat Walsh's adventures, just click the link below.

SIGN UP

https://landing.mailerlite.com/webforms/landing/r4u2m3

TURN THE PAGE FOR A STUNNING PREVIEW OF

ARABIAN COLLUSION

CHAPTER 1

PRINCE TURKI BIN Talal Abdulaziz tried to sit up in an attempt to get out of bed. A bout of dizziness forced his head back down onto the pillow. He was in a king-sized bed in a suite located on the third floor of the Riyadh Ritz Carlton. The surroundings were opulent, the bed soft, expansive and luxurious. The grandeur did nothing to salve the pain shooting through every muscle in his body, especially the throbbing agony in his back. He reached over to the nightstand and grabbed a half-liter-sized plastic Evian water bottle. Unsteadily, he twisted off the cap and with trembling hands brought the bottle to his lips. It took several tries, but eventually, he was able to splash enough fluid into his mouth to quench his thirst before slipping back into unconsciousness.

When Prince Turki awoke, it was morning; he could tell from the sliver of sun brightening the room through the narrow gap in the heavy curtains. The sheets around his waist were moist. He had either wet himself again, or it was the night sweats brought on by his nightmares; he couldn't tell, and he didn't care. Too tired and in too much pain to get up and clean himself, he lay still, helpless, staring at the ceiling, listening for the sound he had dreaded every morning for the past week.

As if on cue, he heard the sound of footsteps approaching his door. His heartbeat went into overdrive. The footsteps triggered another panic attack, and he was struggling to breathe by the time he heard the door open. Then came the familiar South African baritone.

"Wakey, wakey, princeling; time for another meeting with Mr. Van Doren."

Strong hands clamped down on his ankles and he was dragged off the foot of the bed. His back and head thudded against the hardwood floor. He slid easily across the polished wooden bedroom floor and then, with less ease, across the tile of the living room. Eventually, he felt the friction burn of the thick corridor carpet abrading his naked back. The trip ended when he was dragged by his heels into a hotel room at the end of the corridor. Once inside the makeshift interroga- tion room, his bony naked body was lifted by strong hands and he was strapped down to a wooden chair. His feet were shoved into a plastic tub of water. He felt alligator clips bite into his scrotum and a pail of cold water was splashed across his face and chest. After what felt like an eternity filled with dread and fear, a short red-headed man entered his field of view.

"I had a meeting with your cousin last night after you retired to your room. I proposed your offer of fifty-three billion dollars. I conveyed your promise of no retribution and your assurance that fifty-three billion is the maximum amount of liquidity you have. I was very persuasive in making your case. Unfortunately, your cousin is a very stubborn man.

He's convinced seventy-five billion is achievable; he believes I just haven't provided you with the proper motivation." Van Doren nodded his head. A rubber dog bone was shoved into the Prince's mouth. He heard the metallic click of the switch being thrown and then felt the lightning strike. A surge of electricity convulsed every muscle in his body and then a red flash blanketed his vision. He regained consciousness to the familiar copper taste in his mouth and the smell of ozone in the air. Unsure how long he'd been out, he did his best to convince his captors he was still unconscious.

A bucket of ice-cold water caused him to betray his deception. "Your cousin thought it would help if you met with some of the family members who refused his generous offer of restitution. Only the most compassionate of leaders would allow criminals like you to return the money stolen from the Saudi Arabian people to pay for your corruption." The Prince felt himself being unstrapped and dragged from the chair. Naked and wet, he was dragged on his back along the corridor, into an elevator, down several stories and then through a kitchen. He heard a metal latch open and the sound of a vacuum seal being broken. He saw a thick, heavily insulated steel door, and he instantly felt a biting cold. He knew immediately he'd been dragged into a freezer. Lying on his back, looking at the ceiling, he folded his arms across his wet chest and began to shiver. He turned to his left and saw racks of frozen food. With what little strength he still possessed, he turned his head to the right. The sight shocked him. The wall was lined with bodies. He counted seven. He recognized all of them. His second cousin, Major General Hussain Ali, was the first in the line, his features frozen in a scream. Ice crystals had formed in his eyes and hair, making for an eerily grotesque sight. The other six cadavers were frozen in similar states of ante-mortem distress. All appeared to have died in the throes of agony. He screamed.

When he awoke, he once again found himself strapped to the chair, with his feet in the familiar water bucket. The hard pinch of the alligator clips against his badly bruised genitals focused his attention. He felt the water splash against his body and prepared himself for what was to come.

"Your cousin has agreed to come down to seventy billion. This is his last offer, you can either accept it or go into the deep freeze permanently. What's it going to be?" snarled Van Doren.

A feeling of even deeper despair fell over the Prince. He knew if he agreed to seventy billion his life would be spared for the moment, but the reprieve would be short-lived. He would never be able to come up with the money and once the Crown Prince learned he couldn't pay, he would be killed in an even worse way. He simply didn't have seventy billion in liquid assets. Although his net worth as reported by Forbes Magazine was well over one hundred billion, most of those assets were not easily transferable and if he tried to liquidate quickly, the sale would depress the asset price and he would be lucky to get even half. He started to sob uncontrollably. He heard the metallic click of the switch being thrown and then the lights went out.

The next morning, the Prince awoke in a different room. He was clothed in silk pajamas. He felt a heavy object around his right ankle. He reached down to remove it but found it was locked. An Indian servant entered the room and rolled a breakfast service of coffee, juices, fruits, and meats to the lounge chair next to the window. It took all of his energy, but the Prince crawled out of bed and seated himself for his first real meal in weeks. He was starving. He had no idea how much weight he had lost during his ordeal, but if the flesh hanging from his arms and legs were any indication, it had been a lot.

Hours later, Van Doren walked into the room, unannounced, as if he owned it. With him was a tall, middle-aged Saudi Arabian citizen wearing the local dress—a white kandura and red-and-white checkered keffiyeh. The Prince didn't recognize the man.

"The Crown Prince has generously decided to accept your offer of fifty-three billion. He is both kind and compassionate. He asked me to inform you that future corruption will not be dealt with as leniently. These are desperate times, and because of the serious financial crisis Saudi is facing, for the good of the Country he is willing to accept your offer of restitution instead of the retribution you deserve," Van Doren said.

"Talal is here to work out the details with you and your lawyers. You'll not be permitted to leave the hotel grounds until you've fulfilled your end of the bargain. That ankle bracelet you're wearing has an explosive charge inside it. It works like an invisible leash for a dog; if you try to exit the grounds it will detonate, and you'll lose your foot. We also have a guard force monitoring your movements from the signal given off by the bracelet. If you try to escape, you can be sure we'll drag what's left of you into the deep freeze."

Over the next ten weeks, the Prince had his business managers and lawyers generate the documents that allowed him to sign away fifty- three billion dollars from his vast empire to the government of Saudi Arabia. He didn't see Van

Doren again, although the memory of his nemesis was rarely out of his mind. The hotel was swarming with his cohorts wearing the same distinctive black Frontier Security polo shirts as worn by Van Doren. When he was finally released from the hotel, his first act was to lease a private jet, as his Boeing 757 had just been sold, and fly to London. His second act was to plot his revenge.

CHAPTER 2

SARA STRAINED TO find the tail lights of the Toyota Land Cruiser they were following through the thick dust. In the dawn light, the cloud of dust particles had an orange hue that gave the surrounding scenery a sepia-like quality.

"How much further, Saed?" she asked the driver.

"We're almost there Doctor, another twenty, maybe thirty minutes."

Sara shifted her gaze to Saed. He was a heavy-set man in his late thirties, a pleasant laid-back guy, with a ready smile. Saed worked for Shirin International as a combination driver, interpreter, and security provider. Sara was happy for the security; they were driving north from the Syrian city of Homs, through the Idlib Governorate, the last area of Syria still not returned to the full control of the Assad regime.

Sara Salam's official title was Assistant Director of Middle Eastern Antiquities at the University of Pennsylvania Cultural Heritage Center. She was part of a cooperative effort between UPCHC and Shirin International to save the antiquities that were regularly being stolen and ravaged because of the Syrian Civil War.

As the sun rose higher in the morning sky, visibility improved. Eventually, Sara was able to make out a cluster of buildings on the horizon. Above the village on a hill, she could see the stone ruins that marked their destination. The village of Deir Semaan is home to a large Byzantine-era monastery. Prior to the war, it had a population of five thousand, although now it's mostly deserted. In 400 A.D., St. Simeon Stylites, a fifth-century monk, set off a trend among his fellow hermits by living on top of a pillar. St. Simeon climbed a pillar inside the church in 412 A.D. in order to get away from a horde of disciples and onlookers who pursued him after being drawn by stories of his lifestyle of extreme self-denial. St. Simeon once survived the forty days of Lent without eating or drinking anything, an achievement he followed up by standing stock still until he collapsed. Because of his growing popularity, in order to escape the growing masses of followers, he spent the remainder of his life on a succession of ever-higher pillars. After he died, his fame grew even more, and spawned scores of imitators, known as Stylites from the Greek word for pillar, "style."

The monastery, northwest of Aleppo, has been a tourist attraction for centuries, and has come under the control of different groups during the course of the civil war, including the Free Syrian Army, Islamic State of Iraq and the Levant (ISIL), the Kurdish YPG, the Islamist Group Ahar al-Sham, as well as the Turkish Army. It remains close to the front line between rebels, including Jabhat al-Nusra, the local al-Qaeda branch, the Kurdish forces from the YPG, and the Assad regime forces. Located in the Arfin valley, forty miles north of Aleppo, the area is of strategic importance to the Turkish, Syrian, and Kurdish people. Value is never a good thing in a war because it always invites more fighting. In May 2016, Russian bombers weighed in on the conflict and destroyed St. Simeon's pillar and parts of the monastery.

Sara's convoy passed through the battle-scarred village and climbed the winding road up the hill. They halted in front of the ruins of the monastery. Sara stepped out of her vehicle and joined the others who were assembling around the hood of the lead vehicle. She greeted Doctor Wolfgang Boetter and Doctor Felix Reddinger. Wolfgang was a German in his sixties. Tall and thin, decked out in a safari hat and khaki expedition clothing, the genial Bavarian greeted Sara with a smile. Felix was a Swiss citizen in his late thirties. An academic and outdoor enthusiast who was raised in Africa, Felix was armed with both a pistol and a menacing-looking black HK416 carbine. Unlike the affable Wolfgang, Felix wore a serious demeanor.

Wolfgang poured coffee from a silver thermos as they waited for the other two members of the inspection team to join them. Sara sipped the strong, steaming liquid and nodded to Wolfgang in appreciation. Doctor Wolfgang produced a box of chocolates and offered her the open box. Sara studied the assortment and selected a square and then turned to greet the rest of the group. Ole was a Norwegian, former military, and still looked the part of a special forces' operator. Ole, like Felix, wore tactical clothing and came armed. Ole was in his early forties; he was a wealthy man who started out as a donor to Shirin before taking a more active role in preventing the looting and destruction of Syrian history. Adolpho was an Italian, a dapper fifty-year-old professor from the University of Rome. Unlike the others, who were dressed for the field, he wore a navy-blue blazer and shiny Italian leather loafers.

As soon as the five academics and four drivers were assembled, Doctor Wolfgang addressed the group.

"Two days ago, we received a report of looting at the St. Simeon Cathedral. Our task today is to catalog the damage. Because it's not safe to remain here overnight, our time on site will be limited. We'll depart no later than four this afternoon in order to make it back to our compound before it gets dark. That leaves us only seven hours to identify and record the damage to the complex. The Cathedral is vast and expansive. We'll split up into four groups, each group composed of one archaeologist and one armed security member. Make sure you carry your hand-held radios and test them before you depart. Cell service in this area is not reliable. We'll meet back here at exactly three forty-five. Felix, you'll take the nave. Adolpho, you'll assess the eastern and southern basilicas. Ole, I want you to inspect the western and northern basilicas, and Sara, you'll survey the exterior. Are there any questions?" Wolfgang paused for a few seconds and then dismissed the group. "That's all."

Sara attempted to hide her disappointment in her assignment. From where she was standing, she could look into the nave and see the fallen pillar of St. Simeon. Finding something of interest on the outside grounds seemed farfetched. She returned to the SUV and grabbed a small red North Face backpack that held her camera, water, and snacks. The placid Saed was sitting in the driver's seat with his eyes closed.

"You and I are going to inspect the cathedral grounds," she said to Saed, who immediately went to the back of the SUV and retrieved an AK-47 and his own backpack.

"Do you really need that here?" she asked while pointing to the rifle.

"I hope not, but it's better to be safe than sorry."

The massive stone ruins of the church and monastery were copper in color. The wooden roof of the church and monastery buildings had rotted and collapsed centuries earlier. The walls, arches, and pillars that framed the structure were still largely intact. Surrounding the buildings were rolling hills covered with high grass, shrubs, and the occasional hibiscus tree. Large stones, each the size and shape of a small refrigerator, were scattered around the structures, seemingly at random. When it was constructed in 473 A.D., under the order of Emperor Zeno following the death of St. Simeon the hermit, it was the largest Cathedral in the world.

Sara began her inspection at the main entrance and began a slow survey counterclockwise around the cathedral. Waist-high grass sprinkled with red cardinal wildflowers made for a pretty view. The high grass also hid many of the fallen stones. Sara moved slowly and cautiously around the cathedral to avoid tripping and scraping her shins on the stones beneath the grass. She came across a bomb crater. She stopped and took photos of the car-sized hole in the ground, as well as some scarring on the exterior cathedral wall made by shrapnel from the blast.

It took an hour to reach the first basilica, which stretched like an arm two hundred yards from the main church building. Sara sat on a stone and retrieved a bottle of water from her backpack; Saed sat next to her and did the same. The cool morning was turning into a warm spring day. Sara could see a sheen of sweat on Saed's face. From the tip of the eastern basilica, she was able to see across the open field and observe the length of the northern basilica. In between were rolling green hills covered with the ubiquitous red wildflowers. The hill sloped gently away from the cathedral down to a valley where a smaller structure stood five hundred yards from the basilica.

"Those look like fresh dirt piles next to that building; let's go have a look," Sara said to Saed as she placed her pack back onto her shoulders. As the two walked down the hill and got closer to the building, they could see that it was a mausoleum with a small graveyard attached.

"Gravediggers," said Saed.

"Yes, I can see."

Sara athletically vaulted over the stone wall into the small cemetery.

Saed took the long way around through the gate. The headstones were arrayed in lines; some were broken, many were very old, dating back to the fifth century, while others had dates on them that were much more recent. She walked over to the fresh earth and found two gravestones that were knocked over and partially covered with dirt. The writing on the stones was faded, but she could recognize enough to tell the language was Ottoman Turkish. Looking down into the nearest dug-up grave, she found bones and a clay pot. Curious about the pot, she decided to have a closer look. She was dropping her backpack to prepare for the climb down into the grave when she heard a call on the radio attached to her belt.

"Sara, are you there?" She heard Wolfgang's German-accented voice. She picked up the radio and pressed the transmit button on the side.

"This is Sara."

"I need you to come to the northern basilica; we've found some- thing interesting and we need your help."

"I've found two graves that have been dug up in the cemetery," replied Sara.

"This is more important; please come immediately," Wolfgang stated.

Saed was just arriving at the gravesite as Sara was returning her backpack to her shoulders.

"We have to meet Doctor Boettinger in the north basilica."

Saed grimaced as he turned around and started to lumber back up the hill. Once at the top, Sara waited for her security man to catch up. She and Saed entered the basilica together where it intersected with the nave. They noticed a gathering at the far end of the basilica and went to it. Wolfgang met her, while Felix and Ole both remained huddled around a hole in the wall.

"What's going on?" asked Sara.

"Ole has made a most interesting discovery. Inside that niche there once was a series of statues depicting the ascension. The thieves used a crowbar and pried them from the niche interior. What's so interesting is that in doing so, they exposed a storage space behind the niche."

"What's inside?"

"Black lacquer boxes covered in writing. Very intricate gold calligraphy. We haven't opened them yet; we could use your Arabic skill."

Sara stood next to Wolfgang and watched Ole and Felix extract the boxes from within the hidden space. They handled the boxes gently, lined them up, and photographed them. Sara approached the first box on the end and studied it. The box was a perfect cube, two feet in every direction. The lacquer coating had a few cracks but otherwise showed little damage. Sara studied the writing.

"I thought my Arabic was passable, but I couldn't figure it out," Felix said as he walked up beside Sara and studied the box.

"It's Aramaic, East Syriac," Sara replied.

"That explains a few things. What does it say?"

"It says, 'The Holy Quran.'"

"The Holy Quran?"

"Yes, as in 'The' and not 'A' Holy Koran."

"Why would it be written in Aramaic?" asked Wolfgang, who was standing behind Sara and Felix.

"The language around Mecca at the time of Mohammed was

Aramaic, and the first Quran was almost certainly written in the East Syrian dialect," answered Sara.

"This could be a significant find," said Wolfgang.

"Do you think we should open it and find out?" asked Felix, as he placed a second box down next to the first.

"We don't have the tools to open this box without damaging it. We should take it back with us and study it properly," Wolfgang said.

"What about this second box? What does it say it contains?" asked Felix.

Sara moved over to the second box and studied it for a full five minutes.

"This box contains 'The Stone'," answered Sara.

"Are you sure that's what it says?" asked Ole.

"Yes, I'm sure, although I have no idea what it means," replied Sara. "This is intriguing. These boxes may contain important artifacts that have been hidden away for centuries. We'll take them back where they can be studied and safeguarded. Ole and Felix, please have them loaded into the vehicles. We head back immediately," said Wolfgang.

"Don't you think we should open them and confirm they are what you think they are before we abandon the task we came here to perform?" asked Ole.

Wolfgang paused for a minute. "Only if you think you can open them without causing damage," he said.

Adolpho had arrived moments earlier and listened to the conversation between Ole and Wolfgang. He removed a leather pouch containing a small set of archaeology tools from his jacket and approached the first box. Sara watched as he surveyed the box with one tool that looked like a pick and another that was a small mirror that resembled a dental tool.

"The box can't be opened without breaking the seal," Adolpho said. "Break it," replied Felix.

"Yes, break it," said Ole.

"It's up to you," Adolpho said to Wolfgang.

"Go ahead. We would only do the same back at our camp."

Adolpho took a thin razor knife from his pouch and inserted it into the seam at the top of the box. He slid the blade through the wax- like substance sealing the box.

"What is that?" Felix asked.

"Bitumen, I think. It's been used as a seal since Roman times," said Adolpho

Adolpho ran the X-ACTO razor blade all the way around the lid of the box. He then signaled Sara to help him.

The two slowly lifted the top off the box. When the top

separated from the rest of the box they heard the noise of a vacuum seal being broken.

"What's inside?" asked Ole, who was crowded out from view by the others.

Adolpho gently removed an object wrapped in black cloth from inside. He placed it on the box top in front of Sara. He began to unwrap the object. "It's a book, leather bound, probably deerskin or some such animal," he said.

"What does it say on the cover?" asked Ole.

"Same as on the box, 'The Holy Quran,'" Sara said.

"Could this be one of the originals made by Zayd ibn Thabit?" asked Felix.

"We would need to carbon date it to be sure. If it is, then it's

thirteen hundred years old. We should put it back, regardless of who wrote it; it's very old, and the pages are too fragile to touch," said Adolpho.

"Whatever happened to the five original copies of the Koran made by Zayd ibn Thabit which were commissioned by the Caliph?" asked Adolpho.

"Five copies of the one true original were sent to the Muslim regions at the time; the location of three are known, and this may be one of the missing copies," answered Sara.

"Let's check the next box," Ole said.

Adolpho repeated the procedure. The group was expecting to find a stone under the cloth. Only this time, when the fabric was removed from around the object, what they found underneath was another box, this one the size of a toaster. Sara watched Adolpho strain and then signal for Felix to help him remove the surprisingly heavy box.

Adolpho once again went through the process of

opening the box. Sara watched as he unwrapped the cloth from around a black, tablet- shaped stone

"What is it?" asked Ole.

"I have no idea, it's just a square, tablet-shaped stone," answered Adolpho.

"The Quran could be a significant historical find. Let's load up and get these archaeological finds to safety as soon as possible. Cataloguing the damage to the Cathedral is going to have to wait," said Wolfgang.

CHAPTER 3

IT WAS LATE afternoon by the time the trucks were loaded up and the convoy set off on the return trip to the Shirin compound on the outskirts of Homs. Sara was in the third SUV following behind Wolfgang, who was in the second vehicle. Ole was leading the convoy and Adolpho was trailing.

"Why are we stopping?" asked Sara

"Roadblock," replied Saed, as he removed a pistol from the storage console behind the gear shift.

"Are we in trouble?" asked Sara.

"The control of this road shifts all the time; it depends on whose roadblock it is," said Saed.

Up ahead, Sara could see two men pointing rifles at Ole's vehicle, while talking to Ole and his driver. The two men speaking to Ole had heavy beards and wore mismatched military vests and uniforms. Sara watched as the doors to the SUV were opened and Ole and his driver, whose name she did not know, got out. The two men signaled with their weapons for the personnel from the other vehicles to get out and come forward to the first vehicle in the convoy. Sara watched Saed open the car door and tuck his pistol under his shirt in his back waistband as he exited the truck.

When Sara and Saed approached the two soldiers, they were directed to stand with Ole, Wolfgang and the other two members of their team. They were close enough to the soldiers to hear them talk among themselves. The shorter one, who appeared to be the leader, was telling the tall one that, once they had everyone assembled, he would inspect the vehicles. The subordinate would guard the personnel. The tall soldier kept his weapon oriented at the larger group, while the leader kept his weapon aimed at Adolpho and his driver who were still approaching. When Adolpho joined the group, the leader turned his attention to the first SUV and, for the moment, the soldier took his eyes off the group and watched the leader and not his charges.

The sound of a pistol discharging so close to her ear was a deafening surprise. It happened so fast, she didn't have time to react. Sara watched the soldier who was only five feet from her, the one who was supposed to be covering her group, drop like a sack of bricks after a bullet exploded the left side of his skull. Stunned, Sara turned her attention to the leader, who was opening the SUV door when the shot was fired. Before he could get both hands onto his weapon and raise it, five more pistol shots rang out in rapid secession. Sara watched the man fall dead to the ground.

"We need to get out of here, fast!" Saed shouted, with the smoking pistol in his right hand. Although she had trouble understanding the words because of the temporary ringing in her ears, the body language was obvious. All of the others began to run to their vehicles and she joined them.

Driving past the roadblock, Sara stared at the two bodies

on the road as Saed swerved around them to keep up with the other vehicles in the convoy.

"Will you pass me a bottle of water?" asked Saed.

Sara's hands were shaking so badly that she had trouble opening the bottle for Saed. She finally handed the bottle to Saed and it disappeared in his big paw. She looked up at the big man and he looked as passive and docile as ever.

"Who were those men?" asked Sara.

"Al Nusra," replied Saed.

"What did they want with us?"

"Nothing directed at us— they were just collecting tolls, stopping vehicles, and collecting as much money as they can get. If they'd found the relics, they would've confiscated them. They also would've confiscated the trucks and taken us captive. I had no choice," Saed said.

"I just want to get back in one piece. Nothing was mentioned about gunfights when I signed up for this at the University."

Sara found herself focusing on Saed and his neatly trimmed beard and bald head the remainder of the trip back to the compound. He was as relaxed as she was tense. She could feel a familiar soreness in her jaw from a childhood habit of grinding her teeth when under stress.

The sun was setting when they passed through the guarded com- pound gate of the Shirin Headquarters. Sara silently said a prayer as the vehicle came to a halt.

The compound consisted of two villas in the outskirts of the Baba Amir neighborhood of Homs. The city was a major battlefield during the rebellion and had been secured by Assad's forces for more than two years, which was enough time to restore electricity and water to much of the area.

Most of the buildings in the city had been reduced to rubble. Two years after the hostilities had ceased, the city was still mostly deserted, which allowed Shirin International to take its pick of properties offered by the Syrian Government. The villas were comfortably furnished.

Sara emerged from a hot shower, quickly dressed in a pair of jeans and a t-shirt and headed to the communal dining room with a voracious appetite. She grabbed a plate and headed through the buffet, which was stacked with Lebanese cold and hot mezza dishes. She joined Ole and Wolfgang at a table with her plate piled high with chicken kebabs, manakeesh (Lebanese pizza), falafel, tabbouleh salad, kofta meatballs, and baklava.

Ole did a double take when Sara dropped the heavy plate on the table.

"Did you forget you only weigh 50 kilos?" Ole asked.

"I can't remember when I've ever been this hungry or when food has ever tasted so good," Sara replied with a kebab in her hand.

"I think there was a point today when we all felt we had enjoyed our last meal," said Wolfgang. Nobody responded to that.

"Where's Adolpho?" asked Sara.

"He's in the lab with the artifacts," said Wolfgang. "What's he up to?" said Sara.

"He brought a quadrupole mass spectrometer with him. He borrowed it from the University of Rome. He's conducting C-14 measurements," Wolfgang said.

"How long before we'll know how old the Quran is?" asked Sara.

"It will take two days according to Adolpho. His portable

system is a huge improvement over the six weeks I'm used to with the ancient equipment at my University," Wolfgang replied.

"It's a very interesting find. Sara, since you're the only one with the language skills, you should check to see how the text deviates from the Uthmanic Codex. That should tell us a lot," Ole said.

"Like the Sanaa Quran, if there are any differences then we'll know it pre-dates the final approved version crafted by Zayd ibn Thabit at around 650 AD," Sara replied.

"Wouldn't it be marvelous if we discovered one of the early versions of the Quran?" Wolfgang asked.

"The Muslims believe there was only ever one version of the Holy Quran. Mohammed received the first revelation from the angel Gabriel in 610 AD. After each revelation, Mohammed would recite the message verbatim to his companions who would write it down, as Mohammed was illiterate. Because the Quran was revealed in disjointed verses and chapters, a point came when it needed to be gathered into a coherent whole text. There are disagreements among both Muslim and non-Muslim scholars as to when the Quran was compiled. Some believe Mohammad compiled it before he died, while others believe it was collected by either Ali ibn Abu Talib or Abu Bakr. Who knows, maybe the text we found today will help us understand this mystery?" Sara said.

CHAPTER 4

SARA WOKE TO the sound of gunfire. She was frozen in her bed, lying on her back in the dark, unable to decide what to do, too frightened to move. The door to her room flew open and she saw the silhouette of a man. It was a big man with a bald head.

"Come with me, we need to get out of here!" she heard from the familiar voice of Saed.

"I need my clothes." Sara was wearing only panties and a t-shirt.

"No time for that, come on!" Saed pulled at her arm. Sara managed to snag a pair of blue jeans and running shoes from the top of the bureau by the doorway as Saed pulled her into the hallway. Gunfire reverberated downstairs and from one of the bedrooms on the second floor. Saed led Sara down the hallway toward the back staircase when a man exited one of the bedrooms with a rifle. Saed shot the man before he could raise his rifle. Saed and Sara stepped over the man and ran toward the end of the hallway to the staircase.

They stopped, midway down the stairs, to listen, before trying to reach the door at the base of the stairs. Sara used the time to slip her jeans on and to step into her running shoes. They walked down the rest of the way and entered the kitchen. Two bodies were on the floor. Sara hesitated when she recognized them, and then followed Saed out the back door into the darkness of the courtyard. Without warning, Saed fired three shots with his pistol and she heard a weapon fire from inside the villa. She raced after Saed out into the courtyard that separated the two villas and around to the back of the Villa they had just left. When they reached the outer wall of the villa complex, Saed picked Sara up by the waist and lifted her over. Sara felt herself slide over the top of the stone boundary and managed to hang onto the edge before slowly dropping to the other side. Saed followed seconds later.

Out in the street, they ran toward a neighboring villa. The wall of the villa had been destroyed and most of the villa was bombed out. Saed led Sara through a hole in the wall into a dark empty building. The room was illuminated by the moon because most of the roof was missing. They found a staircase and walked down the stairs. Sara put her hand on Saed's shoulder and he guided her down into a basement. They reached the bottom and Saed led Sara to the edge of the room and the two sat down on the dirty tile floor.

Sounds of the massacre could still be heard coming from their villa. The spaces between the cracks of gunfire grew longer, and the ferocity of the violence had slowed. Minutes went by, and for longer and longer periods the only sound Sara could hear was her own breathing. She was too terrified to talk. Saed was quiet; he held the pistol in his hand and his attention was focused on the staircase they had used to get down into the basement. It was too dark to see the stairs, although they were only ten feet away.

Eventually, the gunfire stopped entirely. Sara was exhausted from the stress, sitting back to back with Saed, each leaning against the other, with him facing the stairs and Sara facing a wall. Neither spoke. Seconds ticked away, then minutes that seeped into hours.

"I don't hear anything. I think they've left," Saed whispered. "What do we do now?" asked Sara

"We should go up and get help," Saed said.

"Can't you call someone from here?" asked Sara.

"I don't have my phone. When the attack started, I only had time to get my pistol and then I went for you."

"Are we going back to the Villa?" asked Sara.

"Only if it looks clear."

Saed stood in the darkness and held Sara by the arm helping her up. With the pistol in his left hand and using his right hand as a guide against the wall, he made his way toward the stairs.

As they approached the top of the stairs, they could see sunlight. Sara followed behind Saed with her hand pressed against his lower back as he stepped into the sunlight at the top of the stairs. The crack of three shots echoed in the stairwell. Sara felt her companion's body jerk and then she felt the big man fall backward. Saed's falling knocked her off balance and the two tumbled backward down the stairs. Her head crashed against the basement floor and she lost consciousness.

She awoke in the back of an open truck and could feel a corrugated metal surface beneath her. She imagined it was a pickup truck. Her hands and feet were tied, and she had a gag in her mouth that tasted like motor oil. It was dark, hot, and difficult to breathe under the heavy tarpaulin draped over her; her head was pounding, and her mouth hurt from the tightness of the gag. She could hear traces of a conversation over the road noise. The language came as a surprise; it was Turkish.

After a what seemed like hours, the truck came to a halt. Sara was dragged out of the truck by her feet. Once her body cleared the truck bed, her back and head fell flat against a dirt surface and then someone grabbed her by the arms and, along with the person holding her feet, they lifted her and carried her into a building. She was taken into a room and then dropped hard onto the floor. Her feet and hands were untied. The two men left without speaking.

Sara removed the gag and then picked herself up off the ground. The room had an overhead light, but no windows. The only furniture was a bed. Adjacent to the bedroom was a small bathroom. She went inside and drank from the faucet and then washed her face with water. She tested the bedroom door, but it was locked. Sara sat on the edge of the bed and began to sob.

CHAPTER 5

I PROPEL MYSELF with long, slow kicks through the cobalt-blue water, entering the oval-shaped cave opening with room to spare on either side of me. The filtered sunlight gradually fades to darkness until the only illumination that remains comes from the beam of my flashlight. The limestone walls close in around me as I advance until only a foot of space remains on either side. The dive computer on my wrist indicates a depth of 77 feet. The walls around me are a reddish brown, the water cool. I make a right turn and then have to angle my body to fit through a narrower opening. Beneath me is only two inches of water, and above, I can feel my air tank scrape the top of the cave when I kick. I move forward with my arms fully extended, holding a flashlight to guide my way and using my fins to propel me. I'm committed to the position because the tunnel is too narrow to return my arms to my side. I'm using short kicks because the narrow tube I'm swimming through is too confining for a proper leg kick. The cave twists to the left, this time opening into a large, sphere- shaped chamber.

I take advantage of the opportunity to stretch before

continuing through a triangle-shaped entryway on the far side. The cave is not nearly as tight as before. The absence of light eliminates any possibility of plant life, although there is some black and orange discoloration on the rocks from whatever kind of micro-organisms exist in this environment. I check my pressure gauge and confirm that I still have enough air to continue. The cave drops sharply, and I angle my body into an L and swim straight down until it levels. A boulder is blocking my path. I survey the far side of the narrow opening with my flashlight and then I stow the flashlight. In complete darkness, I unclip and remove my buoyancy compensator and air tank and slip the vest-shaped rig through the small hole and follow behind it. I squeeze my body through; even though it's dark, I can sense I'm in an open area because I can feel a current. I don my BCD and tank by swinging them over my head and clip the straps together. I retrieve my flashlight from where it's been clipped to the BCD and turn it on. The chamber is huge; in the guidebook it was described as cathedral-sized and that wasn't an exaggeration.

My flashlight beam isn't even powerful enough to illuminate the far wall or the bottom. I drift in an upright position in the cavern and turn to look back to where I entered. A flashlight blinds me, and then from behind the light, a neon-yellow wetsuit emerges from the underwater tunnel. The figure is small enough that the person is able to emerge from the tiny opening with equipment intact. The black vest and mask with yellow wetsuit remind me of a bumblebee. The lithe, hooded bumblebee diver swims to me, and in the underwater darkness, we show each other our air levels. It's time to turn back.

The route back is as cramped and claustrophobic as the route in. When I finally see the bright blue water on the other side of the cave exit, I quietly celebrate with a fist pump. With my air running low, I'm anxious to surface. Once the bumblebee catches up, I give the thumbs- up sign and we surface together. A school of sardines briefly surrounds us; it's a mini silver storm for a moment and then it's gone. Unlike the inside of the cave, we're surrounded by a kaleidoscope of color and sea life. Fish, eels, jellyfish, seagrass, and plants are everywhere. It's beautiful. After a brief safety stop, we break the surface and swim to my boat, the Sam Houston.

I toss my fins onto the hydraulic ramp and climb the ladder. Cheryl hands me her fins and air tank with BCD attached. We hose each other off with fresh water while still on the ramp. Cheryl turns her back to me and I help her unzip her wetsuit. She sheds her bumblebee suit and my heart stops. Cheryl turns and smiles. It's a dazzling flash of white, and she knows the effect she has on me. I stay back and clean and stow the equipment while Cheryl showers.

When I'm done with the equipment, I climb the stairs to the fly deck and move into my favorite perch with an ice-cold bottle of Heineken that I snag out of the small fridge on my way to the couch.

Cheryl appears in a bathrobe, sunglasses, and a floppy sun hat the size of a large pizza. She climbs onto the couch and gives me a hug.

"That was awesome; what did you think?" she asks.

"Traveling in tight spaces, moving blindly in the dark, never knowing when you're going to get stuck or lost, use up all of your air and drown. What's not to like about cave diving?"

"It wasn't that bad."

"Yeah, it kind of was."

"Next time, you choose the venue."

"I want to go to that place with the big underwater Jesus Statue." "They put that in when the Pope visited. It's called, Christ of the Sailors, and it isn't far from here; it's midway between the two islands. If we go, there's a shipwreck nearby we can dive at the same time."

"We'll do that tomorrow; open water I enjoy. Caves, not so much."

On the table, my cell phone starts ringing. I look at the caller ID. It's Mike, so I pick up.

"I've been trying to get you for the past hour." "Hi, Mike, how've you been?"

"No time for that. Where are you?"

"Gozo Island, Malta. I'm on the boat."

"I need your help with something."

"Ok, send it."

"We have an American college professor missing, possibly kidnapped
in Syria."

"What's a professor doing in Syria?"

"Her name is Doctor Sara Salam, and she teaches Archaeology at the University of Pennsylvania. She was working with an NGO that was operating out of Homs with the approval of the Syrian Government."

"Homs is solidly under government control. Did Assad's people take her?"

"We don't know. There was an attack, and every member

of her organization was killed. The bodies were found two days ago; hers was the only one not accounted for."

"How long ago was the attack?"

"Three days, tops. We don't have any assets in place. The information we have is coming from Shirin International, a Swiss-based NGO that's working to preserve Syrian Antiquities that are getting lost and destroyed because of the Civil War."

"Dying to save clay pots seems a bit silly, even for an Ivy League college professor. Why's the CIA involved? The only organization that should care about this one is the selection committee for next year's Darwin awards."

"She's not just a Professor; she's also Assistant Director of Middle Eastern Antiquities at the University of Pennsylvania Cultural Heritage Center. They have some clout. One of the board members of the Heritage Center is a big-time political donor and he's pressuring the White House."

"You've been working on this for two days. Have you found anything?"

"Not much. I'll send you what we have."

"Sounds good. I'll get the guys at Clearwater engaged. Can you provide ISR?"

"Satellite only; we don't have anyone on the ground, and all the UAV assets are committed."

"That'll give Dave something to work with."

"He never seems to need much. Some of our folks are starting to think Clearwater's capabilities rival our own."

"I think they may be better. I read an article yesterday in Fortune that said four hundred Google employees resigned because they wanted out of the same business Clearwater is in, which is combining artificial intelligence with intel sensor feeds. They even outed the black project, code name, 'Project Maven', being loyal San Francisco patriots and all."

"That's a Department of Defense project. Dave Forrest is way ahead of them, but he's not ahead of everyone."

"Send me what you have, and I'll start the search. I probably won't be able to go in-country for another day or two."

"Ok."

"Will we get any cooperation from the regime? Will they grant us entry?"

"No, they'll kill you if they find you."

"I was afraid of that."

"Do the best you can. I need to report some progress."

"Vacation's over," I said to Cheryl.

"I was eavesdropping. Forward me what you get from Mike." "We'll head back to the main island and put you on an airplane to Paphos. It'll take me a day to get back with the boat. Hopefully, by then you'll have enough to give me something to work with."